Black
WIDOW

LAUREN RUNOW

Black Widow Copyright © 2016 by Lauren Runow
All rights reserved.

ISBN: 978-0-9966922-5-0

This literary work may not be reproduced or transmitted in any form or by any means. Including electronic or photographic reproduction in whole or in part, without the written permission of the author except for the use of brief quotations in a book review.

Names, places and incidents either are products of the author's imagination or are used fictitiously. Any resemblance to actual events, locales or persons living or dead is entirely coincidental.

Cover Images © Adobe Stock – Slava_Vladzimirska & macrovector
Cover Design © Designed With Grace

Interior design by E.M. Tippetts Book Designs

www.emtippettsbookdesigns.com

For Jeannine Colette
I would never want to be a part of this author world without you!
Thank you for everything!

Books by
LAUREN RUNOW

Unwritten
Rewritten

Black Widow

PROLOGUE

Preston

"Kim, please, don't do this!"

I run up to the side of the Golden Gate Bridge, pleading as I lean over the edge, trying to grab her but she's standing on the ledge and the railing's stopping me from reaching her.

The fog is so heavy that I can't see past five feet in front of me. It's the crazy, thick San Francisco fog that makes the air dense and leaves everything wet.

"I can't go on. Not like this, Preston." Her words are strong but her movements are weak, stagnant in the dark night.

"You don't mean that," my voice stutters in disbelief. "Please, you can't do this. Nothing is worth taking your life."

She's the love of my life. My everything. How could I have missed any sign that she was feeling this way? We've been so happy... at least I thought. Am I truly that blind?

"Yes. You are," she responds as she throws me a glance from over her shoulder causing chills to run down my spine.

For someone who is acting so erratic, I'm taken aback at how every syllable she says is spoken with clarity.

We weren't even fighting. My day was like every other day until I came home from work and saw a note saying she was taking her life.

I've never driven so fast through the crazy streets of San Francisco. The thought that she would actually do this was the only thing that kept me from losing my shit and crashing into the car in front of me. No matter what, I had to get here to stop her.

My black Tesla is still on with the lights pointing right at us, which is making the fog even harder to see through. If I turned them off I would be able to see her better, and maybe even climb over the railing to get her, but I'm not leaving her side. Not a chance in hell until she's safe in my arms. This damn fog is just too much.

"If I can't have you all to myself then I don't want to live," she says as she looks back down to the dark abyss below her.

"I don't know what you mean?" I say, reaching for her again. She does have me to herself. I would never have an emotional relationship with any other woman. Ever.

Wait, holy fuck, is she serious right now?

"Are you talking about the clubs we've been going to?" I ask completely baffled but trying to make sense of it all.

Yes we're married but I thought we would spice up our relationship a bit. I asked her to explore some new passions and I'm hoping that's not what led us here. I've felt all of my needs were being met, and hers as well, bringing our relationship to the best it's ever been.

This just doesn't make sense. I've only gone with her. I've never even thought about going without her and she was involved with every scene I've been in, even seemed like she was really into it.

Now this.

What the hell?

Why didn't she just tell me?

I beg her again, "Please, we can get through this. Just talk to me."

"We can't. You want things. Things I can't do anymore. Will you give that up?"

Give it up?

Shit, of course! I've enjoyed myself but I want her.

If she had just talked to me before coming straight to this then I'd have more time to talk to her about it. Show her that I'm serious and not just saying it to keep her from jumping.

I love her so much. I don't want her to do this. Would I seriously consider denying my own needs instead of living a life without her?

Yes, I would, in a heartbeat.

I reach out to her, "Come on, this is crazy. Please get down from there.

Let's talk about this."

She looks at me. The look on her face is not one of death, or fear, or sadness. It's a look I've never seen before and I literally feel my bones shake when I see it. She's completely unhinged. Her eyes almost shine with delight, excitement even.

After looking down, she looks up, over her shoulder at me again with a smirk on her face as she clearly states, "I'll show you what's really crazy," as she lets go and jumps off the bridge.

I leap forward, jumping over the railing with my arms outstretched in a vast attempt to grab her, yank her back to me but I can't see anything. Not the water below, or even my own hand in front of me. All I can feel is the heaviness in my chest and the loneliness in my soul.

She's gone.

She fucking jumped.

And it's all my fault.

Chapter ONE

Kamii

P artner... I keep saying in my head, over and over again. I did it. I made partner of my firm. It's what I've worked so hard for. What I've wanted for years and I did it. Finally.

A smile spreads across my face as I switch off my computer for the day. But I'm not heading home. No. I never head home. Why? For what? No one's there. That's why I made partner. Because I have nothing else in my life worth doing.

Work. That's it. For the last five years that is all my life has been. I'm ok with it now. I've gotten used to the loneliness. I mean, it's all my fault so I have to be ok with it.

I have my books now. They keep me happy. I don't need anything else. Not anymore.

Not since I lost Nick.

He was my life. My husband. My everything.

But not anymore.

I head to the gym, like I do every night. I'm not a gym rat by any means though. I keep to myself and stay on one machine, the bicycle.

I only come here to read. Spending a few hours on the bike, peddling at a not-so-fast speed so I don't wear myself out but fast enough so I don't draw attention to myself. Though I could care less what people think of me. Not anymore.

I look at this as my happy place, a place where I can escape. Live my life through the characters of my stories. They make my life not so desolate and make me smile, which I tend not to do much of anymore.

That's my life, a whole bunch of *anymores*.

I spot my normal machine, the one back in the corner, alone, where no one will walk by or bother me. Settling in, I pick up my Kindle and switch on the book I just downloaded.

It's a dang good thing eBooks were invented. I read a book about every two days and I would be spending a small fortune on hardbacks if eBooks weren't around.

My favorite part about them is that I can hide what I'm reading. If I actually had to hold the book, showing its cover in my hand, I would be mortified. I don't want people seeing what kind of books I like to read. I'm not a prude by any means, but I'm a little shy when it comes to sharing what kind of books I prefer, for me, the dirtier the better. Give me a good Contemporary Romance or Erotic novel and I'm in heaven.

I don't know why because I have no one to share my excitement with when I get really turned on but that's another reason why I read at the gym. It's weird but I almost like the fact that I get so aroused with people around. It's the closest I'll get to living out my fantasies.

My new book is not disappointing my needs as I set in for my nightly read, um, I mean workout.

A girl I've seen here many times comes up quickly and sits right next to me. I try to stay focused on my book, not paying attention to her but she seems set on interrupting me.

"What cha reading?" she asks, leaning in a little too close.

I look at her and smile, not trying to be rude but I don't want to admit what I'm reading. The title alone would give it away. I reply, "*Bared,*" thinking quickly of a title that is less telling, hoping she'll get the hint by my one word response that I'm not in the mood to talk.

I was wrong.

"Oh, by Stacey Kennedy? I love that book!" she smiles big at me.

I look over and give her a small smile, sighing. Figures she would know that book.

"How far are you? I don't want to give anything away. I knew you were reading books like that though. I just knew it," she bounces slightly in her seat with excitement and I can tell this is a very normal thing for her to be doing.

I eye her skeptically. "How did you know what kind of books I was reading?"

"I could just tell. I see you in here every night. Always on this bike and you have this glow about you. You smile on and off but more telling, I see a flush on your face that I knew wasn't from the bike. I knew it had to be something more…" She leans in, whispering, "sexual."

I look at her, trying to hide my shock but her laughter shows I didn't do a very good job.

"I'm sorry. Too forward? I can be that way," she shrugs. "I'm not ashamed of it. If you like sex, or like to read about sex, then own it. It's fun. Everyone should love it and speak freely about how amazing it can be."

She's smiling from ear to ear and I'm a little jealous that she can be so open, so free about sex.

I've never been open on the subject. Not even with Nick. We had an amazing sex life but I was always afraid to share with him what I really wanted.

My fantasies...

I tried to hint to the fact but I guess it was never enough.

Now it's too late.

I sit silently, not sure what to say.

She smiles, "So what other books have you read? You know Stacey wrote an entire series of Club Sin right?"

I smile, yes I know all about the series, they're my favorite. "Yes, I've actually read them all. *Bared* is my favorite. I lied, too. Sorry. I'm actually reading *Touch Me*." I pause, feeling my face flush, as I'm suddenly very embarrassed.

She must not have noticed my disdain because she acts like it's nothing, "Who's that one by?"

"Olivia Cunning, it's in her *One Night With Sole Regret* series."

"Oh yes, I loved those. Who's your favorite?"

"I love Shade. I can't wait for her to finish the series so I can hear more about him."

"Yeah, I liked his story. It was sweet with his daughter and all, but man, Gabe and those toys got me. Or wait, which one is in the sex club?"

"That's this one with Owen."

"Oh, just wait. You know places like that actually exist right?"

I look at her surprised at first but as the idea sinks in I start to smile, "Really?"

"Of course they do! Everything in every book you have ever read actually exists. Where do you think these authors get their info, their muse per se?"

"I guess I've never really thought about it. This is all just a fantasy world to me." I regret the comment as soon as I make it.

She smiles a knowing smile, "Fantasy, huh?" She winks at me.

What the hell am I doing? I don't even know this girl and here I am sharing my book fantasies with her.

She senses my discomfort and thankfully changes the subject, but to my second least favorite subject, me.

"So, tell me about yourself. What do you do besides sit here and read every night, pretending to workout?" she smirks.

I reach over, my manners and professionalism getting the best of me, so I offer to shake her hand in greeting, "I'm Kamii. And you are?"

She grabs my hand softly saying, "I'm Becca."

"Hi Becca. I'm a criminal defense attorney here in the City. How about you?"

"Wow. That must be crazy. You must hear some pretty crazy stories. Have you ever defended someone you knew was guilty?"

I give her a squinted don't-ask-me-that look that she reads clearly and moves on. "I'm a cosmetologist," she shrugs. "I do hair," she says with a big smile on her face. "I love it. I get to chat all day long with some of my closest friends while making them look pretty."

I can totally see her doing that for a living and I bet she's good at it if her own hair is any sign of her quality. Even though she's at the gym working out, it still looks stylish the way her blond hair is pulled up in a messy bun with a thin black headband wrapped around her head, plumping the front up just a bit instead of slicking it back. She has a body to die for and her beautiful, soft complexion makes me jealous that she can look so natural yet stunning.

"So where's the salon you work at?" I ask just because I can tell she's not leaving anytime soon and I have no clue what else to say. I still don't know why she's even talking to me.

"It's a great place not far from here. Right next to the Transamerica building."

"Really?" I look at her surprised. "I work in that building."

"You do? What a coincidence. You should come in. I can do anything you want."

I stop the bike and think, running my fingers over my hair that's pulled back in my standard bun. It has been awhile since I've treated myself to an actual stylist. My hair is long, straight and I just trim the bottom on my own. Sad, I know. Maybe I should do something new.

"Maybe I'll do that. Do you have a card on you?"

She laughs, looking down at her skimpy, leave nothing to the imagination, workout outfit. "Um, no, not on me. Here," she grabs my phone sitting in the cup holder and puts her contact info in then I hear her phone ding that's attached to her arm acting as her iPod. "There, now you have mine and I have yours."

I smile. *What just happened? Did I just make a friend?*

I don't have friends, but here this girl is programming her number and wanting mine in return…? Why?

"Ok, I'll let you get back to the book. You better call. Enjoy Owen!" She winks as she walks away just as fast as she arrived.

The person reflecting back at me in the mirror the next morning is a mere existence of who I used to be. I'm so plain now. I hardly wear any make-up. My hair is a dull, light brown color that lays flat and lifeless. If I leave it down, no matter what I do it will part down the middle, falling straight down to my mid waist. Sighing, I pull it up into my standard slick bun and spray down any strays.

I have on my same boring pantsuit that hangs on my body, and not in a flattering way. I've lost weight over the past few years but haven't bothered to buy new clothes. Why? I have no one to impress.

I look at my phone and wonder if I should call Becca. Maybe I do need a makeover. I should treat myself as my reward for making Partner at the firm. I know Nick would say I deserve it. Although, sometimes I wonder, would I have made partner if he were still alive? Would I have worked this hard if I had him to come home to?

I push the idea aside. No reason to dwell over something I will never know the answer to and can never change. This is my life now.

As I walk into work, I peek into the salon that Becca works at. Hoping to catch a glimpse of her.

Someone walking up startles me when I hear her say with the most cheerful voice, "You spying on me?"

I turn around, trying to hide the blush that's creeping up my face since I was caught but she blows it off. "Morning," I say, rubbing my hand on top of my head, looking down, ashamed of my looks compared to her.

My palms start to sweat and an uneasy feeling swarms my stomach as I look at her, this gorgeous pin up girl with perfect makeup, an outfit that's fashionable, sexy yet not slutty, and hair that's to die for. I don't know why I even bothered looking in. This girl is so far out of my league, even just as a friend.

"Morning," she says bright and bubbly. "Hey, my 9 am just cancelled on me. Why don't you come in and take her spot?"

I look down, thinking about my day. I have nothing planned. My caseload is actually pretty light right now as I switch everything over to being Partner. Shrugging, I give her a shy smile, saying, "Sure, why not."

"Great! Follow me chica." Her bubbly personality is contagious and I can't help the smile that spreads across my face as I follow her through the door.

We walk into the opulent salon that has pearly white tiles covering the floor of the huge open room with stations in every corner. Tall teal flowers sit in crystal vases in between every station and huge ornate mirrors sit in front of every chair. Trying to act like I belong in a place like this is much harder than I thought when I was just looking in.

To say I feel like a fish out of water is an understatement. Only beautiful women who actually care about their appearance and have men falling all over them come to places like this.

Once I sit down in her chair, I'm instantly reminded of why I never want to get my hair done. I hate sitting in front of a mirror, staring at myself for an hour. It's so uncomfortable and I'm just reminded of the ghost of a person I used to be.

Becca hands me a luxurious white robe and points to a curtain, "You can change in there."

I look down at the robe, rubbing my hand over the softness, "Wow… really…?" I say, confused by the thought of changing.

"Yes, sweetie, we're in a very high-end spa in downtown San Francisco. We want you to be pampered in everyway possible. Can I get you a glass of champagne as well?"

"Um, no, not on a workday. Thank you though."

I come out of the small changing area, glad, actually, to be out of my boring suit jacket, feeling like I'm more on her playing field even though I'm in a robe. I sit in her chair and she wraps the drape around me before taking my hair out of the bun and running her fingers through the length of it.

"Man, you have some hair. How come you wear it in a bun everyday?"

I shrug, "I don't know. I never know what to do with it. It's always so blah, so I just pull it up."

"Do you have anything in mind or can I work my magic?"

Oh God, what does she want to do? "I don't know. I'm not sure I can pull anything else off."

"Stop, yes you can! And I'm the person to do it. Do you have time? I want to put some color on you."

I take a deep breath. I can't believe I'm going to let this girl I barely know *do her magic* on me but here goes nothing. "I guess. Do what you want."

She jumps up and down like an excited school girl, "Oh goodie! I love projects."

Projects? Really? So now I'm someone's project? What have I gotten myself into?

My fear disappears as she washes my hair, only because I'm in pure heaven. The seat has a footrest so I'm almost lying flat as she works her nails through my hair, massaging my scalp.

Yes, I definitely needed to treat myself.

I spend the next two hours in her chair. She cuts, foils and washes my hair again, all while we talk non-stop. I forgot how much fun it is to have simple girl talk where we talk about everything but yet nothing really important. I haven't felt this relaxed since before Nick died and I must say, it's nice.

Any conversations I've had over the last five years have been very deep, meaningful, world politics types of conversations with the men in my office but with Becca I don't feel pressured into these heavy topics. I can tell she's all about keeping things light and it's a refreshing change of pace from my day to day.

She's stayed away from personal questions, which has made me even more relaxed. Our topics of conversations have been books, celebrities and crazy things we've seen people do around the City, which believe me; I could go on for days about. My cheeks hurt from laughing so hard.

She's almost finished and is putting on the final touches of her styling techniques. I told her I don't do hair so whatever she does it better not take any talent for me to duplicate because it's not happening. She laughed at my statement but I was dead serious.

I'm facing away from the mirror because she didn't want to ruin the surprise and just when I think I'm getting a preview of the new me, she grabs my hand, pulling me up out of my chair.

"Ok, now we need make-up," she squeals like a giddy little girl again.

Before I can protest, I'm sitting in another chair with every color of foundation, eye shadow, and things I have no clue even what they are for, in front of me. I'm so overwhelmed I don't even know where to start.

"Don't freak out. I won't over do it. Just a little of everything," she winks. "Bring out your eyes, soften your skin tone and bring out your fuck me lips."

I snort at her words. She laughs and smiles as she explains, "Sorry. I told you I was forward. You'll learn to love it about me. It's true though. You have the most perfect DSLs. I'm sure guys go crazy over them."

I squint my eyebrows, having no clue what she just said, making her laugh out loud.

"D.S.L.… Dick Sucking Lips," she smirks.

"Oh my God, that's hilarious but no, believe me, no guys go crazy over my *DSLs* as you say."

"Girl, you just aren't going to the right places then. Just wait till you see my work. Guys will be tripping all over you from now on."

"Thanks but I doubt it. Besides, I don't go out."

"Well, now you do. Me and you, tonight." I start to protest and she stops me, "No, I won't take no for an answer. I've never been so proud of my work and I want to show it off. You're like a living masterpiece of mine," she says proudly.

Great. How can I turn that down? Sighing, I give in, "Ok, but I have nothing to wear."

"No worries, you'll borrow something of mine and you and I will have a shopping date this weekend."

I'm so confused. Why is she being so nice to me? I understand her wanting to give me a makeover. She's just a good sales person who wants repeat clients but now she wants to hang out and let me borrow her clothes? No one is that nice for no reason.

Are they?

"Can I ask you something?" She looks up from the counter, her eyes giving me permission. "Why are you doing this? Being so nice to me?"

She shrugs, "I don't know. I could just tell you were a nice person and that we would be into the same things." She pauses, pursing her lips together, "Books and all."

I get the feeling there's something more she's not saying but I don't want to push the issue. I'm just happy to have a friend again.

After Nick passed I pushed everyone away, even my family who lives on the east coast. I couldn't look or talk to anyone without being reminded of him. Over the years everyone gave up on contacting me. Besides a call here and there from my parents, I'm extremely alone. Though my life can be lonely sometimes, I was never outgoing enough to try to meet new people.

Applying the last coat of lipstick, she steps back to admire what she called her living masterpiece. Smiling, she finally lets me get up and walks me to the mirror where I see myself for the first time.

She sits back, letting me soak it all in silence before stepping up, playing with my hair, explaining, "It's a balayage color melt. I put these sun kissed strands to highlight around your face. The deep rich roots will gradually fade to light golden ends so you don't have to come in here every few months to keep it up. It's a maintenance free, yet fun, hair color."

I can't speak. I'm still trying to figure out the person reflecting back at me. I reach for my hair, that sits just at my shoulders now, to make sure this isn't a trick and it really is me.

"So...?" Becca's bouncing up and down waiting for my reply. "Do you love it or what?"

"Becca, I'm shocked. I can't believe it's me."

"I know. You're fucking hot!"

I laugh, shaking my head. I guess I am getting used to her forwardness. I lean over and hug her. "I love it. You really did a great job."

"Yay! I'm so glad you like it!"

She goes over styling tips and I purchase some hair products and makeup from her before we set up a time and place to meet tonight before I head for my office. The thought of putting back on my boring suit jacket felt like it would ruin the little high I have going on so I keep it off, only wearing the silk top I have on underneath that normally only shows a tiny bit in the front.

While nervously tugging on my bottom lip, I wait in the elevator to go up to the 11th floor that my firm is on when a tall man walks in. Instantly, I drop my hand from my lip and give him a shy smile hello before looking back down to the ground. He's in his late thirties and when I look up I actually catch him checking me out.

Me!

He's checking *me* out!

He winks and I give him a shy smile again before the doors open and I step off the elevator.

As the door closes I hear him say, "Hope to get stuck with you in the elevator soon."

I get the feeling he was talking about more than just an elevator ride and I clench my thighs together at the thought of being pressed up against the wall of the elevator like some of my favorite scenes in my books.

A small smile creeps up my face as I walk past reception to head toward my office. Stefanie, our receptionist, jumps from her chair, "Excuse me ma'am. You can't go..." she stops once she sees it's me. "Kamii? Wow! Is that you? You, you look amazing!"

I beam from ear to ear, "Yes, it's me. Thank you. A girl at the salon below us had a field day with me. I say she did a pretty good job."

"She did an amazing job. You look gorgeous. I'm so glad to see that smile on your face, too."

I sigh with a heavy heart. She's right. I should smile more often. Stefanie knew me before I lost Nick so she knows more than anyone how much I've changed over the years.

"Thank you, Stef." I turn to walk to my office with a new look and a new attitude on life. From this point on I promise to be different. Or at least try my hardest to be...

Chapter TWO

Preston

I'm just putting the finishing touches on the place when my phone rings and I see it's Becca calling.

"Hey," I answer.

"Hello there. How's the place coming?"

"Almost finished. Just hung the last of the sconces and am about to clean everything up. How's your day going?"

"Great, actually. Remember the girl I told you about that I think has potential for becoming a member? Well, she came to see me today. You should see the makeover I gave her. I'm a genius if I don't say so myself."

I lean over and start putting away my tools. "I'm sure you did great but remember, I don't want to know what she looks like. All I care about is if she's going to join."

"No, I haven't put everything out there yet. I'm taking her out tonight. She needs to break through her shell first. I know there's a crazy sex kitten deep inside though. I just feel it."

An introvert? I raise my hand and rub my forehead. I know many of the members will enjoy the variety, but while many find the shy types sexy as hell, I can't help but be wary. I know what kind of darkness could lie on the other side. Shit, I'm the one living it. I don't want to be friends. I don't want to hang out. I'm here to get my release then go on with my life.

"Ok, well, when she's ready to join let me know."

"Sure. I'd invite you to go with us tonight but that whole no personal contact, names, or faces thing kind of gets in the way of you just hanging out with us. But hey, those are your rules, not mine."

Her zealous tone reminds me why I'm moving forward with this. People don't understand why I don't want any personal connection. This is the world I've been craving. It's been almost a year since Kim died, and for the first time I'm finally feeling like me again. Well, a soulless version of me.

I don't want to date anyone. My wife was my everything and even though I wanted to explore a more sexual lifestyle, I still wanted to be with her. I made a vow to her and I don't plan on breaking it. I know that doesn't make sense, especially since I want to fuck other people, but I don't want to give my heart to anyone else. To me, that's a big difference.

"Damn right those are the rules. Makes it more fun not knowing doesn't it?" I lie, making her think it's more for fun than why I'm really doing it.

"Fine…" Knowing Becca, she's rolling her eyes like a junior high schooler, skirt, knee socks and all. "Yes it does. I just have to give you shit sometimes. You know I'm already on board."

"Ok, well have fun tonight and keep me posted."

"Will do. See ya."

After hanging up the phone, I look around the warehouse behind my newest show room. It used to sit empty but I talked the landlord into leasing it to me for super cheap, told him I needed the extra storage.

There's only a small side door down a back alley as the entrance so no one would ever want to rent it but for every reason they didn't want it, is the exact reason I did.

It's secluded.

My employees who run the showroom floor for our custom built homes and restoration projects will never know it's back here, and any new members of our private club would never put the two businesses being owned by the same people.

It's perfect.

Becca is one of the very few people who know I'm behind the entire place. Everything is a secret and that's the main point.

People who just want to live loosely, find their release, indulge in whatever kink they're into, but in a safe environment, will come here, but with one rule: No identities. Everyone will wear masks to cover their faces and all names will be fictional.

I want to provide a fun, safe place so anyone interested in coming here has to become a member and sign a code of conduct along with submitting fingerprints, background checks and most importantly, STD tests. So yes, it's not 100% anonymous but very close to it.

To get it started, I went to a few clubs wearing my mask and hand picked a few people, Becca being one of them. She was so interested in helping me that I added her on as my partner, well kind of. Though she's not legally responsible, like I am.

So far things are going well and we have thirty members.

We'll only be open Thursday, Friday and Saturday nights with each night focusing on a different kind of kink. There are tons of sex clubs and BDSM clubs around but not one place that caters to everyone. I'm hoping this will be the place to bridge that gap.

Since I'm a contractor by trade, I've created the best, most cohesive space that will work for all nights, with moveable walls to create the space and mood for that particular night.

Thursday nights will be for our couples who are looking to swing or welcome new people into their lives. I've created a cocktail area in the middle of the place with closed off rooms along the edges for people to have fun but in a more private setting. In front of these rooms will be couches for people who like to watch as other people fuck. We will offer a full bar with a two drink limit.

Friday night will be a complete BDSM club with spanking benches, crosses and every whip, cane or flogger anyone could ever want. The walls are removed so the place is one big open room. There will be certain sections set up with couches in front for people to enjoy the scenes. On Fridays the bar will be closed to ensure that everyone is in their right state of mind.

Saturday will be a mixture of both. The room will go back to the center cocktail area with the same two-limit rule on cocktails. Whatever kink the members want is accepted but only light BDSM play will be allowed.

And there you have it, hopefully something for everyone.

I just hope it's what *I* need.

I've been lost since Kim took her life and no matter what I did to ignore it, I still had these needs that I couldn't fight anymore. Forget ever wanting a relationship with another woman. I've already had my forever.

I tried going to other clubs just for my release but once I laid eyes on the woman I was having sex with, it would feel like my heart was being ripped out. As one desire was being met, another was tearing me apart inside and the loss of Kim became even stronger in my heart, making me leave the club in a bigger bundle of nerves than when I arrived.

My life was turning into a slow, downward spiral, hell. This place is my last hope. I need to move on, or at least move on with the part of my life that I can actually change.

After I finish cleaning up, I walk into Rickhouse located on Kearny Street downtown. It's the only bar I'll go to and as I enter, I scan the room to make sure no one I know is here. Like I said, I don't want to hang out or be friends with anyone. I just want a drink.

Becca catches my eye sitting across the room and frustration seeps through my veins. I can see that she's sitting with someone but thankfully my view is blocked to see who, so I quickly turn to walk out.

I don't want to see this woman she's trying to bring into my club. Figures, that she would bring her here. I swear sometimes she just likes messing with me for fun. If she knew exactly why I didn't want to see this, or any woman I'm going to be fucking, she would understand but I don't share my past with anyone.

That's why it's called the past. It's over. Not a damn thing you can do about it but try to forget.

Just as I get to the door a buddy of mine walks in, obviously celebrating something.

"Hey, Preston! My man. So glad you're here," he reaches up, giving me a high five.

"Kevin, sorry, I was actually just heading out."

I met Kevin at another club and we got to talking about the house he just bought and him needing a contractor. I never thought a sex club would bring me business but I'm happy to say we just finished his job and it's an amazing new place for him to start his new life. Alone. If only he knew exactly what that actually means.

He seemed like a cool guy so I invited him to be a member of my club, making him and Becca the only two members who know my real identity.

"No way, shots are on me tonight! I just got word that my divorce is finally final and I'm ready to get fucked up and go to my *new* home with a pretty little thing so I can pretend that part of my life never happened."

"Well, congrats, I think, but sorry, I've got to go."

"Oh no, did you hear me? The bitch is finally out of my life, for good." He puts his arm around my neck, dragging me back to the bar. "We're getting fucked up tonight and you're the perfect wing man."

I don't bother fighting this losing battle as he walks me toward the bar that stands like a big square in the middle of the room. He walks to an open area with two seats and that's when I see her, only from the side but that's already too much.

I'm trying to listen to my friend go on and on about his divorce and how much he hated his ex-wife but my line of vision is straight on them and my eyes keep drifting to her, no matter how hard I try not to.

Becca wasn't lying. She really did work her magic. I have no clue what this woman looked like before but I know now that she is absolutely gorgeous.

She seems to be having a good time with Becca. Her shoulders are relaxed, she doesn't appear to have any nervous telltale signs and she's laughing at everything her and Becca are discussing.

An hour in and six shots later, I'm in a playful mood and my worries of seeing or meeting her seems to melt away. A light and free feeling fills my body for the first time in awhile. Maybe that's all I needed… a lot of alcohol to calm my nerves and forget my troubles.

I feel like fucking with Becca so I walk over, pretending I don't know her.

"Hello ladies. How are we doing tonight?" I say in a flirtatious, drunk tone.

Becca looks up to say something but I wink at her while reaching out my hand saying, "I'm Preston, and you are?"

She smirks, catching on to my game, "Well, hello to you. I'm Becca and this is my friend Kamii."

I turn to face her more and I stop in my tracks when she looks up from her drink and gives me a shy smile. I knew she was pretty but those eyes about do me in.

Oh, this is a bad idea. What the hell am I doing?

Instantly, I sober up and remember why I'm having the mask rule. Her eyes, they pierce right into my soul and I feel my cock twitch in response. I'm staring at her like an idiot when she finally says hello, reaching out her hand to shake mine.

Kamii

Wow. This guy is hot! He's tall with broad shoulders and a dark complexion. There's light stubble on his face making his beard sexy and not overdone on his defined jaw line. His black dress shirt is folded and rolled up at the arms and his dark jeans make his outfit sexy and not like he just left the office.

I'm reaching out my hand but he has yet to grab it, instead piercing, clear blue eyes are fixed on me like they're trying to read my soul. His look is sultry, demanding yet comforting.

I'm reminded of every book I've read about male dominants and I can only imagine the stare they talk about is the same one I'm getting right now.

I feel my panties moisten instantly from the thought as my skin flushes and my spine tingles. When he finally grabs my hand I want to melt, right here into a bed of wet hot sex.

Holy schmoly!

"Hi," he says as he grabs my hand, not shaking it but lightly rubbing his thumb over my heated flesh before he lets go, closing his fist and slowly exhaling.

Goddamn, what just happened?

I bring my fingers up to my mouth where I lightly tug on my bottom lip as I look down at my outfit, running my other hand down the black short skirt that Becca insisted I wear when she showed up at my apartment with it in her hand. I'm so self-conscious in it, especially right now.

I hear him clear his throat lightly and I look up, letting go of my lip when he reaches for my hand again, bringing it up to his lips whispering, "It was nice to meet you, Kamii."

Without saying another word, he releases my hand and turns to walk away. I watch him walk straight to the door and leave without talking to anyone else. My mouth's slightly open in shock as I stare at the closed door behind him.

Becca's laugh takes me out of my dreamland, "Yeah, you like?"

I shake my head, "What was that? I know I'm out of the whole dating scene but what the hell just happened?"

She laughs, "Who knows with men. He was into you though."

I look up, surprised, "You think?"

"Hell yeah, I think! The way he looked at you. Hot damn!"

"God, yes. I felt that..."

"In your pussy?" she interrupts.

"*What*? Um… No… Did you really just say," I lean in to whisper, "the p word?"

She throws her head back laughing, "Yes, I did. Pussy, pussy, pussy. And I bet yours is wet right now."

I put up my hands, waving them in defeat, "Ok, ok. I get it."

"Then admit it. I saw that fuck-me-now look he was giving you. And you were giving it right back to him."

"Ok, fine. Yes, I'm… wet," I whisper which makes her laugh even more.

"Girl, own it. Talk about it. Be it. Fucking is awesome! Don't deny it."

"I know. I won't deny it but it's been awhile so let me get back in the swing of things before I start talking about my," I lean in again, whispering, "pussy being wet."

She claps her hands together in celebration, "Yeah, that's my girl!"

I can't help but laugh. "But explain to me, why did he just turn and walk away? I really have no clue how this is supposed to work."

"Who knows? Maybe he's a hopeless romantic and believes if it's meant to be he'll see you again," she says flipping her hand through the air dismissively as she takes a sip of her drink through the little black straw.

I pick up a nut from the basket in front of us and throw it at her, "Now you're totally fucking with me."

"Hey now, look who just cussed! Am I rubbing off on you?"

I smile, picking up my drink, holding it up, "Well, I guess you are. Cheers to that."

We tap drinks then she says, "Ok good, because there is something I want to talk to you about."

Oh God, what now? Does she want free legal advice? Is this why she's been so nice to me? Here I thought I made a friend...

I sigh, totally deflated when she says, "How open are you, sexually...?"

Whoa, so not what I thought would come out of her mouth.

Since I'm just happy it wasn't a legal question, I answer, truthfully, "Well, it's been awhile, so unless things have changed, I would say I'm pretty open," I pause. "I'm not a lesbian though."

"Don't worry," she crosses her hands in front of her, laughing, "neither am I so that's not where I was going with this. What if I said I could introduce you to a world that you only read about in your books?"

I have to admit, I'm intrigued. I've had many dreams about living out scenes in some of the books that I've read, "I guess I'd have to say tell me more," I smirk at her.

"Yes! I knew it. I knew there was a sex kitten inside that little body of yours."

"Ok, don't get carried away. I said tell me more. Not take me away right now."

She laughs, "Ok, so what if I told you I belong to a private sex club and we're looking to bring in new members."

"Wait, what?" I ask totally shocked to hear that she not only is a member of a sex club but she's actually inviting me?

"You heard me. You can bring all those book fantasies to life and more."

"How? I mean where? I mean who?" *Is she kidding me right now? Could this really be happening?*

"Ok, don't freak out on me now. That guy," she pauses, tilting her head to the door, "there are guys just like that guy there. All hot as hell and offering you things you only imagined in your dreams."

"Is it safe?"

"Yes, actually, this new place is going above and beyond to make sure it's safe. Everyone has to sign a code of conduct, a background check and take a STD test."

"Ok, but is it safe, like word wise?"

This time she picks up a nut and throws it at me. "Yes, it's a safeword type of place but there's more to it. It fits whatever kind of kink you're into, depends on the night you go. Not just BDSM every night. It will be the best time of your life. Trust me."

"How long have you done this?" is all I could think to ask.

"A few years now."

"And..."

"And what? I love it. Believe me, I don't share this lifestyle with everyone, only a selected few," she winks.

I'm so overwhelmed. Never, ever did I think I would be having a conversation like this. There are so many things running through my mind. Every time I wondered if I would have the nerve to join a club if I had an opportunity and here it is, right in front of me. Then the thought hits me like a stab to my heart, "But I don't have a guy to go with. How does that work?"

"Oh, don't you worry about that. With your hot little body guys will be lining up to play with you. There's one catch with this place though."

There it is. *I knew this was too good to be true.* Wait, did I really just think that? Wow, could I really do this?

I shake my head, focusing on this little catch first. "Oh God, what?"

"It's all anonymous."

"Ok, what do you mean? I can't use my real name?"

"No, and you have to wear a mask covering your eyes, like you're going to a masquerade ball or something."

"Why? Wait, so you don't know who you're, um, playing with?" Is she serious right now?

"No, you don't. It adds to the fun of it. Everyone is there for the same reason, to get off. This way it takes all the drama, real life shit away from it."

"Oh, I don't know. I don't know if I can have sex with someone when I have no idea who they really are."

"I get it. I do, really. But just come with me. You'll see what really goes on and I bet you change your mind."

"What? I can just come and, um, watch?" The thought alone makes my chest tight with excitement.

"You know you want to," she smirks. "Place opens tomorrow night. Say you'll come with me?"

I can do that. Just watch. Shoot, that will fulfill enough of my fantasies to hold me over for a long time. I shake my head up and down, "Ok, I'll come with you. Just to watch, though."

"Uh huh, and sign up by the time you leave," she winks.

Chapter THREE

Kamii

Just breathe. *In through my nose, out through my mouth.*

I can't believe I'm doing this. I'm going to a sex club. Me. This is crazy.

I look at the reflection in my mirror and see a completely different person staring back at me. Becca and I met today to go shopping at Union Square. I bought clothes I've only dreamed about wearing but never thought I would have the chance.

I have on a sexy little black dress that comes up around my neck and has capped sleeves. The dress is tight around my waist then flows out with a little sheer lining at the bottom, giving a little peak-a-boo from under the end of the short skirt.

I also bought the sexiest lingerie I've ever seen though I don't dare have it on. The bra and panties are black with lace and a garter belt that's hooked up to stockings that run up my thigh with a black line running down the back of my leg where I would wear a stiletto heel with them.

Really, Becca made me buy it, though I'm not sure exactly why since I'm not a member and have no idea if I will actually become one.

I stare at the bag lying on my bed and think about the last time I had lingerie on. I was with Nick…

"Come here gorgeous," Nick says with nothing but sex in his eyes and his tone.

I stare at him, naked on our bed. It's official. I'm Mrs. Nick Schafer. I wore sweet, innocent but sexy, lingerie under my wedding dress. I just slipped the dress off and now I'm standing here, giving myself to him as his wife.

I walk toward him and he takes me by surprise, pulling my hand down to him and flipping me around so I'm lying on my back with him partially on top of me.

He takes his fingers, starting at my face and sliding them down my neck, over my stomach and down to my mound. He hasn't taken his eyes off of mine and I melt at his expression.

I love him more than anything in the whole world and he just stood up, in front of everyone we know and said he would love me for the rest of my life. Could life get any better?

He starts to run his fingers up and down my slit, teasing me through my panties and I realize yes, life is about to get that much better.

I grab my chest and sit down on my bed. It's been awhile since I've thought about Nick that intensely and now I can't breathe. I vowed I would love only him, for the rest of my life. Now here I am going to a sex club. Without him. What the heck am I doing?

There's a knock at my door and I know it's Becca.

Shoot. I can't do this. What am I going to say to her?

I answer the door and she reads it all over my face.

"Oh no, girl. You're not backing out on me. Look at yourself. You're hot! Guys will be all over you and you'll break their hearts when they realize you're just there to watch and you aren't a member yet."

I'm reminded of my own broken heart but I don't dare go there again. I've already relived too much for one night, so I keep it to myself. "I'm just not sure. This is all just nuts."

"Yes, nuts, balls, cocks, whips, chains," she leans in smiling, "and wet pussies. It will all be there. Come on, you're just watching. No harm, no foul, right?"

She has a point and I have to admit, I felt a twitch in between my legs when she said the wet p word. I may be a widow but I still have needs. Needs that my rabbit vibrator are just not serving any more.

I shake my head in agreement and she jumps up and down, "Great. Now where's your mask and purse before you change your mind again?"

We drive for a few minutes and after she parks we head toward a dark alley.

"Wait… Now this is really crazy. Don't you know to stay away from dark alleys? Where are you taking me?" I was worried before but now I'm terrified. Everyone knows you don't go down dark allies in any big city.

"It's ok, it's just down a little ways. There's a bouncer standing at the door so I promise we're safe. Now put on your mask."

Taking a deep breath, I feel my hands start to shake and I can't remember the last time I was so nervous and anxious at the same time. I grab my mask and slide it down my face. It's soft and flexible against my skin, forming perfectly to my face.

I went with a black mask with an intricate design. It reminds me of the Hindu culture and henna designs, which I've always thought were very beautiful.

Tight swirls design the mask that covers half of my face, only leaving pointy, cat-like openings for my eyes and coming to a low point that slightly hangs off the tip of my nose. The top rides high above my eyes then dips low in the middle of my forehead before meeting in the middle with a crown like display that grows up my forehead.

Having the mask on helps settle my nerves tremendously and I'm suddenly very thankful for what I thought was a very crazy rule. Wearing this mask almost makes me feel invincible. Like I'm not even me, the woman who already gave her heart to the only man she'll ever love. Now, I feel like I can be anyone I want to be, even the craziest characters in my favorite books seem possible.

The thought excites me more.

We come across a bouncer who stands tall, wearing a suit and a plain black mask. Becca smiles sweetly, "Hello sexy, I'm Baubo and this is my friend Eurydice."

We had to pick "code" names and when I suggested using Greek Goddess names Becca was totally on board. When we googled for suggestions Baubo fit Becca to a T since Baubo is the humorously indecent Goddess who lifted her skirt in front of the Greek God Demeter.

Eurydice was a simple one for me to choose because it's referenced in one of my favorite books, *The Edge of Never*, so it's perfect for reliving my own book fantasies. Eurydice was the wife of Orpheus and after Eurydice unexpectedly died Orpheus played beautiful music, which allowed him to work his way into the underworld to bring her back to life. I know that is how Nick loved me and if I could play music to bring him back, I would in a heartbeat.

Music was our passion together. Now that passion is gone.

The bouncer finds our names on the list and opens the door, allowing us to enter a dark hallway. I hear people talking in the distance and we follow the sounds. My heart is racing and my chest is so tight, I'm having trouble breathing.

Becca turns around to me, grabbing my hand, saying, "Just breathe. This is your fantasy, remember?"

I do remember, and I envision myself as one of the heroines the first time they encountered their new sexual destiny. I try to really zone in on that thought and focus on what I'm about to see.

I turn the corner and it's exactly what I envisioned a sex club to look like. The walls are painted black with black leather couches placed strategically throughout the room. There are areas set up with some walls in between sections but you can clearly see each zone set up like a scene for whatever sex wants to go on there.

I feel like I've died and fell into every sex club book I've ever read.

The room is lit with wall sconces and dim lighting overhead. To my right, I see a fancy bar with every drink option you can imagine. "You can drink in here?" I ask in surprise as I grab Becca's arm.

"Yeah, but only a two drink limit. Just enough to calm any nerves and get you more in the mood." She looks at me smiling, "You look like you could use a drink."

I nod, "Nothing sounds better right now."

"Nothing?" she smirks at me.

I laugh, hitting her arm, "I'm watching tonight, remember?"

"Yes, I hope you remember that, too. Unfortunately you haven't filled out your membership info yet so even if you wanted to, you can't. Sorry girl," she taunts.

"Don't worry. I know it won't be a problem tonight."

"Uh-huh, we'll see."

We walk to the bar where she orders two shots of tequila.

"Oh, no, I can't do shots," I protest.

"Come on, you only get two drinks. You need to loosen up. Just this one shot then you can get something you would normally drink."

I shrug, giving into Becca yet once again. This is turning into a trend between the two of us. It's amazing what this woman has gotten me to do in the very short time I have known her.

She hands me the shot and I go to take it when she stops me. "Um, hello! We're in a sex club for God's sake. Put on a little bit of a show for the men. You may not get fucked tonight but I fully intend to."

I laugh, not sure what she has in mind but knowing I don't really have a choice.

She takes the lime, places it in my mouth backwards so the fruit is facing her and slowly tilts my head to the side. Licking me slightly before she pulls back and sprinkles salt on my neck.

I stay, completely still, mesmerized by her motions and the way it felt when she licked my neck. We catch eyes and she winks as she leans in, licking the salt off my neck while moving her hand up my body, gripping my breast and holding on while she takes the shot with her other hand, throwing it behind me and then pulling me close, sucking the lime out of my mouth while grinding herself against my body.

I'm not a lesbian, by any means. I like dick, shoot I need dick, or at least my vibrator, which is the only form of dick I've had since Nick passed, but goddamn that was hot.

She pulls away from me and I have to admit, I'm sad she did.

She gives me a small smirk before I hear a man approach her from behind.

"I see we're getting the party started off right," he says in the most manly, deep, sensual voice.

I'm still in a haze from her kiss. *Wait, did I just say her kiss? Holy schmoly!*

I shake my head, opening my eyes wide and that's when I see him. He's tall with broad shoulders and he's wearing a thin, black mask that wraps perfectly around his face, making his eyes nearly invisible. He has on dark designer jeans and a thin, dark blue button up shirt with the sleeves rolled up to his elbows.

Becca smiles at him, placing her hand on his chest saying, "Well, hello there. This is my friend, Eurydice. Eurydice I'd like you to meet."

He interrupts her, holding his hand out to meet mine, "Eros."

I smile, "Eros huh? That's fitting."

"And why do you say that?" he responds, lightly rubbing my hand.

"Eros is the Greek God of sexual desire."

He tilts his head slowly up and down. "Why yes he is."

"So are you just arrogant or can you prove your names worth?"

Becca looks at me, giving me a look that I know means she's proud of me. Shoot, I'm proud of me. It's this mask. I feel like I can be anyone I want to be and say things I've only dreamed I would have the nerve to say if I was ever in a situation like this.

"Well then. I think I have to prove myself to someone tonight," he smirks the sexiest smile I've ever seen through his sexy stubble that covers his jaw line.

Becca interrupts us. "Sorry, Eros, but she's not officially a member yet. Owner's rules and all. If you don't like it, bring it up with him. But she's off limits tonight, only here to watch."

He smiles at her, "Maybe I'll just have to do that then." He looks back at me. "That shot looked mighty good. Do you mind if I have a taste?"

Oh God, yes, please. "By all means," I reply with a slight smirk on my lips.

He grabs the salt from the bar and walks dangerously close to me. I lean my neck to the side, inviting him to me. He leans in, placing a sweet kiss on my neck before licking me slightly. I feel my body start to quiver and I swear I hear his breath shake.

He places a lime in between my lips before shaking a bit of salt on my neck. He pulls back to look straight into my eyes and stares for a few seconds before leaning down, licking my neck slowly from well before the salt to well after, then taking the shot and leaning in and demanding the lime from my mouth.

He sucks the lime clean before dropping it to the floor and pulling my body in tightly, kissing me, taking from me every ounce of breath I have.

Slowly, he lessens his kiss and his hold of me before pulling back, giving me a sexy smile and turning to walk away after whispering, "Thanks for the taste."

I can't help but keep my lips slightly parted as I lean toward him, wanting more and sad he's walking away. I look over at Becca who's smiling from ear to ear. She starts to laugh when I try to talk but can't get the words out.

When I look back at him, I see a woman trying to get his attention and I can't help but smile at the fact that he's looking over at me. Not her.

Becca breaks my staring contest when she grabs my arm, "And that's only the beginning. You'll be begging to be a member by the end of the night. I promise you."

I start to nod my head up and down, "Ok, for the first time I might have to agree with you on that one."

"Yay! I knew my girl liked it kinky. Come on. Some people are starting a scene. Let's grab you your drink and go find you a place to watch before I get me some."

I turn completely away from him and order a Captain and Seven, which they serve in a tall skinny glass with two small black straws, before we walk over to a black couch with a few people in front of us, who are starting to strip each other.

I can't help but glance around the room for Eros and I notice he's still with the same woman, but if I'm reading him right, he doesn't look too into the idea of being with her.

After Becca makes sure I'm ok, she walks over to join the scene that's unfolding in front of me. Just like that. She joins them all having sex, like it's a totally normal thing to do. I don't have the confidence to join in on a conversation sometimes, and here she is joining a sex ring with people she doesn't even know.

I sit quietly, shocked at where I am, hoping I'm not looking like the most prude virgin sitting here by myself.

I'm both very thankful and extremely upset with this rule that I can't join in. Then I wonder how is it that I can be both upset and thankful for the same rule? If there wasn't this rule could I really just walk up like Becca did and join them?

The answer is no. I couldn't. I'd never have the guts to do that. The thought saddens me more than I'd like to admit.

What am I even doing here?

I bring my fingertips to my mouth and start to slightly tug on my lower lip when I suddenly feel the heat of someone sitting next to me. When I turn I see it's him. Eros. And he's alone next to me. *Where did the other woman go?*

I drop my fingers from my lip and start to play with the straw in my drink, looking forward, watching the show unfolding in front of me.

There are three guys and three girls. Two of the girls have been stripped of their clothes and are starting in on one of the man's clothes. Becca is lying down on the bed. One man is stripping her clothes while she already has another man's dick in her mouth. She's up on her elbow, leaning to the side, working his dick between her lips as the other man finishes taking off her skirt.

She's completely naked now and the man leans in, licking her folds and the familiar ache in between my legs heightens as I continue to watch.

I can't believe what I'm seeing. Right in front of me...

I close my legs tightly, shifting in my seat, trying to ease the need I'm feeling.

Heat starts to overwhelm my body and I realize it's Eros; he's sliding closer to me, pushing his body against mine. A shy smile slips from my lips before turning my attention back to the scene.

Becca is still on her back but now a female is straddling her face and the guy who was licking her before is now doing her slowly as he watches her devour the female. My vision locks on him as he slowly pushes himself in and out of her while she licks the woman who she doesn't even know.

I'm shocked.

I'm mortified.

I'm more turned on than I have ever been in my entire life.

My chest is tight and my stomach starts to ache as my breathing gets so erratic, I can't hide it anymore.

To change my focus and try to calm down, I look around the scene to see the other two guys with one girl. They're sitting on a couch with the girl bouncing up and down on one guy while sucking on the other who stands next to them. He's leaning down, rubbing her breasts as the other guy rubs her clit.

I hear her moan in ecstasy around the guy's dick and I feel myself get wetter than I ever thought was possible from just watching people.

I can't just sit here. I have to do something.

The glass I was holding is still in my hands so I open my legs just wide enough to slide the glass down in between my thighs, suddenly very thankful that Becca made me wear this short skirt.

The feeling of the cold glass up against my soaked panties is pushing me further than I imagined. The coldness along with the hardness of the glass pressed against me is causing my clit to tingle, releasing pure ecstasy.

Slowly I move my hips from side to side, trying to hide my movements and not make what I'm doing obvious to anyone around. With my vision stuck on the body of a woman I don't know as I watch a man's dick slide in and out of her, I feel myself start to almost drool from my lips that are slightly parted.

I think I'm getting away with my own private little scene until Eros slides closer and I hear him whisper in my ear, "Let me help you."

I jump, surprised to hear his offer and embarrassed that I was caught. "I'm sorry. It's the rules. I can't do anything but watch."

"It's not breaking the rules. Just keep your panties on. Then it's no different than kissing, really."

I take a deep breath, agreeing with his logic as I move the glass and open my legs a little wider, inviting this stranger to touch me once again. I don't know why but just his presence comforts me. In a place where everyone is wearing masks that shade their eyes, his are a piercing blue that shine through like they're lighting my way.

His sexy smile sends tingles down my spine as he slides his fingers across my lap. Chills cover my entire body as I shiver before taking a sharp breath in to calm my nerves.

Tightness in my chest is making it hard to breathe and I'm dying for him to move faster to his point of interest. He doesn't though; he takes his time rubbing my leg, my inner thigh, my lower abdomen, the top of my mound, everywhere except the one place I am yearning for.

So I don't get more frustrated from the sexual charge his fingers are causing, I llook up to watch the scene in front of me some more for a distraction.

Becca is now on all fours with her butt in the air. A guy is behind her, doing her hard while smacking her butt just as hard. She sucks on the other guy's dick while he holds her hair back so he can watch the view. The other two girls are with the last guy. He's laying on his back while one is sucking his dick and the other is straddling his face, rocking her hips back and forth while rubbing her breasts and tugging on her nipples.

My breath picks up as Eros finally reaches his destination. His fingers run on the outside of my panties, rubbing up and down my mound on either side but not hitting my lips or my clit. The feeling is pure torture, but oh so good.

I tilt my hips, hoping to guide him exactly where I want him to be but he stops his movement instantly. Dejected, I look at him as he shakes his head, telling me I can't do that. The smile that is covering his face is telling me that he likes this little game, too.

I take a deep breath, turning my attention back to the show in front of me, trying not to explode from desire.

Though I'm trying to stay still, it is incredibly hard with his fingers so close to heaven. They're right where I need them but he's not giving it to me. I tilt my hips again and swiftly I'm picked up, moved between his legs and stabilized to where I can't move, my back to his front. Now I'm stuck as he holds me tightly between his thighs.

This man, who I don't know, and in any other situation I would be terrified, but here and now, there's nowhere I'd rather be. All I feel is comfort wrapped around me like angel wings keeping me from floating away.

I'm so freaking turned on right now that I would let him do me right here. Shoot. Becca was right. I'm about to beg him to do me right here.

I lean back, whispering in his ear, "Please."

He lets out a small laugh, "I love to hear a beautiful woman beg for me."

He holds my hips tightly between his legs and finally touches me. Sliding his fingers up and down my slit. My clit is so engorged it's giving him easy access and he teases it through my panties. Rubbing up and down before pressing hard against my clit.

He whispers in my ear, "Give it to me."

I explode, throwing my head back on his shoulder, twitching internally from my orgasm, feeling like I'm releasing around every inch of my body. I can't even begin to hide it as I scream out in pleasure.

It's been years since someone else has gotten me off and I've forgotten how unbelievably amazing it can be.

After I catch my breath, Eros picks me up, turning me around and kissing me even harder than before.

Preston

Holy Fuck. That was so beautiful. This woman has to join. God, I would do anything to be able to fuck her right now.

I lean down to kiss her shoulder, moving her to the side so I can stand. I don't even look at her when I walk straight to the back toward my office. It's tucked away behind one of the walls. No one knows it's there so I sneak in, grab the paperwork for new members off my desk and head straight back to Eurydice.

She's looking down, tugging on her bottom lip with her shoulders slumped forward. The sight doesn't sit well with me and I'm not sure how I feel about that. It's like I care. But I shouldn't. I can't. But why this feeling is turning in my stomach I'll never know.

I shake the feeling away and sit back down beside her, placing the folder containing the paperwork on her lap. Before she says anything, and before I question this feeling any more, I lean in whispering in her ear, "Here's your membership paperwork. Fill it out, give it to Bec… Baubo and she'll make sure it gets to the right person."

She turns to me, starting to say something but I place my finger over her lips quieting her, "Shh… I'll see you next week sweet Eurydice."

I stand up before she can say anything and walk to join in on another scene in front of us. There's two guys and three girls already naked and having a good time. One guy is fucking a girl from behind so I walk up to stroke her hair and see how she feels about me joining their scene.

The girl is nothing but beautiful with pale white skin, dark long brown hair and a bright red, soft lace eye mask. She looks up at me with the corners of her mouth tilting up to a smirk as she raises one hand to rub my cock. I drop my head back, enjoying the feeling of her hand on me as I watch her getting fucked, hard.

My cock lifts to action as she zips down my zipper like a pro.

Reaching inside, she springs it free with a huge grin on her face. She's hungry and my cock is the exact candy she's looking for.

Wetting her lips, she licks from base to tip before swirling her mouth around my tip. Her mask is covering her face but I see her eyes look up to me before reaching up and taking me in deep.

I growl in response looking from her out into the rest of the scene but my vision is stuck. I see Eurydice looking back at me and I can't move. I'm frozen, staring at her as she blatantly stares directly at me.

A feral woman is deep throating my cock and I'm lost in a staring contest with someone else. I try to look away but the harder I try, the more I can't.

A smirk grows on my face as I signal for her to come toward me with my index finger, long and slow.

She jumps, like she's shocked I noticed we were staring at each other. Like she didn't even know we were staring. After a second she shakes her head *no* but doesn't look away.

I frown slightly and mouth the words to her, *come here.*

She shakes her head again and I firmly tilt my head to the side and command her to come to me mouthing, *now*.

Timidly, she sets down her drink and slowly starts to make her way toward me, stopping at the threshold of the mock up room that I've created for these separate scenes.

I point my finger toward her again, motioning for her to come closer. She shakes her head again and I reach out to her, grabbing her hand. "It's ok. You aren't going to join us. Just come here."

Thankfully, she grabs my hand and I pull her into me, kissing her without abandon and blowing my load almost instantly once our mouths meet. I place my hand on the head of the woman sucking on my cock to warn her before I do but she doesn't seem to care. She takes it like a champ and I never lose contact with Eurydice's lips.

It's so fucking hot.

It's so fucking intense.

I'm in heaven only quickly to realize, I'm actually in hell.

Our lips part and reality hits me harder than a wrecking ball. No, this chick is way more than a wrecking ball, knocking down walls meant to stand up for five lifetimes. In a matter of an hour, she's not only knocked down my wall, she slammed into it, tearing it apart with no care in the world yet she has no idea all the damage she just inflicted.

I lean down, making sure the girl who had my cock in her mouth is ok, even though there isn't a drip to clean up and she swallowed everything I offered. Normally I'd be even more turned on by the sight but I'm not. Not tonight. I need to get out of here.

Now.

Chapter FOUR

Kamii

"Ok girl, what happened to you last night?" Becca slides in front of me at the corner Starbucks the next morning.

She text me multiple times last night and this morning trying to figure out why I left without saying anything to her last night. I told her I was fine and we could discuss it over breakfast but she wouldn't drop it. After her fifth text I turned off my ringer, curled up in bed alone, trying to get the image of Eros out of my mind but who was I kidding? It was never going to happen. After an hour of trying to sleep, I put on a movie and finally dozed off around 2 a.m.

Now I'm here, right where I said I'd be and I don't even get a simple hello before I'm being drilled again. I wish I could tell her why I left. What really happened but I'm just as confused as she is.

I was so lost in the heat of the moment. Still reeling from my orgasm, then devastated when he left me so suddenly. I was so embarrassed and felt totally alone with no clue what to do.

When he returned warm, comfort covered me all over. The sound of his voice, alone, made me melt inside, with a feeling of security once more. When he got up to join the scene, jealousy worked its way over me.

Even though I hated what I was seeing, it was like a car crash, no matter how much I didn't want to see what was happening in front of me, I couldn't help but sit and stare. But yet he stared right back.

When I joined him I felt a sense of happiness overcome me, even though some other girl had her mouth wrapped around his dick. I felt it and I knew he felt it, too. He came as soon as he kissed me.

Me.

Not her.

Me.

I beamed with pride until he pulled away from me, quickly checked on the girl and bailed without looking back. There I stood, in the middle of five people having sex all around me while I was fully clothed and in no way involved with them.

I've never felt so stupid and out of place in my life. I turned and ran out the door, catching a cab and heading straight home. So to say I'm totally confused would be an understatement, which is why I was avoiding Becca's texts. I wasn't ready to deal with any of it yet.

I don't want to be having these feelings. I need to step back and look at this like the law, black and white. Just sex, no feelings.

"Good morning to you, too. I'd ask how your night was but I saw it with my own two eyes," I hit her arm, teasing, trying to put the focus on her.

"I have a grande non-fat dirty chai on the bar for Becca," the male barista yells out.

Becca gets up to grab her drink and I watch as she obviously flirts with the guy. I'm in awe that she can be so sure of herself to flirt so openly. He's a little younger than us, with tattoos running up his arms that you can see under his long sleeve shirt rolled up to his elbows. If it's not his lip ring that tops off his bad boy look then it's his longer hair that's spiking out from under his Starbucks hat.

I can't help but laugh as she joins me again at our table.

"What?" she smiles knowing exactly why I'm shaking my head in disbelief. "He's cute, isn't he?"

"Yes, he is. And of course my dirty friend would order a dirty chai."

She winks at me with a silly smirk before starting in on me again, "Ok, spill it girl. I looked over and Eros had his arms all over you. What happened?"

I sigh before spilling every hot detail, which is weird since I've never spoken this openly about sex but for some reason with Becca it feels totally normal. She smiles like I'm telling her about a new movie I watched, even though the movie I was watching was her, in real life, getting done from behind.

I still can't believe it.

"So you're going to join right?" she spits out once I've told her the whole story.

"Hello? Weren't you listening? He just left. I stood there like an idiot."

She waves her hand dismissively, "That's no big deal. You better join though. He wants you to. I just know it. He was probably just pissed he couldn't fuck you."

I shake my head. "What's the point? All I've done since I left was think about him, and yet I really have no idea who he even is? Or what he really looks like. This is not what I want."

"The point is for fun. That's it. Enjoy life's little pleasures. Unless…" she stops squinting her eyes, "I guess I should have asked you, are you looking for a relationship? Like real, get together on weeknights to make dinner together and take him home to mom and dad, relationship?"

Without hesitation I answer, "No!"

I guess I should have tamed my response back a bit because now she's wondering why I'm *so* against it.

She sighs, her lips tilting down to a frown. "Is there something I should know? I get it. I'm not really looking for a relationship either but I get the feeling it's more than that for you. When was the last time you've been in a relationship and what happened that you're sooooo against it?"

My eyes instantly tear up. "It's been a while. Can't we just leave it at that?"

"No, sorry. To be involved in this world it's important that you're open and honest, especially with yourself. This world is built on trust and if you can't trust yourself then you definitely can't trust someone else and that's when things get nasty. I've seen it happen. The human factor. You join us for a fun release, not an escape. There's a difference. I need to make sure you know the difference."

I sigh, "I know the difference. I'm not escaping from anything. Well, I mean, not really. I don't want a relationship that's all. I already gave my heart to someone and vowed I would only love him." I grab a napkin dabbing the tears falling down my face.

Becca grabs my hand, holding it softly, saying, "So what happened?"

"It's been five years. Don't worry about it."

"No, Kamii. I'm your friend now remember? Tell me what happened."

I close my eyes, bringing back my last memory of Nick.

"Well Mrs. Schafer, how does it feel to be a married woman?"

I run my fingers through his chest hair. It's the perfect amount of hair. Just enough to be sexy, where I can run my fingers through it but not enough to make him look like a bear. "I feel like this is going to be the best day of my life, Mr. Schafer. Knowing that I get to wake up in your arms for the rest of my life is truly a dream come true."

He leans over, kissing my forehead, "I fully agree. Our flight for Hawaii leaves in a few hours. I thought I would go get you breakfast in bed from your favorite bakery. How does that sound?"

"Only a few hours of marriage and you're already spoiling me rotten. You know the way to my heart."

He leans down kissing my lips, "Yup, a maple donut with a lavender latte coming right up."

I grab him before he can get up, kissing him as I whisper, "How'd I get so lucky?"

"You said yes. That's how."

He kisses me softly before getting up and putting on some clothes and slipping out the door. Lying back down, I roll over, grabbing the covers and pulling them up high with a huge smile on my face.

Not even thirty seconds later my smile was gone.

Forever.

"Oh Kamii, I'm so sorry," is all Becca says.

I'm sick of people saying they're sorry. Sorry for what? They didn't kill him. They had nothing to do with it and nothing to be sorry for. I shake my head. Wiping the last of my tears, sternly saying, "So this is why I'm not looking for a relationship. They're nothing but heartache."

Becca grabs my hand again, "Not always."

I see the pain in her eyes. Pain for me. Pain I have seen in everyone's eyes since that fateful morning and I'm sick of it. This is why I don't have friends. Why I buried myself in my work and my books. That was my escape. This will be my reality. I think it will be good for me and now that I really think about it, the fact that I don't know who he is probably is even better.

"No, this is exactly what I need. When I said this is not what I want I didn't mean it in terms of a relationship. Exact opposite actually. I don't want to be thinking about him, which is exactly what I've been doing. I just want the sex part. That's it."

"I get it. I do. Just please, promise you'll talk to me if you need to at any time, ok? I'm sure things will be normal after he fucks you. It's just because that was probably the first time he's been in a situation where he really wanted to but couldn't."

"Ok. You're probably right."

"Besides. You have to fuck him. Mmm, it's so good," she smirks.

Now my interest is piqued, "Really? You have?" I smile.

"Oh girl, just wait. And he's in your same boat. No relationships so you have nothing to worry about. So, now, where is that paperwork?" she smiles, winking at me.

"I have it right here. I did fill it out last night. How well do you know this guy?"

She smirks, "I've known him for about six months now. He's pretty secretive and I promised I would keep his secrets so don't ask me anything else. I hate to keep secrets from you but I owe him that. Just know that you're in for a world of fun. But not only with him. There are new men in this group that I have yet to taste and I'm sure we will have our fill of many different options. After you're with someone else he won't be more than a rating on your fuck scale. Those who you've done, would do again and would try to do every time you see them," she winks as she sticks the paperwork in her purse.

My heart flutters with excitement as she fills me in on more of the rules, what each night is meant for and we make plans for next week. Since the club is new, they are rushing my test results and I have an appointment already scheduled for tomorrow. Becca told me they made the appointment last week knowing that I would want to sign after my first night of just watching. Pretty presumptuous of them but I guess they knew once I walked in I'd want to belong.

They were right.

Chapter FIVE

Kamii

My week has been insane. We're working on a new, high-end case at my firm that has taken control of my life. I can't say I'm sad about it though. I've had no time to think about Eros, what happened last Saturday night or more importantly, what's going to happen tonight. I had work as an excuse to get me out of last night, which was more of a couple's night. I didn't want to be a part of that. Not for my first time.

Tonight is Friday and Becca said she would drag me kicking and screaming if she had to, saying I would fit right in since it's BDSM night. I know she was kidding about fitting right in with the kicking and screaming but not about dragging me down there.

She won't need to though. I'm ready. I want this.

I went to bed every night this week reading my favorite kink books, trying to psych myself up and, let me tell you, it has totally worked. I'm nervous but, at the same time, excited. This is what I've wanted. What I've dreamt about. And knowing now that I have an extremely sexy guy to do it with makes it even better.

The more I've thought about it, the more I love the fact that I don't know what he really looks like. He can be Christian, Master Aidan or even Kellen, all my favorite book boyfriends. He's really anyone I want him to be and I'm more than ok with that.

More importantly though, I can be whoever I want to be. I don't have to be the widow, the woman who is responsible for the murder of her husband. The idea frees my soul for the first time in years, lifting the weight I carry around just a little bit more.

Excitement of my plans for tonight had me playing a little secret game with myself where I wore my lingerie I bought under my skirt to work today. My black lace garter belt attached to my nylons made me feel sexy all day and I have to admit, I loved every secret minute.

When I was in a meeting with four men, all I could think about was what I had on underneath my new, more sexy outfit and what each one of the men sitting next to me would do if they found out. The thought of them ripping my clothes off, throwing me on the table, all taking their turn with me was the best part of the meeting.

I must have been blushing because after awhile one of them asked if I was feeling ok. I had to excuse myself to the ladies room to splash some water on my face to cool off.

After turning off my desktop light, I lock my office door and walk down the quiet hall toward the elevator. It's nine o'clock at night and everyone has long gone home. The elevator door dings its arrival while I'm off in lala land thinking about the possibilities of tonight.

As the doors open my gaze meets the eyes of a gorgeous man standing tall in the elevator. I'm not sure if I should be afraid or thank the gods above for bringing him to me. Channeling my inner Becca, I go for thanking the gods and give him a shy smile while fluttering my eyelashes at him.

Becca's gone over all different types of make-up techniques and my non-existent lashes now look long and luscious thanks to the help of Chantecaille mascara. It costs a fortune but worth every penny when I see the man's eyes light up.

"So we meet again?" he says slow and lusciously as his eyes move up and down my body. I'm feeling sexy in my black high heels, black pencil skirt with a tight, dark teal sleeveless shirt that is low cut showing the perfect amount of business appropriate cleavage.

After I step onto the elevator, I look to the side, over my shoulder, smiling at him, "Excuse me…?"

"This is the second time I've had the pleasure of riding in the elevator with you. I'm surprised you're here so late. A beautiful woman like you, don't you have a hot date on this Friday night?"

I can't help the blush as it creeps up my face. I turn forward as I scrunch my shoulder up with a small smile. "No hot date. Just meeting friends," I lie. "How about you?"

"Same here, um, meeting friends. Maybe I can be your *friend* sometime…?"

"Maybe," I smile as the elevator dings its arrival to the bottom floor and opens to allow us to exit. I walk away from him, trying to be elusive and keep him wanting more. *I can't believe I'm being so brave right now.*

"Can I at least get your name?" he asks, still standing in the doorway of the elevator.

"It's Kamii," I answer as I push the door to our building open and walk to where my car is parked.

With a huge smile on my face, and my newfound confidence streaming through my veins, I drive to the dungeon, my name for this place. I felt it just made things more dreamlike. The actual name of the club is Bridge but I'm not sure why.

I told Becca I would meet her there since I would be coming straight from work.

Becca is waiting in her car as I pull up so I park behind her on the street. Upon seeing me she jumps out of the car and runs to my door, throwing it open.

"I was beginning to think I was going to have to come get you!" she yells at me.

"Sorry, I told you this case is kicking my butt. Don't worry, I'm here and I'm ready," I wink at her, giving her a small smile.

She jumps up and down in her Becca way, "Ohhhhh, this is going to be so much fun!"

We walk arm-in-arm to the side door, giving our names and entering to the building only to strip our clothes at the front door. I laugh at the sight of the "coat check" and how really it's an entire wardrobe check.

Even though there are people around, I somehow feel totally comfortable stripping my clothes off right at the front door. I swear it's the mask, giving me super powers I had no idea I had.

Becca whistles as she examines my attire and when I go to hit her arm to stop her someone grabs me from behind, holding me tightly.

I shutter at first then melt into their hold when I hear Eros whisper into my ear, "Are you ready?"

Oh yeah, game on, "Whatever you want, Sir."

"Fuck me. Did you really just call me Sir?" he forcefully whispers in my ear.

I question myself, "Yes I did, Sir. Is that not ok?"

"It's more than ok. It shows me you really are here to play tonight and that you have done your homework. Have you done your homework my sweet Eurydice?"

"I have, Sir. I've wanted this for a while. I just never thought it would actually happen."

"And why did you think that?"

"Because I work too much. I don't put myself out there and I never thought I would meet someone like Baubo or anyone else here, Sir."

"Does that mean you never thought you would meet anyone like me?"

"Yes, Sir."

"Are you happy that you've met me, Eurydice?"

"I'd like to say yes, Sir. And so far I can say that but I guess I won't really know until tonight."

"Oh really... Do you have doubts in my ability?"

"No, Sir. Absolutely not."

"Then how come I have to prove my worth?"

"Sorry, Sir. It's my job. I doubt everything until I have proof."

"Don't be sorry. I like the challenge you've presented. So you're a member now?"

"Yes, Sir. I'm officially a member and can play with anyone tonight."

"Anyone?"

"I meant you, Sir. I can play with you tonight."

"That's better."

He finally turns me around and I see he's wearing a tight black shirt with dark jeans and his facemask. He looks casual yet demanding. Really, he's pure sex I'm staring at and I like what I see.

"Have you filled out your hard and soft limits?"

I look at him, not backing down. "Yes, I have."

"I thought you said you've done your homework my sweet Eurydice. How come you're looking at me?"

"Because I want to, Sir. We're not in a scene. Is that not ok?"

"For right now I guess I'll allow it. When we are in a scene. No."

I'm a little taken aback by this. I mean I know it's part of the scene but it's not settling with me right now. I close my eyes, pushing my thoughts away and looking down to the ground, shaking my head *yes*.

He places his finger under my chin, tilting it up. "I said right now was fine."

"Sorry, Sir. Please, be patient with me. I'm still learning." Nerves and doubt slip their way into my secret bubble I've put myself in as I pretend to be someone else.

"I know you are and believe me, that's what I like about you."

I look into his crystal blue eyes, hopeful, "You like me, Sir?"

"I do. And I want to play. May I take you into a scene? Are you ready?"

"I am, Sir."

"I want you to be comfortable, do you want Baubo to join us tonight?"

My eyes open widely, looking to the side, completely forgetting Becca was standing next to us this entire time, watching our interaction with a huge smile on her face.

I look from her back to him, "I've never been with a girl. I would like that but maybe not tonight. I'd like to experience each new thing on its own before I put everything together. But... I would feel safer if she was near. Maybe, watching us?"

"Sounds good to me!" Becca jumps up and down not trying for one second to hide her excitement.

I shake my head with a small smile on my face as I look back to Eros who is reaching out his hand to me, "Well, please, follow me my sweet Eurydice."

I place my arm in the nook of his elbow and follow him as we enter the room where everyone is gathered. The place is more open than when I was here last Saturday and the rooms are equipped with more, I'd like to say furniture, but it's not really what it is. Well, unless you call spanking benches, a flat table top with polls on either side or a big X with places for your hands and feet to tie to the structure. Thankfully, there is still a bed so at least I know there is something I've done before in here, even if it is a boring bed.

As we cross the room, a woman walks in front of us, stopping to talk to Eros. She tilts her head to the side with a slight smirk on her face as she states clearly, "Already wanting to scene? But she just got here. Are you looking for two submissives tonight *my* Eros?"

It's not lost on me the way she says *my* and I wonder who this woman is, or maybe I should be wondering, *what* she is to him?

Eros looks at me then back to the woman. She's tall and thin and from everything I can see, very well manicured. Her long, brown hair flows down her back with a few strands pulled forward and falling over her shoulder.

Before I can say anything, Eros replies, "Thank you my dear but Eurydice here is new, so I think we'll keep to just the two of us tonight."

She looks at me and, even though I can't see her eyes through her mask, I can feel the death stare she's giving before she changes it to a slight smile, saying, "No worries, have fun tonight you two," and walks away.

We walk to the corner where a smaller area is set up. No one is currently using the space and he claims it before anyone else can.

Becca kisses me on my cheek, whispering, "Enjoy, I'll be right here if you need me," before she leaves us to sit on the couch in front of our scene.

I watch as she walks away and Eros grabs my chin, turning my focus back to him. "Tell me your safewords, Eurydice."

"Yellow for I'm close to the edge and Nick for stop immediately," I say with no emotion.

"Nick? Why is a man's name your safeword?"

"I'd rather not say, Sir, if that's ok with you?"

"What if Nick is my real name?"

I tense, never thinking of the possibility. I chose it because I truly never want to have to pull a safeword, and I never want to have to say his name either, so I felt it fit for my needs.

The thought of it possibly being his real name hits me like a stab to the heart and he must have noticed.

"Don't worry. It's not. Good to know that it affects you the way it does though. Don't worry. I won't ask again and I promise to not have you say it either."

"Thank you, Sir."

"Now, go lean on your knees for me by the bed while I prepare our scene and gather your paperwork so I can learn your soft and hard limits."

I look down, whispering, "Yes, Sir," as I walk to the bed and kneel.

My heart is pounding with nerves and anticipation. Becca slightly jumping with excitement in her seat catches the corner of my eye. The sight calms me down as I giggle to myself.

Eros is gone for a few minutes and butterflies fill my stomach the longer he's gone. Taking deep breaths, I imagine my favorite scenes from my favorite books and really let my imagination run wild making my nervous butterflies change to dancing ones filled with excitement. Moving my hand over to my arm, I lightly pinch myself to make sure this is all real.

Eros leans down, whispering in my ear, "No need to pinch yourself, this is really happening. I promise you."

I look up, surprised by him standing there as a small smile reaches my lips. "I know it is, Sir, I just wanted to make sure I wasn't dreaming."

"Well then, stand up and I'll prove to you that you aren't."

I do as he says. Standing in front of him, offering myself to him, trying to show confidence in what is happening. I stand tall, shoulders back, head high and chest out with my hands to my side.

He circles my body, looking me up and down. "I love a woman who holds herself with confidence. Have you always been this way?"

"No, Sir. I lost my way a few years ago but Baubo has brought me back to life and made me feel sexy again."

"Has she now? I will have to thank her for bringing you to me."

"Yes, Sir. She is the only reason I'm here today. May I tell you something, Sir?"

"Please do."

"This is my first time, um, experiencing something like this. I'm not a virgin but I've never done anything this… something so freeing. I'm excited but please, be gentle with me."

"You have nothing to worry about my beautiful Eurydice. I want this to be a pleasurable experience and I want you to want to play with me again. I've taken note of your hard and soft limits and I thank you for telling me you're new to this. I will take things slow, ease our way into the scene. Know that it is my job to read you, your body language, and your subtle movements. I need for you to hand me your trust. Can you do that?"

"I will try, Sir. I must admit I don't trust many people. In my line of work it's hard to trust anyone. Everyone has secrets, things they're trying to hide." I hate that I just brought this up. I'm supposed to be someone else in here.

"There's no hiding in here. From either you or me. For this to work, both of us have to break down any walls we hold up and let everything go. I can't do this unless you trust me."

"Then earn it, Sir. Go slow, show me how this works and earn my trust." His words oddly ease my fear and my bubble starts to fade, allowing me to be a little bit more myself, and, more importantly, being ok with it.

"Is that a challenge sweet Eurydice?"

"Yes, Sir. If that's ok with you, I mean."

He wraps his hands around my face, his long fingers cupping the back of my head as he leans down, kissing me with control, demanding me to submit to his touch, which I gladly do, as he whispers, "I accept your challenge."

He drops his hold from me and walks toward the spanking bench. "Come here."

I follow and stand still in front of the bench, not sure how to proceed so I wait for his direction. Silently, he walks around me again, placing his hands on my shoulders, running his hands down my arms, around my waist then smacking my rear end, hard.

The sting sends a sensation straight to my, dare I say, pussy, that was hard not to notice. I always thought I would be into this but now there's no thinking involved. That feeling alone told me this is exactly what I want.

"Well… I like what I see. Your skin turned a beautiful flush all over from that spanking. I think you might like this."

"There's no thinking about it, Sir. I know I liked it. I'm glad you can tell. That just earned you more trust from me."

He leans in to whisper in my ear, "Glad to know I'm doing so well," before kissing down my neck, reaching around and gripping my nipple through my thin lace bra.

I lean my head back, giving him more access as he kisses my neck more thoroughly while moving his fingers down, rubbing my slit through my lace panties.

"You weren't kidding, I can feel how wet you are through your panties," he whispers.

I respond by opening my legs slightly wider, allowing him more access. A deep moan escapes my lips as he slides a little deeper between my thighs.

"Bend over, let me see that beautiful ass on display for me," he demands as he lightly pats me again.

I crawl onto the bench with the center padded in a soft leather cover with arm and foot rests to match making it surprisingly comfortable. There are handles for me to grip onto and leather cuffs to keep me there. I glance down, hoping to see Eros but he catches me by surprise when he grabs my ankle, strapping me down tightly to the bench.

"Remember your safe words, Eurydice."

"Yes, Sir. I don't plan on using them though, I want to trust you, Sir."

"And you will," he kisses my forehead as he straps my arms in tightly.

Tingles race through my body as I feel something very soft moving across my back. What feels like a hundred very soft fingers is touching me all over. The feeling sends shivers up and down my spine, sending a thrill all over my body and I'm taken by surprise when he pulls the little fingers off my back and smacks me hard across my ass.

I jump slightly; surprised by his swift movement. The sting is real but not bad. My head spins for a second until he wraps his large hand over my ass and rubs it tenderly, bringing my skin back to life. I drop my head down, loving the feeling his hand brought deep inside me, even though he's just touching my backside.

He removes his hand and I sigh, sad to feel the coldness left without his touch. That is until I feel the smack again, a little harder. It stings a little more but when he rubs his hand over the area it's so much more intense. He continues this movement over and over again, harder and faster with every smack until I find myself literally panting. I can't even hold up my head I'm so lost with desire. My eyes are heavy, my breathing is labored and I'm dying for him to touch me more.

I wiggle my ass at him, trying to lift it up so his hand goes lower, touching me where I need it most. My head spins as I start to pull on my restraints. My chest is tight and I feel a faint layer of sweat forming on my lower back.

I need to feel something, anything, between my legs but no matter how I try to move, I can't get it.

Eros learns down, whispering in my ear, "Do you need to cum my beautiful Eurydice?"

I shake my head up and down, unable to actually speak.

"Let me hear you say it and I'll give you what you need."

"I… Yes… Please… I… Need…" I drop my head, breathing even more heavily now.

"You need what love? Do you need me to touch you?"

"Yes…"

"How do you need me to touch you? Do you want my fingers, do you want my mouth or do you want my cock?"

My eyes literally roll back in my head at the thought of any of those options. I want, I mean, I need it all. "All of it, Sir."

"Hmmm… you're a greedy little thing aren't you?"

"Yes, Sir. Please," I barely get out.

He leans down, kissing my back, "Please what?"

"Please touch me. I need to cum, Sir."

"Do you trust me now?"

"Ye…yes, Sir. Please."

"Since you want it all, I will make you cum three times, one time with each part of my body. Do you think I can do that?"

My entire body quivers at the thought. I shake my head *yes* but don't respond. He smacks my ass hard with his bare hand, saying, "I want to hear you say it."

"Yes, Sir. I know you can. Please show me."

He wraps his fingers around my lace panties, pulling it to the side and sliding his fingers up and down my wet folds. "Beautiful Eurydice, you're soaking wet. I made you that way. Remember that. Me," he says with intense emotion as he slides his fingers inside, rubbing his thumb over my clit, making me erupt instantly in an intense orgasm.

I feel my body clenching around his fingers as I start to convulse, pulling on my restraints and dropping my head down. I've never cum so fast in my life. I've also never been so turned on before. Ever.

My breathing returns to a somewhat normal state when he removes his fingers, striping my panties down to my knees and climbing under the spanking bench. Before I can even think about what he's doing, his mouth wraps around my clit, making me scream out in pleasure.

He moves his tongue up and down my folds, lapping up every ounce of my juices and sucking softly on my clit. I'm still tied down, not able to move since he's now wrapping his arms around my waist, holding my hips down to the bench. I'm at his complete mercy as his tongue dances around bringing me higher and higher.

Pleasure rips my world apart so much that I'm having trouble breathing. My eyes roll back uncontrollably making it hard to see straight and I'm totally stuck to feel nothing but the bliss he's putting on my body.

He pulls away from me slightly only to say, "Give me number two," licking me softly between each word.

Just hearing his words along with him slowing down his movements make me want it even more. Sweat starts to form on my lower back again as my breathing thickens and just as I feel myself coming to the edge, he sucks on my clit, pressing his face firmly against me making me erupt for the second time in mere minutes of each other.

Continuing his leisurely licks, long and slow, he calmly brings me back down to reality, helping to return my breathing to normal.

"You're so responsive, so beautiful. Are you comfortable here? Can I fuck you from behind?"

I take a sharp breath in, not sure if I can handle much more.

"I'm staying true to my word. I have to earn your trust, remember? I've made you cum twice so far, once with my hand, once with my mouth. Now I'm going to make you cum harder than you ever have before. Are you ready?"

"Yes, Sir. I'm ready," I say through panting breaths.

He easily lifts from the ground. Rubbing his hands over my body, caressing all of my curves.

I hear the crinkle of a condom wrapper and he walks around to show me what I hear. "I promised I'd keep you safe. I want you to watch me put this on, so you know I've kept you protected. You know I'm clean from the rules of this place, but know that I will do everything in my power to keep you safe from pregnancy as well."

I shake my head, whispering, "Thank you," as he zips down his pants in front of me. He's already removed his shirt and I'm dying to see more of him but with this mask on, and the fact that I'm still tied to the bench, I can't see much.

Once the condom is secure, he walks around to the back of me, rubbing my body from my shoulders to my ass. Leaning down, he wraps his strong arms around my waist, kissing the back of my neck, sending shivers down my spine.

"Are you ready for me Eurydice?"

I feel him holding his cock in his hand, rubbing it up and down my slit, wetting himself with my moisture.

"Yes, Sir. Please, take me."

"As you wish."

He slides into me with a slow motion, filling me a centimeter at a time, allowing my body to welcome him in. Once he's fully inside, he pauses, pushing against my body, holding still.

I wiggle against him, needing to feel some kind of movement, but he grabs my hips, holding them still once more and pulsating a fraction of space inside me.

Groaning, I hear him take a breath before pulling out and slamming back inside me with the most intense pace, pounding his sexual attack. Shocked by his fast pace, but loving the feeling it's building within me again, makes me scream out in pleasure.

With my arms and feet still tied down, along with the pounding of him inside of me, it's hard to focus on anything but the feeling running through my veins. Pulsing up my body, putting all my nerves on high alert, tingling my toes and fingertips. The fine sweat starts to cover my back again as that familiar pull tugs on my insides.

Eros' fingers dig into my sides, not letting up his attack. I hear him grunting through his teeth as he says things like, "So good," and, "So tight," and, "So wet."

Just when I can't take enough, he slams into me harder, "Come for me – now!" he blurts out and like he flipped a switch, I convulse around him as an orgasm rips through my body and I scream out my release.

"Yes, sweetheart, yes. Give it to me," he grunts when his own release rips through him as he grips my hips even tighter.

After we both recover, he quickly unties my legs, then my arms, and easily grips my entire body, lifting me up, flipping me around and holding me tightly to him. Before I can even protest, he has my lips locked to his, kissing me passionately, not letting go.

I'm taken aback by the intimacy of his kiss. I try to pull away but he just pulls me closer. *No, no, why are you doing this?*

When I'm finally able to break away, he keeps his hold on me and whispers to me, "That was amazing. How are you?"

I put my hand on his chest, lightly pushing him away. "That was great. I think you met your challenge head on. Thank you."

"Thank you?"

"Yes. That was perfect for my first scene."

"I'm glad to hear it. Let me help you." He leans down to pull up my panties.

Embarrassed that I didn't even realize I was sitting there with my panties wrapped around my knees, I lean down, pull them up saying, "It's ok. I got them."

I turn to walk away and he grabs my arm, "Where are you going?"

"What do you mean? I'm going over to Baubo," I say totally confused.

"You can't just walk away. There's aftercare. I need to sit with you. Make sure you're ok."

"Oh, no you don't. It's ok. I'm doing fabulous! You just made me cum three times in a matter of twenty minutes or so. Believe me. I've never been better."

I'm not lying. The feeling of euphoria is still tingling inside my body and I just want to go sit down and enjoy this high.

He pulls me in closer, "Are you really going to just bail on me? I must say. I'm a little shocked."

"Don't be. That's what this entire place is for isn't it? For a good time with no ties… I don't want aftercare. I don't want to mix emotions. I got what I wanted. It was seriously the best in my entire life so, thank you," I shrug. "Maybe we can do it again. Is that how this works? Does everyone try each other, see who they like in that way?"

"Whoa, wait a minute. I mean, I guess that's how this works but I thought we had something going here?"

"We did. And it was fabulous. But it wasn't more than this… Was it?" The thought almost makes me nauseous. *Did he think there was more to this? I'm so confused.*

"Yes, I mean, no, I guess. I'm just a little shocked you're so flippant about it."

"Oh, I'm sorry. I didn't mean to offend you. I just, like I said, I don't want to mix my emotions. I don't even know who you are, what you really look like or what your real name is. I don't want to know either. I want this. What we just did. Is that ok?"

"Yeah, I guess, as long as you're ok."

I lean up to kiss his cheek, "I'm more than ok. Thank you for caring enough to make sure I was. We'll definitely do this again."

I walk over to where Becca has been sitting watching our interaction. "Is everything ok?" she asks when I sit down next to her.

"Are you kidding me right now? Were you paying attention at all? That was the most amazing experience of my life. I can't thank you enough for introducing me into this lifestyle. It is definitely for me!" I grab her hand, jumping up and down on the couch just like she does every time she's happy about anything. I guess she is rubbing off on me more than I thought.

"Yay! I'm so glad to hear. But what happened afterward? Why is he over there and you're over here?"

I explained my feelings to her just like I did to him and she shrugs, saying, "Hey, I'm not one to judge, and neither is anyone else in here. If that's what you want. I get it. Just glad you enjoyed yourself."

I give her a big hug, "I really did. This is exactly what I needed in my life. Thank you!"

Chapter SIX

Preston

It's Saturday morning and I'm lying in bed with a fucking hard on thinking about last night and how amazing it was with Eurydice. I don't know why I can't get her out of my mind. I'm the one that set up the rules. No real names, no identities, all so I wouldn't get attached and here I am, laying in bed, thinking of her.

The worst part, I know everything about her. Even though Becca is the one who did all of the research on each member, I still have her application which means I know her real name, what she does for a living and her fucking phone number. It's staring me in the face, screaming for me to dial it but I can't. It breaks every rule that I put in place to protect me.

This fucking blows!

I can't even think about her real name. It's Eurydice and I have to keep telling myself that's all I know about her.

I keep thinking back to the way she walked away from me. Like she got what she needed and was done. Is that why I can't get her out of my mind? Because *I* didn't get the aftercare? Or is it because she blew me off?

No, I know it's neither. I felt it. When I had my cock inside her I felt something different. It was amazing but fucking intense! If she hadn't cum on my command I might have died trying to hold back. My orgasm shot down to my toes and I almost lost my balance as it ripped through me.

I've never felt that before. Even with Kim.

The thought stabs a sharp needle into my chest, which is exactly what I needed to kill the hard on that seemed like it was never going to go away.

Note to self: when your cock won't go down just think of your dead wife and how your actions made her kill herself.

Shit, now I feel like I'm going to be sick.

I hop out of bed and head straight to the shower. Becca and I are meeting at her salon. I had some things to discuss for getting new members and since she cuts my hair now, it worked perfectly to meet there since I was due for a trim.

She's her bubbly self, standing at the front desk as I walk in. Her smile makes me laugh as she slightly bounces up and down saying, "So, she's good right?"

I smirk, "Good morning to you, too." I kiss her on her cheek, "Can I at least get my robe on before I'm drilled about last night?"

"Oh, come on, you know me better than that. You're lucky I didn't call you last night." She leans in, "I'm digging this Mr. Black guy. He kept me there very late and let me tell you, I am not complaining one bit at how tired I am this morning."

I hug her, "I'm glad, now come on, walk me to your station."

We walk back and I change into the robe before she walks me over to wash my hair. She stays quiet while other people are around but as soon as we are safely away from everyone and tucked into her station she lets loose, "Ok, spill it. She's perfect for us, huh?"

I try to hide my true feelings and keep my monotone expression. "Yeah, it was pretty good. Kind of weird how she just bailed on me afterward though."

"She said she explained it to you. Did I tell you she's a lawyer? Her brain is very black and white. She doesn't want to mix emotions. Makes sense really." She tilts her head to me in the mirror, "That bothered you didn't it?"

I shake my head, "No, no it didn't. Just thought it was weird. Maybe it was because it was her first time. I was fine."

"Liar," she hits my shoulder.

"What?"

"Stop ok. I know it bothered you. I saw you standing there lost like a little puppy."

"I was shocked more than anything."

"Yeah, ok. So, what about tonight? What if she plays with someone else?"

I jerk my head up, "Did she say she was going to?"

"Ha! See, I knew it. You like her."

I shake my head, upset I let myself be that transparent, "No, I don't. I just want to make sure our new members are cared for and I hoped I could train her some more."

"Train, collar, make her your very own…" she laughs.

"Stop," I sternly say, "That will never happen so please drop it. I don't want anything like that and you know it. Please, drop the subject." Heat fills my face as I grip the handles of the chair I'm sitting in, not exactly sure why I'm so pissed off all of a sudden.

"Whoa, ok. Subject dropped," she blurts out as she turns to grab her comb.

"Look, I'm sorry. I know you don't know me that well but the last thing I want is a relationship. That's why I wanted this place to be anonymous. No ties. Just fun, remember?"

"Yeah, first week in, how's that working out for you?" she taunts.

Silence fills the area between us as she finishes the cut and has me stand to go re-wash my hair to get rid of the little hairs that find their way everywhere. Once everything is complete, she removes the drape from around my shoulders and without looking at me or saying another word, she turns to look at her phone, "Crap, my next client just cancelled on me. Talk about late notice."

I reach out for her with a small forgive me smile on my face, "Hey, I'm sorry if I just upset you and I'm sorry your client cancelled on you. Please, let me take you to lunch."

She sighs before smiling, "Ok. I'm sorry, too. I know I don't know your past but I get the clue that it's not something good so I won't ask or tease you again. Friends?" She reaches her hand out to me.

I reach out, grabbing her swiftly and pulling her in for a hug. "Believe me, you don't want to know my past. That's why it's in the past. Nothing I can do so I just try to forget, ok?"

"Ok," she leans up, kissing my cheek. "Where are you taking me for lunch?"

"Come on, I know a place around the corner."

We walk to one of my favorite little hole in the wall places. Kim and I ate here a lot so I guess it's a little weird that I'm bringing Becca here but it's not like she's my date or anything. Sure, we've fucked, we've fucked a few times actually, but that's all it is and it was always at a club, never on our own.

Becca has become a friend of mine, a good friend actually, over the past couple of months. Though I've still kept her at a distance with my personal life and my past, I've trusted her to help me build my place and she's brought on some amazing people. I'd say she's as close to a business partner as I'll ever get so it's fun to hang out in the outside world. I need someone like her in my life, someone to bring some sense of normalcy back to it.

If I had to explain our relationship to anyone I'd say she's more like a little sister to me. Wait, oh God, no, that's gross. Ok, I'd say she's more like my best friend's wife. Fuck, that's not ok either. Um, let's just say, I feel really comfortable with her and feel like I can completely be myself. Totally laid back with not a care in the world. It's nice to have someone like that. I get the feeling she feels the same way about me. Just good friends.

We have lunch and then I walk her back to the salon, giving her a hug as thoughts for tonight enter my mind, making me genuinely smile for the first time in what feels like forever as I walk away.

For whatever reason I know I have to be with Kamii again tonight. Hopefully then I can get her out of my head and go on with this club like I had planned. I know Kamii will be right at Becca's side. She may have blown me off after we played last night but I know she's not brave enough to venture off on her own yet.

Visions of taking both Kamii and Becca together make my cock so hard I can barely walk straight. It's perfect; I get to have Kamii again without coming out and saying it. I'll start with Becca, acting like she's all I want at first then see if Kamii wants to join in with us.

Later that night, I walk into the club seeing that my plan is already well into action without having to do anything. Becca and Kamii, I mean, Baubo and Eurydice are at the bar taking body shots again but this time it's Eurydice licking Baubo's neck.

This is going to be easier to pull off than I thought.

I walk up behind Eurydice, placing my hands on her shoulders as she takes the shot back. When she goes in to suck the lime out of Baubo's mouth, I rub my hands down her arms, grabbing the back of her hands and moving them to rub Baubo's breasts.

After leaning back to spit out the lime, Eurydice looks back to me, smiling sweetly but not moving her hands away from Baubo's body.

I smirk at her and tilt my head back in Baubo's direction and she must be able to read my mind more than I realize because without hesitation she turns to Baubo and kisses her again.

I'm lost, staring at these two delicious women kissing with open mouth. I watch their tongues twirl as they both take a breath and turn to deepen their kiss.

Pulling them in closer to me, I make sure to show Eurydice how hard I am and how much I love what's happening in front of me. By the looks of it though, I'm thinking she wants this with Baubo just as much as I do.

I whisper to both of them, "Come, let's go play."

Eurydice stops her kiss with Baubo and looks to me before looking back to her. I wish she didn't have that mask on and I could read her expression more. It's dark in here so her eyes are almost completely hidden. I wonder what's going through her head? Fear, hesitation, anxiety…?

Then she surprises the hell out of me saying, "Can Baubo join us, too?"

Fuck me. I guess I won't have to do any convincing for my plan to happen. She just flat out asked to have a threesome and I'm more than happy to oblige her command.

"I'd love for her to join us. Do you want more people to join or just the three of us?"

She shakes her head, "No, just the three of us. I told you, one new thing at a time."

"Sweet Eurydice, I love your inhibition and willingness to try new things. Come," I say, grabbing her hand along with Baubo's.

I catch a glimpse of Baubo as I do and the smile on her face makes me laugh slightly as I walk toward the more private room in the back. People can still watch, and there is an area for them to do so, but it's a smaller place and not much room so it's really only made for three people max. Before I enter the room I notice a woman walk in and sit on the couch in front of us and, since I'm one for people watching me, the thought of her being there turns me on that much more.

I can feel Eurydice's hands start to tremble lightly so I hold her hand tighter, giving her a small smile before pulling them both together, standing facing each other with me in between but off to the side. I'm in awe as I take both my hands, rubbing them through their hair as I stare at the beautiful women in front of me.

"Baubo, why don't you get this started by giving our sweet Eurydice a kiss," I say, as calmly as I can, trying to set the mood for a slow, methodically fucking session.

I watch as Baubo smiles slightly and Eurydice returns her smile. Both haven't even looked my way and seeing the calmness in Eurydice is making my dick hard. I can tell she wants this and, fuck, it makes me want her that much more.

Baubo leans in, lifting her hands to Eurydice's face as she slowly leans in, placing her lips softly to hers, holding her position. I watch as Eurydice's body calms, her shoulders relax and her arms come up, wrapping through Baubo's hair as she turns her head to deepen the kiss between them.

I watch in complete lust as they pull each other closer, pulling away just to breathe and move their heads to the other side. As they do I see their tongues entangling with one another and I feel a tinge of jealousy boiling low in my chest.

I can't help it, I place my hand under Eurydice's chin, breaking their kiss apart and pulling her mouth up to mine. I'm thankful they both go along with the new plan and Eurydice is instantly turned toward me, pressing her body against mine as Baubo wraps around her back, cupping her breasts with both hands.

I feel her squeezing them between us then her hands move lower as she grabs the bottom of her black, lace tanktop, pulling it up and over her head. I break our kiss just long enough for the thin shirt to pull over her head before I'm grabbing the back of her head, pulling her into me again. I can't get enough of her taste right now and I'm not ready to move on yet.

The feeling of her tongue is so soft, the way she swipes it around mine, pulling in and out, teasing me before she lightly nips my bottom lip. It's so fucking good and all we're doing is kissing.

I move my hands down her black leather skirt that's so short I'm sure anywhere else it would be considered more like lingerie but walking in here it works perfectly. Her ass cheeks are just below the rim of the skirt and I run my fingers lightly around the curve of each side.

Her ass is so fit, lifted and perfect for my hands to grab.

Baubo watches as I do this and runs her hands along the top of the skirt, unzipping the zipper and slowly moving the leather down her smooth legs, revealing the thinnest g-string I've ever seen.

I can feel Eurydice's breathing pick up but can tell by the intensity of her kiss that it's more from excitement than fear. I love the fact that she's almost naked and Baubo and I are still fully clothed. This night is for her. It's all about her and we're going to treat her like the goddess she's named after.

Baubo must be reading my mind because without any guidance from me she wraps her fingers around the thin straps of her panties and pulls them down. Eurydice doesn't hesitate a second or break her lips from mine as she steps out of them.

Baubo drops to the floor and I part just my lower body, allowing her to move in between us, sitting with her face right at Eurydice's pussy. Eurydice moves slightly, opening her legs and I feel her body almost give in as I'm sure Baubo just licked a sweet, slow lick across her pussy.

I break our kiss, just long enough to look down, getting a visual of Baubo's face buried in Eurydice before diving back in and furiously kissing Eurydice.

A moan breaks our kiss before she moves back in to bite my lip. Holding it there like she's holding on for dear life. My arms wrap around her waist tightly, feeling her body start to shake as Baubo holds her hips, keeping

Eurydice prisoner against her mouth and applying a pressure that is sending Eurydice to her knees.

I pull back slightly, knowing I have to watch her completely fall apart. Her eyes are closed, she's holding on for dear life right before her head falls back and her mouth opens, letting out the best sounding moan as her entire body convulses. Her arms drop from my shoulders to Baubo's hair as little tiny squeals release from her mouth.

Fuck me.

I've been with other girls and have been a part of other girl-on-girl action before but nothing I've ever seen even comes close to how sexy it was to watch Eurydice cum, while holding onto Baubo's hair as she sat in between her legs.

Reality starts to come back to Eurydice and a slow smile grows on her face as Baubo turns around, unzipping my zipper and pulling my hard cock out. Before I can even think of what's next, Eurydice drops to her knees, right next to Baubo and both of them start to lick up and down either side of me.

I wrap my hands in both of their hair, encouraging their movement, moving my hips slightly back and forth, teasing their mouths with my movement.

Baubo moves down, sucking one of my balls into her mouth as Eurydice takes full advantage and wraps her entire mouth around my cock, taking me in deep, shaking her head slightly as she takes me all the way back in her throat and pulling back out with a *pop* of her mouth.

I look down to see her wet lips, sweeping their way over the tip of my cock and I'm done for. Reaching down, I grab her chin again, pulling her up to me, kissing her softly before moving her over to the bed.

"Take off your bra," I demand in a low voice. "I want you completely naked." I look over to Baubo, requesting her to do the same thing.

Grabbing Baubo, I pull her to me once she's undressed, motioning for her to get on the bed. I lift my hand behind me to the top of my back and pull my shirt off then remove my pants the rest of the way before leaning to the side table where a basket of condoms lay; grabbing one and ripping it open with my teeth.

"I want to watch you lick Baubo my sweet Eurydice while I fuck you. Are you ok with that?"

She looks up, smiles sweetly and lays down on her back, grabbing for Baubo to move over her face, not saying a word as she opens her legs wide for me.

Fuck. Me.

I'm stuck, watching her guide Baubo to where would be easiest for her and slowly opens her mouth, sticking her tongue out and slowly licking from back to front. I look up to watch Baubo arch her back slightly, tilting her head back as she wraps her hands around her own breast.

Reaching down, I rub Eurydice's clit softly and she wiggles against me, welcoming me more.

Pulling the condom down my length, I grab my cock with one hand and lightly move it around her opening, just barely sticking the tip in and out. It must have a good affect on her because she's moving her hips around more and more, trying to push down against me, trying to work my cock into her but I'm not allowing it.

She hasn't pulled away from Baubo and the more I tease her, the faster her tongue moves around, savagely licking like she can't get enough. Her chest rises and falls with every breath, and the intensity I'm seeing unfold before me is fucking unreal.

I wait until she can't take it anymore and I know it will only take seconds to make her cum. Finally I give her what she wants, sliding fully inside. She takes a break from her licking only to scream her response to me being inside of her.

I pump in and out, holding her hips tightly in place as she returns to Baubo. I watch her movements of what she's doing to Baubo and do the same to her. She goes fast, I go fast, she slows down to long, slow, teasing licks and I do the same.

Her body starts to really move along with the movement of her mouth and I follow suit. Pumping hard into her, fast and with no abandon.

Almost instantly, I watch as both Baubo and Eurydice tighten up and explode at the same time, both screaming their release around each other. The sight makes me cum almost instantly.

Chapter SEVEN

Kamii

I'm sitting at my desk the next Wednesday when Stefanie buzzes me through our intercom system, "Oh Kamii… You have a delivery…" she sings through the line.

I have a what? "Excuse me? Did you say I have a delivery?"

"Sure did. Why don't you come out here to see what it is?"

Just by her tone alone I can tell it's not a normal document or something I need for a case but I have no clue what could be waiting for me. I walk through the hallway to reach the reception area where I'm greeted with a huge bouquet of white roses.

When my eyes meet Stefanie's, her face lights up as she jumps from her seat, "Get your bootie over here. I'm dying to see who these are from. Give me the dirt sweetie."

I'm stuck. I don't know whether to smile, throw up or run back to my room. Who could these be from? Eros? No, he doesn't know who I am. Does he? That's the whole point of the anonymous thing.

"Um, I have no clue…" I finally answer as I put my hand to my chest like I can stop my pounding heart just from the simple touch.

She pulls the card from the bouquet holding it out to me. "Well, open the card!" she smiles big.

My feet finally start to move from where they'd begun to grow roots and I walk forward to grab the card from her. With trembling hands, I flip the envelope open to read:

> *I've missed running into you in the elevator this week. How about being my friend tonight for a few drinks after work? Meet me in the lobby at 6?*
>
> *Kevin Foster*

I can't believe it. I'm being asked out. Like on a real date. I haven't gone on a date since my first date with Nick…

Two long years I've waited for this night. Every class, every lecture, every paper I wrote with him on my mind, never thinking I would ever have a chance to get to know him outside of class yet here I am, nervously getting ready for my first date with Mr. Schafer, Nick…

I had no idea he felt the same way about me. It wasn't until earlier today, at my graduation from University of San Francisco with my Law degree, that he found me, pulling me to the side and saying he's waited two years for this and couldn't wait one more day to take me out on a proper date.

I thought I had died and gone to heaven. All of those times we sat next to each other, going over law briefs, wishing his hand would move those few centimeters to touch mine and here he was hoping for the same thing the entire time. Tonight is our time to be boy and girl, man and woman and not teacher student.

I can't wait.

The doorbell rings and I run to answer, not caring how anxious I look. The time has come where I can finally share my true feelings for him.

The door swings open and we stare at each other.

"Kamii," he whispers through his gorgeous lips.

"Nick," I breathlessly respond before his arms are wrapped around my body in our first of many wonderfully, intense kisses.

"So… who are they from?" Stefanie asks, breaking through my thoughts of a time when I thought life was simple and didn't have a care in the world.

Shaking my head I answer, "I guess his name is Kevin. I met him in the elevator last week. He wants to meet for drinks tonight."

"Are you serious? That's awesome Kamii!" she jumps up, grabbing my shoulders in a small hug.

Her joyous attitude takes me out of my daydream funk and back to the realty that I'm actually being asked out.

"So you'll go right? Tell me, is he cute?"

I smirk at her, "He's gorgeous. Tall, dark hair, slight five o'clock shadow, strong jaw, bright green eyes... yeah, he caught my attention," I pause, letting out a big sigh, "but I don't know."

"Oh Kamii, I hope you go. How can you turn down a man that buys you these amazing flowers?"

"I know. I'll think about it. Right now I'm not sure if I can even carry them back to my office," I laugh.

She helps me maneuver them over her desk and I walk nervously back to my office, with the thought of dropping them along the way the least of my worries.

Could I really go out with this guy? I promised myself that I would try to be different, and Becca already told me she has other plans tonight, and it's only Wednesday so the club is closed.

Oh man, am I really going to do this...?

I sit nervously in my chair, tugging on my lower lip, trying to focus on work but not doing it very well. What will I say to him? Will he expect anything? I can't go home with him. Club rules. No sex outside of the club and I'm such a new member, I don't want to mess up my chances until I try everything there is to offer.

Six o'clock finally comes around and I decide to go for it. Live a little. Enjoy this new life I'm trying to lead.

As the elevator doors open, I'm thankful when I see it's empty. Riding down with him again would have been a little awkward.

Unconsciously, I start to tug on my bottom lip while staring down to the floor, completely lost in a bundle of nerves and thoughts. The elevator stops at the 5th floor and I don't pay any attention to who gets on until I feel the heat of someone standing tall over me.

His hand reaches up, removing my fingers from my lip and tucking his finger under my chin, tilting it up to meet his eyes.

"Hi Kamii."

Gorgeous green eyes meet mine as I watch my name slip off his lust filled lips. My mouth has lost all function as I stare at his eyes, then his lips, wondering what they would feel like pressed against my breast. *Oh jeez, I can't think this way. Not with him.*

"I'm Kevin," he says deep and drawn out.

"Hi... hi, Kevin. I'm Kamii," I nervously stutter.

He smirks, "Yeah, I know that. Are you planning on joining me for drinks tonight?"

"Yeah... I mean yes... I mean sure," I look down feeling like a complete idiot.

He tilts my head up once more, "Great, let's go."

He steps off of the elevator, grabbing my hand as he leads us through the elevator.

Once outside, I finally gather my bearings and come back to reality, "Um, thanks for the flowers, they're beautiful."

"Beautiful flowers for a beautiful woman," he replies. His voice has a very small hint of a southern accent, which makes me smile as I think of some of the cowboy romances I've read about.

We walk in silence a few blocks to the bar, Rickhouse, and I laugh at the coincidence that he's brought me here. I've never been here until Becca brought me the night that she first told me about the club.

He finds us a small, private table in the corner and orders us a bottle of Caymus Cabernet Sauvignon that arrives fast as we get situated in our seats.

"So Kamii," he pauses as he pours the wine and hands me a glass, "tell me, how was your night out with your *friends* last week?"

I almost choke on my wine at the thought of what I did with my *friends*. "Um, it was a fun night. How about you?"

"Very interesting. I enjoyed myself to say the least. I hope you did as well."

Why does this conversation feel a little odd all of a sudden?

He smirks and quickly changes the subject, "So, tell me about yourself. What do you do on the 11th floor?"

"I'm an attorney for Whitman, Osborn and Steinhorn, just made partner actually."

"Wow, impressive at your young age. You must be very good… I'm sure you're good at all things…"

My face instantly flushes as I pick up my wine to take another drink. "And how about you. I've seen you going above the 11th floor a few times now but yet tonight you entered the elevator on a lower floor."

"Ah, so you have been paying attention to me. I wonder just how much?"

"Excuse me?" I tilt my head to the side in question.

"Oh, I'm a CPA. I work for City Financial on the 15th floor and was dropping off paperwork to a client on the 5th floor as I left the building. I was lucky enough to run into you in the elevator again. I seem to be running into you a lot lately… in the elevator I mean."

I smile, not sure what to say so I grab my glass and take another drink of wine.

"What else can you tell me about yourself? Where are your friends tonight?"

"Oh, um, they're busy I guess. It's Wednesday so it's kind of odd to go out on a work night."

"But yet you're here with me," he smiles.

"Well yes, I wanted to thank you personally for the flowers."

"Yes, you've already done that."

I smile as I pick up my glass, looking at the bar to try to think of what else I could possibly say. He's sure not making this easy on me. Is this really how dating is now? More of an interview with weird questions?

"So do you live in the City?" I finally think of something to ask to break the silence between us.

He sits back, more relaxed as he answers, "I do. In Noe Valley. Just restored a place."

Finally, something we can talk about. "Really? I'm thinking of doing the same thing. Was it an entire gut job or a just a little remodeling?"

"Complete gut," he takes a sip of his wine. "A ton of work but I hired the right construction firm so it turned out exactly as I wanted."

"Really, I've been looking at contractors. Who did you use?"

"Babcock Construction."

"Hmm, I haven't heard of them. So you would recommend them?"

"Sure you have. You know, Preston Babcock..." he says the name slowly, like if he pronounces every syllable it would have more meaning.

I scrunch my eyes, trying to think, "Um, no, I'm sorry I don't."

"Are you sure? You've never heard the name Preston Babcock or Babcock Construction?"

"Um, wait, is that the company that is re-doing that entire building complex on Van Ness, turning it into a high rise apartment building? I didn't know he did smaller jobs?"

"Yes, he does *jobs*, he would *blow* away the smaller ones."

Why is this guy annunciating the weirdest words? Is he trying to drop some kind of weird sexual innuendos with jobs and blow? Are men that immature?

I try to ignore them hoping that wasn't his intention. "Well, thank you for the recommendation, I'll have to look into him."

"I'm sure you'll have no trouble finding him or getting *in* with him," he smirks as he leans back taking a drink of his wine.

Well, this has been fun and all but if I had to choose between this or a night at the club I would chose the club anytime so I think I'm ready to go. I lean sideways to reach for my jacket on the back of my chair, "Well, this has been nice but I really must get going now. I appreciate the flowers. My office smells amazing thanks to you."

Thankfully, he doesn't stop me from wanting to leave, "It was my pleasure. I'm sure I'll be seeing you soon, hopefully not just in the elevator."

"Um, yes, well, thank you again. Have a nice night."

"You too," he pauses, "Kamii..."

The way he says my name sends chills up my spine. I have a feeling I might be taking the stairs from now on.

Chapter EIGHT

Kamii

"I have a dirty chai for Becca…" the male barista calls out.

"Watch this…" Becca winks at me before getting up. "Hi there…" she says to the barista as she reaches over the counter that he purposely put very close to him so she had to reach for it.

He grabs the drink, holding it hostage while giving her a sexy smirk. "Why is it you order a dirty chai and not just a chai latte with an add shot?" he asks.

"Because what's the fun in that? As my friend over there says, 'a dirty chai for a dirty girl.'"

"So you're a dirty girl?" He pulls her a little closer over the table.

"You find my club and I'll show you all kinds of dirty. Or maybe you'd have to show me."

"Club? What do you mean by club?"

She grabs her drink from his hold, and as she walks away she looks over her shoulder, "I can't tell you, it's a secret. Too bad though, I can only imagine the noises you make when you cum."

There's a loud bang as the metal container that he uses to steam milk in hits the counter, spilling milk all over the floor. I'm laughing so hard I have tears running down my face. Poor guy. I don't think he saw that coming.

Her smile is priceless as she sits down in front of me before taking a drink of her dirty chai and smiling from the delicious taste that permeates her mouth.

"I think you either made that guys day or ruined it. I'm not sure," I smirk, hitting her arm.

"I definitely made it. Do you think any girl has ever said that to him? No. Maybe now he'll think of me next time he jerks off."

She looks his way, giving him a small smile and he winks back at her.

Yup, she made his day. I only dream of being like her some day. So free, so sure of herself.

"Why do you flirt like this though? Do you ever go out with these guys? Isn't it against club rules?" I ask.

"I can go out with them I just can't fuck them. Most of the time I wouldn't want to though, I get all I need from the club. A normal fuck in a normal bed would probably bore me to death. I don't know," she looks back to the guy, "he looks like he could have some potential in that department."

"Speaking of, someone asked me out last night."

"Shut up! Are you kidding me? Details. Tell me everything."

"At first I was shocked. I haven't been asked out since… since," I look down trying to hide the thought, "never mind, let's just say it's been awhile. He sent me a huge bouquet of white roses asking me to meet him in the lobby of our building."

"Wait, he works in your building?"

"Yes, I first met him in the elevator. Actually, the day you gave me that make over was the first day I saw him."

"See, I worked my magic and got you a date like that," she snaps her fingers with pride.

"Yes, it was all because of you," I smile.

"No, no, no, don't mix things up. I just worked with what was already there. You are sexy as hell and don't ever forget that."

I smile sweetly at her before continuing, "So we met in my lobby and he took me to Rickhouse for drinks."

"Oh cool!"

"Yeah, I thought so. Made me feel a little less out of my element with it being my first date in years and all. He was really sweet but kept dropping these weird comments or questions that were, I guess, a little sexual but just odd. Not really sure what they meant."

"Like what?"

I sigh, "I don't remember, it was nothing big that stood out, just odd is all."

"Well, I'm sorry. Hopefully your next date will be better."

I scrunch my fist into a ball, "No, if anything it just proved that I really don't want anything with anyone. Like you, I think the club is all I need."

"That's my girl. So what else is new?"

"Oh yeah, I haven't told you. I'm thinking of buying a new place and having it gutted and completely redone. I think it's time that I move on from my place that I shared with Nick."

"That's cool. Where are you looking?"

"I found a few places not far from here but need to talk to some contractors first to get some bids. Funny thing is the guy last night actually recommended someone to me, a company called Babcock Construction."

Becca chokes on her coffee and covers her mouth trying to clear her throat before she replies, "Um. Yeah, I think I've heard of them."

"You have? Jeez, I must be out of the loop. This guy acted like I should know exactly who the owner is, some guy named Preston Babcock. I told him I didn't know who he was. Do you?"

"Um, not sure but the name sounds familiar…" she says taking another drink of her dirty chai while looking at the barista again.

"Well, he highly recommended him so I think I'm going to give him a call, get a quote, see if what I want is even possible."

Becca looks down at her phone to check the time, "Sorry babe, I've got to run, I have a 9 am appointment. I'll see you tonight though right?"

"You know I'll be coming!" I smile as I wink in reply.

"Ha! I love the way I'm rubbing off on you!" She gives me a hug as we both stand up, "Later, girl."

As I walk into my work, Stefanie stands instantly, greedy for information about how my night went. "Oh, tell me, tell me, tell me. You know I have two little kids so the excitement from my life is gone. I have to live vicariously through you single people now."

I laugh, "Believe me. Being single is not like it used to be. Everything seems more like a weird interview full of sexual innuendos."

"Ugh, really?"

"Yeah, sorry. I didn't stay long. He was cute but things were just a little off. Sorry I don't have better news for you."

"It's ok, here's your mail," she hands me a stack of envelopes before sitting back down at her desk.

"Thank you, Stef,"

"Yeah, yeah, yeah. Get to work," she smirks.

Before I start my work for the day, I call Babcock Construction to make an appointment to go over my ideas. I'm bummed when I hear the owner is out and though they would love to meet with me, they are about a month out from starting any new projects due to time restraints. I make the appointment anyways figuring if I can't find anyone good by then at least I have a backup plan.

Ever since I met Becca many things that used to be important to me but I completely pushed out of my life have started to come back, and I'm wondering if I should, for the first time in years, play some music while I work.

Music used to be a huge part of my life both before and during my time with Nick. We would go to any concert we could get tickets to and music constantly filled our home. We both were never big with the television so music played any time we were there. The DJ at our wedding had the easiest job ever because I gave him the exact playlist I wanted played. Every song that Nick and I would dance to or sing in the car had to be played.

After his death, every song reminded me of him. No matter what the genre, what the lyrics were or if it was fast or slow, I would find something there that would crush my soul even more. So eventually I turned it all off and learned to live my life in silence.

But like everything in my life now, I'm trying to change my *anymores* into *yes I wills*.

I look around my office and wonder if there is a radio around here that I can borrow. Pressing my intercom to Stefanie I ask, "Hey Stef, is there a radio around here I can borrow?"

"A radio? For what?" she asks, completely confused by my question.

"Um, to listen to music. Why else would anyone want a radio?"

She laughs even harder, "You have your computer, don't you have a Pandora station set up?"

"A what?"

Her laughter gets harder and I'm starting to feel stupid that I have no idea what she's talking about. "I'll be right there."

I'm shocked at how much the music world has changed in just the past five years with technology. Stefanie showed me how I can stream music straight through my computer and now I'm trying to think of which band I should play as my station.

My taste in music has always been eclectic and really just depended on my mood. I used to listen to pop, country and classic rock but my favorite was modern rock with my favorite band being Three Days Grace. Adam Gontier's voice did things to me that should be illegal.

My heart warms at the thought of his voice as I click their station and *Lost In You* plays bringing back memories of Nick singing this song to me. The thought still hurts but, thankfully, seems more manageable now. His voice still has the same affect on me as I sit back in my chair, closing my eyes and singing the lyrics like I just listened to them yesterday, not five years ago.

Warm thoughts fill my body as the thought of finally having myself back settles in. I'm more than thankful and know that I have Becca to thank.

My workday flies by with the help of Pandora and the Three Days Grace channel. I've found some new bands and liked as many songs as I could. I'm embarrassed to say that I've probably spent more time researching bands than I did actually working today. I was shocked when I learned that Adam Gontier left Three Days Grace but thankfully started a new band, Saint Asonia, so of course I had to listen to their songs as well.

Deciding to call it quits for the day, I shut off my computer and head to Becca's to get ready for the night. I'm not sure what to think because I've never been on a Thursday and tonight is more of the swinger's night.

Thankfully, Becca's place is not far from mine and both are close to our work so I don't have to go far. I hop in my black BMW and head to Russian Hill and her place on Hyde Street.

"Hey girl!" she greets me with a big hug as I walk through the door.

"Yum, it smells good in here," I reply after smelling the garlic and onion radiating from her kitchen.

"Good! I made us dinner. I hope you're hungry." She has an apron on and walks to the stove stirring whatever she has on the stove.

"Well aren't you Miss Suzie Homemaker. I didn't think people actually cooked in the City, just always ate out. At least that's what I always do."

"Well, now you don't. It's not healthy to eat out all the time. And I love to cook so you'll have to join me for dinner more often."

"You got a deal. Can I help in anyway?"

She gives me a snide look, "I thought you said you don't cook."

"Oh believe me, I can ruin boiling water. I guess I meant, can I run to the store to get us a bottle of wine?" I laugh.

"Already done," she winks as she hands me a glass and pours the grapes from the gods filling it to the top.

"Cheers," I say holding up the glass before taking a sip that instantly warms my body and lightens my soul.

"Ah, guess what?" Becca asks as she puts the spoon down and does her little girl excitement bounce.

"What?"

"I went shopping today and bought you something!"

"Oh Becca, no, you shouldn't have," I say shaking my head no, both because she doesn't need to be buying me anything and also because I'm a little scared at what she bought.

"Oh stop, look…" she says as she pulls out a black dress that I'm afraid to look at because I know no matter what, I'll be wearing it tonight.

After taking a big gulp of my wine, I walk toward her and get my first glimpse of what's in store for me. To my surprise, I'm actually in love with what she bought.

"Becca, I, I love it. It's perfect!" I say as I run my fingers down the black lace arms. It's a short dress that has a tight waist and tulle under the dress to make it more girly. It's not super sexy but it's totally me. The new me.

I give her a big hug, "Thank you so much!"

"No prob girl. We're going shopping this weekend and getting you a whole new wardrobe as well, just so you know," she winks as she walks back to the kitchen.

"I can't thank you enough. You've helped me in so many ways and I feel like I can't do anything for you in return."

"Oh stop. You have done a ton for me as well. I've never really had a friend that I wanted to share this lifestyle with. It's a blast for me that I have someone to go with and to talk about sex with. Everyone is so stuffy on the subject and I've never found another female that I wanted to be friends with so I should be thanking you. I knew you were different than the others."

"The others?" I ask confused.

"Yeah, you know. Girls can be major bitches. I've been going to a few other clubs for a few years and lord I can tell you all kinds of drama."

"Are you serious?"

She shakes her head, "Believe me, you don't want to know. That's why I was so on board with this place. I like the fact that it's all anonymous. I've had girls stalking me at my work, waiting for me outside of clubs and don't get me started on the guys."

"I'm shocked. I guess I never thought about this side of these clubs."

"Yeah, unfortunately, feelings always get involved and one person will think they have something going on with the other person and then that other person will be fucking someone else the next week and things just get messy. I actually had a girl walk up and slap me while I was riding who she said was her man. I had to laugh, I mean, we were in a fuck circle with I think eight people total. Talk about ruining your orgasm. It was like she waited until I was coming to slap me."

"Holy schmoly!" I say completely shocked.

Her laugh rumbles throughout the room as she puts her hands down on the counter to brace herself. "You crack me up. 'Holy schmoly.' Do you cuss at all? Say it with me, holy fuck."

"Yes I cuss," I laugh, embarrassed by her remark.

"Say it, holy fuck," she raised her arms like a conductor to a symphony.

"Holy fuck…" I say under my breath.

"Louder," she eggs me on.

"Holy Fuck."

"Louder."

"HOLY FUCK" I scream making her laugh. "Are you happy now?"

She shakes her head sternly in confirmation, "Yes, that's better. None of this schmoly shit. Say fuck like you mean it. Like you love it. Like every time you use the word your pussy tingles and you can't wait to get *fucked*," she says up close to my face before kissing my cheek. "Now let's eat."

After dinner, we get dressed for the night and when I see myself for the first time in the dress she picked out I can't help but stare at the woman who is reflecting back at me. My hair is wavy, brown with the blonde highlights she put in and sits right on my shoulders. The dress is lace down the arms and comes up to a small button at my neck but leaving a big hole for my cleavage to show brightly against the all black material.

I'm still in shock of what I've become and that I'm the person looking back at me. Never in a million years did I ever think I could be this beautiful, this sexy, this womanly yet here I am. Tears fill my eyes as I glance at Becca who's putting on her mascara next to me.

When our eyes catch she stops instantly, "Wait, whoa, why are you crying?"

"I just can't believe it. I can't believe this is me," I point at the mirror.

"It's you girl. I knew you were underneath there. We just needed to peel back the leaves to let the beautiful rose bloom."

Wrapping my arms around her for a big hug, I thank her before running to the bathroom for a tissue to blot my eyes without smearing my makeup.

Chapter NINE

Kamii

When we arrive at the club we both grab a drink and scan the room looking for possibilities. I'm not sure how this is supposed to go. This is my third time here and though I know I am supposed to venture out to other people I'm not sure if I'm ready yet and to be honest, I'm not comfortable enough to do so.

Eros has been great to me and I think once I experience *everything* I'll be ready to venture off some more.

Warmth covers my side as I feel a man's hand grip around my waist and pull me close to him. Automatically, I drop my head to his chest but am slightly frightened when I hear a voice that isn't Eros' whisper in my ear, "Do I get to play with you tonight or are you with your friends?"

Turning around in a flash, I see a tall man with a slight five o'clock shadow covering his very strong jaw watching me from under his simple, black mask.

Butterflies fill my stomach as I think of the possibilities with this man. I can tell by the tight fitted Henley he has on that every muscle is perfectly sculpted. Imagining the feeling of his barely there beard between my legs brings tingles to places I've become very fond of recently.

Channeling my inner Becca again, I try to think of what she would say when I feel the warmth of another hand grab my waist from behind. I place my tiny hand over his large fingers, wrapping mine around his and knowing instantly that it's Eros by the feeling of the calluses that just barely cover his hands. Thoughts of being with Eros and another man enlighten my desires as I lean back on Eros and tug on the pants of the man in front of me.

"Hello there Eros," I say tilting my head slightly to see his face before leaning up to kiss his neck, keeping my hands on the man in front of me.

"Hello my beautiful Eurydice. Who's your friend?"

I look to the man in front of me that has a slight smirk on his face as he stands there watching me with his mouth slightly parted. "Not sure yet. Should I even care?"

I feel Eros shrug, "Totally up to you, sweetheart."

I haven't taken my eyes or my hands off the man's pants as I ask, "Do I care who you are?"

"No, ma'am," he responds and I'm instantly turned on by his slight southern accent and the way he said ma'am.

I look to Becca who's standing a few feet away, talking to another man but I don't care, I want her to join me if I'm going to go through with this. "Hey Baubo..." I say as sweet as possible. "How about you join me and these two handsome men tonight?"

She pats the man's chest in front of her before turning to walk toward us, "You don't have to ask me twice." She cozies up to the man that I still don't know his name and smiles, "Hey sexy. You want to fuck me tonight?"

"Well, I'd like to fuck both of you if I can."

My chest tightens from his words and I feel Eros tighten his grip around me in response, which is odd because I didn't think I moved at all but he must have sensed it. Leaning down he whispers in my ear, "You don't have to if you don't want to."

"No, it's fine," I say rubbing his hand that I still have a hold of. "I told you I want to try everything so this is the next step. I'd like for both you and Baubo to join us. I think I would feel better this way."

"Of course my sweet Eurydice, there is no place or no one I'd rather be with."

His lips meet the back of my neck and my head drops instantly from the heavy lust filling my insides just from the feeling of his tongue licking up behind my ear to my pulse spot.

"I can tell she likes what you're doing by the way her eyes just fluttered back and her skin became a beautiful flush of rosy flesh. You are very responsive my lovely. I can't wait to have my turn," the man says.

With that, all four of us turn to claim a room. Eros leads us to a more private area of the club where there is both a bed and a small couch in the room.

I feel my pulse start to thud through my veins as we enter the room. Becca thankfully takes control and grabs me away from Eros, kissing me softly as she puts on a show for the two men.

Her hands run through my hair as I lightly feel up her waist and grab her breasts with both of my hands. It's amazing how comfortable I've gotten with kissing my best friend but, to be honest, I've actually started to enjoy it, turned on by it even. It's the fact that I know the two men are watching us. I could never imagine wanting to kiss her in any other setting but here, now, knowing what I'm doing is turning these two men into ravenous alphas turns me on more than I could ever explain.

Eros walks up to me as the other man comes to Becca from behind. His hands meet mine at her breasts but instead of rubbing her, his hands grasp mine and his fingers run in between mine like we're holding hands.

My kiss with Becca breaks as my eyes meet his, making his fingers grip mine even more, rubbing softly over my fingers. This little act makes me feel more comfortable with him and what we're about to do so I bravely reach over Becca's shoulder and kiss him softly which instantly turns into a much more passionate kiss as Becca slides out of the way but Eros never lets go of my side, just moving with me as I move closer to the other man.

Our kiss breaks when I feel Eros reach between us to unbutton my dress in the front as he starts to slide it down my arms and off completely.

"Damn," I hear the man whisper as he looks me up and down, appreciating my black lace bra and the fact that I had no panties on.

"Naughty girl tonight, I see," Eros says from behind before he swings me around, staking his claim against my lips, tongue and body. I enjoyed the kiss of the other man but going from him to Eros is nothing but phenomenal. The way our mouths blend perfectly, the tingles that shoot through my body as his tongue brushes against mine feel one thousand times better than it did when I was kissing Becca or the other guy.

Totally lost, my arms wrap around his neck, needing to feel his body against mine. Two manly hands gripping my breast from behind take me out of my lust filled haze as I feel my bra straps fall down my arms and to the floor.

Leaning against him, I start to unbutton the shirt of Eros in front of me as Becca removes his pants from behind before dropping to her knees and taking Eros' cock in her mouth.

The other man's breath brushes against my neck, sending chills down my arms as he whispers, "I'd love to watch you suck on my cock like that."

Without a word, I turn, drop to my knees and unbutton his pants, reaching in to free his already hard cock. My tongue works its way up and down his shaft while looking up to the mask of the man I have no clue who he is. The thought both turns me on and frightens the hell out of me.

His lips turn up to a sexy smile as I try to focus on how hot he is and not the fact that I don't even know his name. Opening my mouth wide, I take his entire cock in deep, pulling back and forth, running my tongue over his tip every time I pull out. Strong hands grip my hair, yanking me roughly to and away from him as he starts to fuck my mouth.

Feelings of both shame and lust grip my chest and stomach, and I'm not sure which one I should focus on more.

Eros reaches around Becca, running his finger down my face, instantly calming my nerves and wanting all of my attention to go to him. I stand up, turning toward him, pulling his hand to the bed and pushing him to lie down before I straddle him, suddenly greedy for the feeling of his cock inside of me.

Becca throws me a condom from the basket and I rip it open as fast as I can, sliding it on and sinking down on him slowly, enjoying as he fills every inch of me inside.

With my hands gripping his chest, I feel my eyes roll back in my head as I lift up to sink down on him again. The bed moves and I see Becca climbing on all fours to meet Eros' face. I watch as their lips wrap around each other but I quickly look away, trying to ignore the sudden jealousy gripping my chest, not sure where this feeling is coming from.

Instead, I look to the man as he covers himself with a condom and starts to ram Becca from behind roughly. Becca screams out, enjoying the sudden surprise attack before reaching to kiss Eros again.

Sounds of ecstasy fill the room as slapping skin and moaning grunts fill the air around us. I'm not sure what is turning me on more, the fact that I'm in control, riding Eros however I want or watching as the guy's dick pulls in and out of Becca.

My orgasm builds quickly as I slow my in and out on his dick and rub my clit against his body.

Eros' lips pull away from Becca as his gaze meets mine, "Yeah Eurydice, that's it, give it to me." His hand reaches in to rub my clit and instantly brings me over the edge, making me scream in my release as I stay completely still, feeling my insides clench against his hard length in its release.

"Fuck that was hot," the guy says as he slaps Becca's ass in a way that says *I'm done with you* and moves toward me. "My turn," he smiles.

Eros' hands instantly wrap around my waist possessively and I grab them, assuring that it's ok and climb off to offer my body to the other man.

Trying to be someone else, I find the strength to tease him, "Yeah, you think you can make me cum like that?"

"Damn girl, just wait," he responds as he throws me down on the bed, pushing my legs open wide and I finally get to feel that tickle I dreamed about when I first laid eyes on him.

Laying down on the bed is actually exactly what I need as the warmth from my orgasm fills my body and the feeling of his tongue playing softly with my clit is working perfectly to bring me back to now if he's going to make me cum again.

He takes his time, moving and licking long, slow licks and I can't help but wrap my hands in his hair and pull hard as I try to put him exactly where I need him. I hear and feel his laugh as he steadies my hips with his strong hands; keeping me in the exact place he wants me, driving me crazy from inside.

I turn my gaze away from him to try to calm down and am surprised to see that Becca is sucking on Eros instead of fucking him. I know that neither one of them came yet but they seem to be enjoying themselves so I turn my attention back to the guy just as he pulls away and grips his cock making sure the condom is still secure.

This is it, I'm going to fuck a man that I just met and I have no idea what his name is. I turn to look at Becca but my gaze is caught on Eros as he watches the man enter me slowly. The feeling overwhelms me but I can't close my eyes or even want to, I just stare as Eros stares at where this man is ramming inside of me and his stare is anything but lust filled.

Thankfully, Becca breaks his attention as she pulls away from his cock and pushes him down on the bed, trying to mount him herself but before she does, he flips her over, kissing down her body before licking her to a quick and fast orgasm.

My own orgasm has been slowly building again but not until watching Becca cum all over Eros' face did I feel the need so deeply. My hand comes to my clit, rubbing right were I need it and sending me over the edge as the guy never stops his assault and finding his release shortly after.

Sounds that filled the room now quiet down and heavy breathing is all that's left. The man pulls out of me and I instantly turn to the side, more relaxed than I've been all week and enjoying the high filling my veins.

Rustling around takes me out of my sense of heaven when I hear, "But you didn't cum…" from across the room.

I open my eyes to see Becca reaching for Eros as he stands up, pulling his pants on. "It's fine," he says trying to blow her off and she doesn't ask any more questions, just leans over to lay next to me, both in our sexual bliss.

The bed dips down next to me and I feel the warmth of someone leaning down toward me from above. I turn my head slightly to see it's the other man leaning to whisper something in my ear. "Thank you. You have no idea how bad I wanted to fuck you. I hope to see you again in the elevator soon, Kamii."

Quickly I turn to the side, shocked that he knows my name as what he just said computes in my brain. *See me again, elevator, he asked about my friends earlier, he knows my name. Oh my god, this is Kevin from my building that I went out with the other day.*

Fear fills my body as he leans down to kiss my lips softly, shushing me from saying anything before getting up and leaving the room without saying anything to anyone else.

I sit up, scared shitless and not sure what to do. *What does this mean? How did he know it was me? Did he know when he asked me out? Holy fuck!* Yes I said it, in this case there is nothing else that fits more than *holy fuck!*

"You ok girl?" Becca's hand rubs my back, trying to reassure my sudden freak out.

Eros is instantly at my side, obviously concerned as well. After taking a deep breath I push all my thoughts down, trying to hide them and act like nothing's wrong because there is nothing I can say to Becca in front of Eros.

Chapter TEN

Kamii

Becca and I leave together and drive back to her house. I still have no clue what just happened and how I feel about it. I mean, I guess I should be happy that I do actually know the man I just let fuck me but really the fact that I did actually know him is what is bothering me. Backwards, I know.

"Ok girl, what's up? You were all in lala land from what I can only assume were two amazing orgasms and then you seemed to freak out. What's going on in that lawyer, black and white brain of yours? Are you freaking out because you don't know the man you just fucked or what?"

I let out a short laugh, "That's the problem Becca. I *do* know him."

She turns quickly in her seat to me, "You *what*? How do you know that?"

"He leaned in and whispered in my ear, 'You have no idea how bad I wanted to fuck you. I hope to see you again in the elevator, Kamii.'"

"Wait, what? I don't get it?"

"It's the guy, Becca. The guy I told you about, from my building that I went out with the other day."

"No way!"

I look and nod at her. "Once he said it everything clicked in my head. He must have seen me last week though I don't know how he could tell. That's probably why he asked me out and kept dropping all those weird questions and sexual innuendos. He knew I came here. He was probably trying to get me to play along."

"Holy fuck."

"Yes, holy fuck," I say deadpan and she laughs.

"Hey, at least you said that right," she hits my shoulder. "So what does this mean?"

"I don't know. At first I was weirded out that I was having sex with a guy I didn't know and now that I do know who he is I'm freaking out even more."

She grabs her stomach, laughing in hysterics. "Oh the irony. Never thought you would be freaking out because you actually knew a guy you just fucked, huh?"

My glare stops her laughing as she playfully hits my arm again, "Oh relax. It's no big deal. Part of the membership is to keep a secret so you don't have to worry about him telling your whole building he fucked you or anything."

"I know that but it just doesn't sit easy with me. I wanted this to be my escape from reality and now I have to worry about running in to my escape *during* my reality."

I turn the corner to her street when flashing lights fill my car. There are four police cars and one ambulance wheeling an injured person out of her building.

"What the hell?" Becca says as I pull to a stop and put the car in park.

We look at each other in question as we both unlock our seatbelts.

"Do you want me to come in?" I ask.

"Um, yeah, why don't you. Until we find out what's going on," she says as she opens the car door.

We walk up to a police officer who is blocking the entry way and Becca approaches him in a way that seems a little too familiar, "Hey Nicholas, what's going on?"

"Good, I wondered where you were. Becca there's been a home invasion to an apartment in your building. Thankfully no one was hurt and the man was home and was able to apprehend the suspect. Things got a little messy but it looks like he's going to be ok. I'm glad you weren't home but I wondered where you were, especially dressed like that?"

She hits his chest, "Stop. I'm fine, see." She holds out her arms to show that her body is indeed intact. Thankfully, she has on a jacket because if this man thinks what she's wearing is bad he would definitely not like to see what's under her jacket.

"Well, I don't think you should stay here tonight. How about you come back to the station then you can come home with me?" he asks.

"Um, no," she points her finger at him. "Here, I'll go home with my friend," she turns to point at me as I sit a few steps down from her on the entryway.

He gives me a questioning look and then gives her approval and we walk back to my car.

"Who was that?" I ask.

"Him? Oh, he's no one. Just someone I know is all."

Preston

Last night has me in a twist of nerves and rage. Why is this woman getting to me so much? I left there with the worst case of blue balls but for some reason that was better than cumming in anyone that wasn't Eurydice.

I'm so fucked.

Seeing that other man fuck her felt like I was being stabbed in the chest with every thrust he made. I never got this way when I watched Kim with other men so I have no clue why I'm so affected now.

My workload has been insane lately and I know I should be thankful my business is doing so well but since we're having to push new clients back a month, I'm feeling like I should look into hiring more people. As I look over and crunch some numbers, I hear a knock at my office door and a lively as ever Becca bounces her way into the room.

The calmness she's brought into my life recently is like a welcome beam of sunshine on a cold day, so I set my pencil down, "Well hello there. To what do I owe this honor?"

"Hey cutie!" she smiles as she sits down in a chair in front of my desk. "Fun time last night," she says with a knowing look on her face and a small wink.

"Fuck Becca, really? Not now…" I say turning my attention back to my spreadsheet. She may bring calmness but she's also annoying as shit wanting to pry into my personal life.

"You're totally falling for her, I know it," she sings with a little girl grin on her face.

"I said not now. Are you here for anything else or just to torture me?"

"Well, you know you're my favorite person to fuck with but I do have a purpose for being here. Something that I thought you should know about."

Thankful she's going to drop it, I turn back to her to give her my full attention, "Ok, what's up?"

"So you actually know that guy from last night, don't you?"

"Yeah, a little I guess. I just remodeled his house but that's about it. Why?"

"Well, he knows Kamii, too and made it known last night."

"He what?" I say grinding my teeth and almost breaking the pencil I'm holding in my hand.

"Yup. Turns out he's been hitting on Kamii before she was even a member and then recognized her at the club. They went for drinks a couple of nights ago and he was dropping hints but she didn't catch on. He whispered it in her ear after they fucked. That's why she got all weirded out."

"Is she quitting?" I say, panicked.

Becca gives me her knowing smile again which I want to permanently remove from her face. "She hasn't mentioned it but she's not feeling good about the situation. She didn't want her real life interfering with this life, which I'm sure you can understand Mr. Secret Pants," she taunts.

I look down. *No, she can't quit.* The thought grips my heart making it feel like it's being ripped straight out of my chest and dying slowly in front of me, but if anyone understands not wanting to mix the two lives, it's me. "Yeah, I get it."

"Don't get all scared on me. I'm sure she'll stay, we will just have to wait and see what happens today at work and if this guy makes it known." She gets up to leave before turning around again, "Oh and one more thing. There was some drama at my building last night so I'm staying with Kamii for a little while. Just so you know," she winks as she blows me a kiss and leaves my office.

I try to go on with my day but the thought of Kamii leaving down right freaks me out so I take matters into my own hands before that can happen.

After looking through my client list for Kevin's number, I dial it on my phone, knowing exactly what I have to do.

"Preston, my man. What's up?" he says as a greeting to my phone call.

"Hey Kevin. I'm sorry to do this," I get straight to the point, "but I have to revoke your membership to Bridge."

"What? You've got to be kidding me. Why?"

"It's been brought to my attention that you revealed yourself to a fellow member and that is against all rules of keeping everything anonymous," I say still trying to hide my anger toward him and the jealousy that is ripping through my veins knowing that he had his hands and cock all over Kamii last night.

"Come on. That's all bullshit. Everyone will find out sooner or later. Come on, don't kick me out," he pleads.

"Sorry. I can't risk you telling other members who you are or, more importantly, who I am. You are only one of two who know my identity and I can't risk it."

"You're a fucking prick. This is bullshit. You're just jealous because you have a thing for this chick. I've seen you all over her every time you're together.

You're just jealous because she liked my dick, maybe even more than yours."

With that I don't even bother to give him a response. How could I? He's knows the truth no matter how hard I fight it but I don't regret revoking his membership. He broke the rules and that's the only reason why.

My phone dings with a text message:

Kevin: Fuck you, you fucking prick. You better watch your back because it's fucking on. You'll regret doing this.

I definitely don't respond to that and just click the messaging app closed, trying to go on with my day.

Kamii

I arrived at work much earlier than normal just to avoid any awkward elevator rides. So far so good and, thankfully, I haven't heard anything from Kevin.

The day drags on and any moment my brain isn't enthralled in a case I'm working on it instantly goes to the look on Eros' face as he watched Kevin have sex with me and the feeling I got when I watched Becca kiss him.

This is all not ok. I need to stop these growing feelings, what did Becca call it, the human factor, before things get out of control. This is not what I want. This is not why I'm going to this club. I'm going to forget about Kevin, not let him bother me and go on, continuing my mission to become the new me.

Since the incident happened at Becca's apartment building last night, we decided that she's going to be staying with me for a few days until they figure out everything that's going on. So I turn off my computer early, excited to finally have a real reason to go home.

The building is still bustling with people eager to leave for the weekend so the thought of running into him escapes my mind as I weave my way through the crowded lobby.

Just when I thought everything was clear, I feel a strong palm grip around my arm, pulling me to the side and pressing me up against the wall.

"Hi Kamii," he whispers as he pushes his body against mine.

My arms instantly go up in defense as I try to push him away. "Excuse me, but I don't appreciate you doing this here, now."

"But you sure loved it last night?" he responds, turning my chin so I'm forced to look at him when I was trying to look anywhere but. "You have no idea how surprised I was to walk into Bridge last week and see the woman I just wanted to fuck in an elevator stripping her black skirt and teal top right in front of me."

Knowing this man had sex with me last night isn't sitting well with me now. His demeanor and the look in his eyes are frightening me to be honest. His eyes graze over my body and I know he's imagining my body naked. My arms wrap tightly around my chest, like I'm trying to cover his image and a chill runs down my spine as his lips tilt up in an evil smirk.

"Please, just leave me alone. Nobody is supposed to know anyone for this reason alone. I'd like to keep it that way," I say as sternly as I possibly can.

"Well, you don't have to worry about that anymore. My membership has been revoked and I have a feeling you had something to do with that."

What? What did I do? "I don't know what you're talking about," I say, completely confused. *Did Becca tell the owner what happened?*

"Don't worry. He'll pay for cancelling my membership," he says as he pushes off the wall, walking away, leaving me shattered, standing there, questioning everything that just happened.

When I arrive home, Becca's not there so I quickly strip my clothes, in sudden need for a hot shower. My emotions are all over the place. I'd be lying if I said I didn't enjoy having sex with a man I didn't know. But is it possible to get away from this *human factor* that seems to be leering around?

Once out of the shower, I throw my wet hair up in a sloppy bun and put on my favorite lounge pants and tight tank top, grabbing a glass of wine and opening a new book I just downloaded on my kindle.

I hear the door open and feel the unmistakable happiness that Becca radiates as she walks through the door, "Honey, I'm home!" she teases as she shuts the door behind her.

She gets one look at me on the couch and starts in right away, "Whoa, whoa now. What are you doing? We're going to the club in an hour? Come on, get dressed."

I sigh, "I don't think I can go."

"Oh no you don't. That guy won't be there, I promise."

"I know, he made that very clear when he basically assaulted me in the lobby of my building."

"Shut up!" she says as she bounces down on the couch.

"Well, I guess *assault* is a harsh word. But he grabbed me, pulling me to the side and made me feel more than uncomfortable so I don't know. Can we just have a girls night in?"

She rubs my leg that's sitting next to her on the couch. "I get it girl. Let me get in my cozies and we'll do whatever you want, ok?"

I give her my thank you smile as she gets up and heads to change her clothes.

Surprisingly enough, the night turns out to be a blast with just the two of us. We stay up all night talking about boys, sex and more boys. She's told me more crazy stories about clubs she's been to and reassures me that this is all just part of the gig, the human factor, she keeps referring to.

She says it will get easier and gives me some warning signs to look out for, and more importantly, what to stay away from.

We get the brilliant idea the next morning that we both deserve a day of pampering in Napa so she calls her clients to reschedule her day and we head off to Calistoga for a day of mud baths and massages.

I honestly do have plans to go back to Bridge but I think taking a few days off will make me miss it and help me deal with all the emotions I have over Eros and the place in general.

As we go to walk out the door, I turn to ask, "Do you want to drive or should I?"

"Nope, you drive so I can control the radio," she replies as she holds up the keys for me that were sitting on the counter.

"Excuse me, I thought the driver always gets to decide what's on the radio," I fight back.

"Um, no. Not nowadays. Now we listen to Pandora or your iPod and you're not allowed to look at your phone while you drive," she says in a lower tone like she's a father scolding his child. "So the passenger takes control."

"Ok, but you have no idea the affair I have with music so you better play something good," I say as I grab the keys from her and walk toward the door.

Once in the car, she instantly hooks up her phone to my connector that I didn't even know I had in the car. "Ok, so let's test your music knowledge. Who's this?" she asks.

She plays a beat that definitely gets me moving and nodding my head along but I have no idea who it is. "Ok, I suck. I have to admit. I just recently started listening to music again," I pause thinking I need to explain why I wasn't listening to music. "It was an important part of Nick's and mine relationship," I pause again as I try to blink away the tears that are forming, "Never mind. But no, sorry, I've never heard this one."

Without notice, Becca turns the radio on full blast and sings at the top of her lungs, "I'm gonna love ya, until you hate me."

Just like everything she does, her actions instantly lighten my mood to my pre-Nick memory moment and I can't help but laugh as I listen to the song that slows down to a female rap beat.

I must admit, I'm digging this song. It's a mixture between a rap song and a slick reggae beat with a steel drum. Once it's over, I turn down the speakers and ask, "Ok, I liked that. You've earned your DJ status in my car. Who was that?"

"Yay! See I told you I'm good! It was *Black Widow* by Iggy Azalea. It's one of my favorites. I can't believe you've never heard it. It's been out for about a year now and they play it all the time on 94.9."

"I told you. I just recently started listening to *any* music again and though pop/rap songs weren't my favorite, I really liked that. Play it again."

"You got it," she says as she plays the song again which quickly becomes our theme song for this entire trip as we bounce around the car, dancing and singing at the top of our lungs.

Chapter ELEVEN

Kamii

It's Thursday and I can't wait to head back to Bridge. I've found myself having a hard time breathing today I'm so excited. Taking the few days off was exactly what I needed to miss and realize I definitely want this in my life.

Every time the thought of my plans for tonight crossed my mind, I instantly felt my chest tighten with anticipation.

It's like the club is a drug. I've become so addicted; almost blind to anything else and tonight I only want more.

I'm in such a good mood that I decided I needed a little tunes in my office while I cleaned up. Streaming Pandora through my computer is probably the best thing that was ever invented. I jump up when I hear the clapping and steel drum beat from the intro to *Black Widow*.

Instantly, I turn up the tiny speakers, bouncing around the room to the fun dance beat that reminds me of my weekend getaway with Becca.

My office door opens then quickly shuts as my assistant, Angie, walks through the door, clapping her hands and dancing to the beat as well.

As we switched everything over to my partner status we gave her two weeks off and you should have seen the look on her face the first time she saw me and how much I've changed.

Instantly, I stop dancing, embarrassed that she caught me dancing around my office but then relieved when I see she's here to dance along with me. The smile across her face makes me laugh as we both sing, "I'm gonna love ya, until you hate me."

A freeness I haven't felt in years overcomes my body as we both dance around my office singing at the top of our lungs. Once it's over, we both fall into the chairs in front of my desk, laughing.

"That seriously is my favorite song," she says, still laughing through her hard breathing from the serious dance club we just created.

"Me, too! That beat gets you moving," I laugh.

She grabs my hand, squeezing it tightly. "Hey, I'm so glad to see you happy. I'm not sure what you're doing, but keep it up. I've missed this side of you."

"Thanks. Me, too." We look at each other, smiling, not saying anything else but saying more in those unsaid words than what have been said in the past five years.

"Ok then. That was fun. Anytime you want to dance you let me know!" She gets up and walks out of my office as I laugh at her response.

It's been a three weeks since I've joined Bridge and I can honestly say it has been the best couple weeks of my life. I've done more in this small time frame sexually than I have in my entire life. Not only have I enjoyed it physically, but I can tell mentally my life is turning for the better as well.

I smile all the time now. I even feel more clear and focused on my work. Things that used to be daunting tasks don't feel that way anymore. My entire life feels lighter and I know I owe everything to Becca.

Even though Bridge is only open three nights a week, we've spent every night together now that she's staying with me. No longer am I dreading going home to be alone. Now, I actually look forward to getting off of work and whatever crazy plans we have going on for the night. To say she has taken me out of my shell would be an understatement.

I've done crazier things this week than I have in my entire life and I'm not just talking sexually.

We've hit up every club or bar around my area it seems like. Flirting shamelessly with the bartenders and patrons. Meeting the most amazing people I never would have dreamed of talking to. Though it never goes further than talking or flirting. Everything sexual happens at the club. It's an honor system but one that members take very seriously. If you have sexual encounters outside of the club, with non-members, they ask that you get tested again.

It makes total sense to me and really, I'm so over satisfied with what I'm receiving there that I don't even think about wanting something from outside.

But tonight, I think I'm ready for a little more *inside* the club. Eros has been amazing, bringing me to orgasm more times than I can even remember, but I'm ready to venture off without him. I think it's what I need to get him off of my mind.

I'm thankful he has taken me under his wing but tonight I want to explore the other members. See what everyone has to offer. I mean, that is what the club is for, sharing…

The thought excites me even more. I noticed a few other members that caught my eye and tonight I'll make my move. I haven't even talked to Becca about it. I didn't want her help. I wanted to prove that I could put myself out there, go after what I want and actually get it.

There are two in particular that have caught my eye when I looked around the club on my past visits. I haven't seen these men attached to one specific woman and even if they are, I'm learning the more the merrier has more meanings than I ever knew.

Once home, I go through all the clothes that Becca helped me pick out on our shopping excursions and I now have a completely new wardrobe. I pick out an all black romper that's short shorts with long sleeves, backless and a plunging neckline making it impossible to wear a bra. I pull my hair half up, showing off my neckline more and grab a thin, black leather string necklace, wrapping it around my neck like a choker and tying the ends so it hangs down my cleavage then finishing the outfit off with strappy, three inch black heels.

Becca walks in my place like she owns it, which brightens my day even more. "You ready girl?" she yells as she shuts the door.

I walk from my room into the hallway not saying a word, waiting to see what her reaction would be to my chosen outfit.

"Holy shit, girl! You look fucking hot! Damn, I couldn't be more proud of myself right now. I'd say my work is complete."

I laugh, "Thank you! You like?"

"Like? Girl, I know we've done things at the club together but I kind of want to do you right now. You look *that* good."

I know she's kidding and I can't help but laugh at her response. "Well, thank you. You look pretty hot yourself."

"Seriously, Eros is going to lose his mind tonight."

"Hmm, about that…" I walk into the kitchen to grab my purse. "I was thinking I might look around tonight. Maybe sample someone else."

"Whoa, really? Look at you… I couldn't be more proud right now. Oh man, Eros is going to be pissed once he finds out."

"You think? I mean, is it weird that he's always with me? I've seen you with many other people but he's only been with me and me with him. Well, besides you," I laugh. "I thought the point of this place was to be with other people? Shouldn't I want to venture out more?"

"Oh yes, don't get me wrong. You are more than welcome to be with whom ever you want but I've noticed the way Pr… shit, I mean Eros has kind of staked his claim on you."

That's not the first time I've heard her almost say his real name. I try to ignore it. I don't want to know his real name. I don't want anything of this to be real. This is all for fun. No faces, no names, no strings attached.

"Yeah, that's why I want to try someone else. I don't want him to think I'm always just going to be with him. I'm very thankful he's showed me the ropes and all, no pun intended," I hit her arm laughing, "but I want to play with someone else tonight. I'm ready."

"Well, good. So who do you have your eye on?"

"I'll show you when we get there. I want to do this on my own."

"Damn, you have made me so proud. I've turned you into a sexual deviant and I fucking love it!"

We walk in and I'm thankful that my target men are here, both standing at the bar, talking to one another. I wasn't planning on both of them but my mind goes into overdrive as new possibilities fill my brain and, before I can chicken out, I walk straight up to them, working my way in between their conversation.

Leaning back on one while placing my hand on the other's chest, I seductively whisper, "Hi. Are you guys here with anyone tonight?"

I feel the guy behind me place his hands on my hips, pulling my back into him and whispering in my ear, "No, we aren't. Are you looking for some double trouble tonight?"

I turn my head slightly to look at him while running my fingers down the shirt of the man in front of me until I'm tugging on his belt buckle. "Maybe. I'm still new to this. Will you guys be gentle with me?"

"I've seen you around. I thought you were with Eros. You've never ventured beyond him," the man in front of me says while moving his arms out of the way to allow my advance.

I slowly start to unbuckle his pants while rubbing my ass against the man behind me. "I want something new tonight. You both were on my mind but I wasn't thinking together. Maybe you can show me my way?" I reach in, grabbing his cock.

Yes, I said it. Cock, pussy, fuck, moist… I say it all now. I'm much more open with my language now thanks to Becca.

As I slide my hands up and down his cock his head falls back as the man in back wraps his arm around my waist, reaching my pussy, rubbing gently from side to side. "Why don't we take this in the other room? By the looks of my friend here, I think he's down with your little plan, I'm…,"

I stop him, "Shh, no names." I turn my torso around, kissing the man behind me while continuing to rub the cock of the man in front of me.

"Eurydice…" I hear a voice to the side of me saying my name. I ignore it until I hear him again more loudly, "Eurydice, baby."

I don't stop my rubbing but break the kiss only to see Eros standing in front of us.

The man I was kissing thankfully speaks first, "Hey Eros."

Eros doesn't look at either men, just stares at me. I wish I could see his eyes but the mask is blocking them more than usual. Something is not right though. He doesn't seem mad but if I had to guess I would say he seems hurt. Why? I don't even know the guy. I feel a very awkward moment coming on so I try to ease the tension.

I let go of the guy's cock I was rubbing and put my hand on Eros' chest. "These two are going to show me something tonight. You're off the hook. I really appreciate you taking the time to teach me all you have. It's been a lot of fun."

I swear I saw his face wince when I said the last part. I'm so confused. I thought that was the point of this place. No ties, no connections. Just plain, free fucking.

After a beat he shakes his head, "Of course. Just wanted to make sure you were safe." His jaw is tight as he places his hand on the back of the guy in back of me, "You take good care of her tonight."

In unison they both reply, "We will," as each of them grab my hand and we walk to an area a little more secluded.

When I look behind me to give Eros a small thank-you smile, I notice the same woman who wanted him last week walk up behind him, staking her claim like a cougar on the prowl. I turn quickly trying to ignore the pang of jealousy that hit my chest.

As we enter the room, I notice there's no door but three walls standing up, giving a little more privacy. If someone wanted to though, they could sit on the couch in front of our scene and watch.

Little flutters of butterflies fill my stomach but quickly go away when I feel one of them come up behind me, kissing the back of my neck while pulling my romper down my shoulders. The other man comes up in front of me, leaning down to kiss my bare nipples once they're exposed.

Sensations from all over my body make my head spin and my pussy ache. The feeling of two men's mouths on me at the same time is different than anything I have ever felt.

I feel the silkiness from my romper slide down my thighs as they pull it all the way down to my feet, leaving me in just my black thong panties. Their hands rub all over, from top to bottom. Rubbing my breast, my ass, my pussy. My eyes start to glaze over as I succumb to the feeling their hands are rewarding my body with.

I've had threesomes. Shit, I've had foursomes. But never have two men been wrapped around me like this where every bit of attention is on me.

Having two strong, manly hands touching my body like this is lighting my insides on fire with possibilities and, more importantly, excitement of the unknowns of what's to come.

The man in front of me tugs on my panties, pulling them down my legs while licking the tip of my clit, making my knees instantly buckle. Thankfully, the man behind me holds me upright, allowing me to slightly lean on him, opening my legs more so the other man can lick a little further.

He reaches around, rubbing my breasts while I put my hands in the hair of the man in front of me, tugging hard like I'm holding on for dear life.

The man behind me stables me more so I'm fully on my feet and starts to remove his own clothing. I reach around, grabbing his cock and stroking it up and down.

I'm taken by surprise when the first guy picks me up and quickly tosses me on the bed before removing his own clothing.

All of us are naked besides my strappy heels but I feel sexy as hell keeping them on so I don't dare remove them. With my body on display like a sexy painting, I lay back on the bed, waiting for them to take me as they wish. I look out to both of them but am startled when I see Eros standing right outside of our scene by himself, watching us intently.

My eyes are glued on him until one of the men spreads my legs further, leaning down and licking slow circles around my clit before sucking slightly, while the other guy climbs up, straddling my head and offering his dick to my mouth, which I'm willing to take with a greedy need I've never felt before.

I've done the threesome thing with Eros and Becca and even though I was slightly turned on by Becca, now I fully know that deep down I am all about men.

Men. Cock. All of it. This is what I like. What I love.

Having one lick me while I get to suck off another is so hot. I feel my temperature rising and I think tonight is going to be a multiple night in more ways than one.

And I was right. I bring his cock out of my mouth only long enough to scream my release, gripping my legs tightly around his head as the ripples flow through me. Once it's passed, I slowly pull his cock into my mouth, wanting it even more now.

I'm so focused on licking and sucking this amazing cock in my face that I don't even notice what the other man is doing until I feel his length push inside me. Filling me with the most amazing surprise of my life. So not what I was expecting but it turned me on so much that three pumps in and I cum hard around him thrusting inside me.

"Holy shit, sweetheart. Watching you cum twice like that was so fucking hot since my cock was in your mouth," the one guy says while running his fingers through my hair.

I let it go with a *pop* as my head falls back in disbelief as I'm overcome with ecstasy from the other guy continuing to pound me hard.

"Flip her on top of you," I hear the guy that doesn't have his dick in me request.

The other one moves me around with ease and the angle hits my clit hard, almost sending me into another orgasm as he continues his motion in and out of me.

I feel the other one climb on top of me, whispering in my ear, "I'm going to take you from behind. Are you ok with that?"

I tense; I've never done that… "Um, I've."

He kisses my back to stop me, "Don't worry. I'll go slowly. Stop me anytime. It's so much better if you have someone in your pussy, too. Takes your focus off what's actually happening. I have a condom on and will use plenty of lube. Just sit back and enjoy sweetheart."

The man underneath me rubs my clit in just the right way, making me moan in response as I feel the other man's tip press against my tight hole. I try to tense but really, after just a second, I realize actually how good it feels and just let go, continuing to ride the man underneath me while the man on top slowly enters.

Once he's in they both pause, filling me to the brim, allowing me to get used to the feeling. It's so unreal, so intense and all I know is if one of them doesn't move quickly I might explode with the most intense need to cum.

The guy below me moves first, sending a rippling sensation through my entire body as I scream in response. They both start to pull in and out at a different pace sending my body into an overload of sensation. I almost can't take it it's so intense and so good.

My eyes feel like they're permanently rolled back in my head and I can't seem to focus on anything but this need to cum, explode, ignite and crumble all at the same time.

The bed moves slightly to one side but my mind is in a complete fog until I hear his voice. "Here, you're losing yourself to sensation. Suck on this so you can focus and enjoy what's happening inside of you."

I look up to see Eros, naked with his dick next to my mouth. I open wide, greedily taking it in and he's so right. The feeling calms down to manageable and I let go of him only to sigh and moan my release as it builds up inside of me until fireworks run through my body, exploding out of every inch of me. I can't help but scream at the top of my lungs with my release.

Both men pulse inside me a few more times, releasing their own orgasm as Eros bends down, wrapping my lips with his while he runs his fingers through my hair in an emotional kiss that he's never given me until now.

I unwrap myself from the other men and fall down on the bed, exhausted but with a huge smile on my face. I'm in a total mind-blown sense of sensation and emotion.

That was hands down the best experience of my life and I can't do anything but lie here in the afterglow.

Chapter TWELVE

Kamii

I feel and hear the men kissing me goodbye, thanking me for the good time as they both exit our area. I sense Eros still standing over me, just looking at me with a simple stare. When I finally feel like I have the energy to open my eyes, I look up as our eyes catch.

He leans down, kissing me again but this time holding me tightly while he slowly moves his tongue around mine.

This kiss feels different. I'm not sure if it's because of what just happened but suddenly I want to be wrapped in his arms.

His arms only.

He lies down, turning me to my side and pulling me in close to him. Reaching to the side, he pulls a blanket around us as we lay, close to one another, naked yet not in a sexual way. I'm so comforted by his touch. He's not trying anything with me, just holding me as we lay in silence.

I've never felt more secure, more alive and more comforted than this moment and I don't want to fight it. Nothing matters more than the relaxation that I feel in my soul. It's something I haven't felt in years and I don't want it to end.

I must have fallen asleep because I don't remember anything until I see light peaking through the window shade that, to be honest, I didn't even know was there. I'm still wrapped up in Eros with nothing on but my shoes and my mask that's slipped up on my forehead.

"Mmm, morning," I hear him whisper in my ear.

I don't over think it, just do what's feels normal by grabbing a hold of his arms and holding them tighter to me, whispering, "Morning."

He leans down, kissing my shoulder, "How are you feeling?"

I grip him tighter, "I'm fine. Thank you for staying with me. I didn't realize I needed it until you were here."

"I want to be here and make sure you're always safe."

He continues his kisses on my back and neck. Reaching around, I feel his hands move to my front, between my legs, opening me up and rubbing softly.

I can't help but moan as I open my legs wider, allowing him more room to explore.

He moves to be on top of me and I reach up to pull my mask down in place, closing my eyes, just incase his mask is off.

"I think you can remove the mask. It's morning."

"No, no. I don't want to. Please tell me you have yours on. I don't want to ruin this. This place has saved me. I don't want anything to change," I say, almost begging him.

He pauses and I hear him wrestling with something before he leans down, kissing my neck, "Ok. I wanted this to be us but I understand and will take you any way I can get you. It's on, you can open your eyes now."

I do as he moves down my body, kissing everywhere he can, caressing my naked body. After he slips on a condom, I feel him slowly slide inside as he lies softly on top of me. Moving in and out at a very slow pace while he holds me tightly and leaves soft, tender kisses on my lips.

We lay like this for a while, totally lost in each other as we slowly fuck ourselves into intense orgasms at the same time. I want to kiss him, I want to hold him tight, but most of all, I want to get up and run. These are not feelings I should be having and I need to get out of here.

Now.

After he gets up, I quietly dress, making sure not to look at him as I say, "Thanks for last night and this morning."

"Wait, don't leave like this," he pleads.

I don't stop or turn around. I walk out as fast as I can.

Thank God my workload is light today because there is no way I could go to work right now. My head is rocked from what just happened and how it made me feel so as soon as I'm in my car, I pick up my phone to call Becca, needing to talk through what happened last night and this morning. On my screen I notice there's a text from her that came in last night:

Becca: Hey girl! I saw you wrapped up in Eros and didn't want to bother you so I decided to go back to my place. I'm sure everything's fine by now. Starbucks in the morning?

I try to call but when she doesn't answer I drive to her place and knock on her door but there's no answer there either. I try to call her phone again but still no answer. Looking at my phone I see it's 8:30 in the morning so maybe she's still asleep. I take out my key she gave me to her place and let myself in. I need to talk and I have no problem waking her up to do so.

Not paying attention, I walk through her door, calling, "Becca. Are you asleep? Sorry, but I need to talk."

I shut the door, mindlessly locking it like I do every time I enter a home before I turn around, letting out a scream that crushes my soul to the core.

I run over to Becca who's lying on the floor, bleeding everywhere. Grabbing her shoulders, I lift her head to my lap, shaking her, trying to wake her up, touching her everywhere, trying to do something, anything.

There is so much blood. She's still in the same clothes she had on last night but her entire body is covered and I can't tell where the blood is coming from. Screaming at her, I beg for her to wake up, crying as I shake her harder.

I scream, "HELP," at the top of my lungs, not having a clue what's going on but no one can hear me. Reaching for my phone, I dial 911.

"911 what's your emergency?"

"My friend. She's bleeding. I don't know what happened. Please, come. Help me!" I'm starting to hyperventilate.

"Try to breathe. What's your address?"

I give them the address as she tries to talk me through mouth to mouth. I'm going through the motions but there's just too much blood. The dispatcher keeps asking me if I know who could have hurt her but I really have no clue. How could I not know anything really about her? We've spent all this time together yet I know nothing about her past, her family or any other friends.

"I don't know," I scream as more tears run down my face. "I found her like this in her apartment. She's not responding. Please help!"

She stays on the phone with me waiting for an ambulance to arrive. I'm screaming Becca's name, crying into her face as she lays limp in my lap. I know deep down she's dead but I don't want to believe it yet.

I've been here before though.

I wait, praying, saying over and over, "Please, please make her ok."

I feel like I'm in a nightmare. I've already lived through something like this with Nick and here I am holding the lifeless body of the closest person in my life on my lap. Again.

I hear the paramedics arrive and someone removes me from the scene but I'm in such a fog that I have no clue what's actually happening. I can't breathe. I can't move. I'm going to be sick.

I run to the bathroom and do just that, throwing up and barely making it to the toilet.

How can this be happening? To me? To her? Again?

The next hour is a complete whirlwind of people asking me questions that I don't know the answer to. I'm limp, lifeless, sitting on her couch, watching helplessly as they zip my best friend up in a bag and roll her out of her apartment.

Chapter THIRTEEN

Preston

My head has been a cluster fuck ever since I watched Eurydice walk out the door after I made love to her this morning. I'd like to say I fucked her but I didn't. That was something different and fuck me, it felt so good.

Then she just got up and left without another word. I left the club after she did, wanting to get out of there and rid any memories of what just happened. If only it could have been that easy.

As soon as I started my Tesla, *Comatose* by Skillet blared over my speakers with its violin intro and my chest instantly ached when I heard him talking about how she takes the pain away and waking up to her never felt so real. The entire song sent my head into a spinning frenzy. I don't want to have these feelings but fuck, I feel like I need her like I need air.

My day sucked worse than it has in years and now I've been sitting here at Bridge, waiting for either her or Becca to show up tonight and both of them are a no show.

I tried to call Becca today, just needing to talk to her but she didn't answer, which is not like her. I'm afraid she's upset with me, too. I feel like I might have crossed a line. Broke my own no emotions rule with this place and I hope Becca's not mad at me, too.

That would just blow. She's been a good friend to me through this journey.

She's helped me achieve my goals of this place and we've spent a good amount of time together doing so. I'd like to say she's my girl best friend, however lame that sounds. I just hope I didn't fuck that up as well.

It's midnight and I'm finally giving up. They aren't showing so I'm out of here.

Once I'm home, I drink myself into a drunken, self-loathing stupor and pass out on my couch.

I'm awoken to someone banging on my door the next morning, yelling, "Police, open up!"

My mind is spinning and with each pound on my door, my heads screams in pain. I stumble to the door, bracing myself against the frame, opening it to see three policemen standing guard.

Instantly I stand up, "Can I help you?"

"Are you Preston Babcock?"

"Yes, that's me. What's going on?"

"Will you please turn around and place your hands behind your back? You're under arrest for the murder of Rebecca Anderson."

"Wait, WHAT? I'm What? What are you talking about? What happened to Becca? Murder? Is she ok?" *No, no. This can't be happening. Where's Becca?*

"Sir, don't make us get rough with you. Put your hands behind your back."

"Rough with me? What's going on? Why am I being arrested?"

"Sir, don't resist arrest."

"What? Will you please explain to me what's going on?"

"You're being arrested for the murder of Rebecca Anderson."

"Murder! I didn't murder anyone. What's going on? What happened to Becca?"

Before I know it, I'm thrown on the ground with my arms being pulled from, what feels like, their sockets and handcuffed behind me.

"Now stand up!" the police officer yells as they pull me up, force me out of my apartment and down the front steps of my complex.

Thankfully, my neighbor is just walking in the building, "John, John, please help me. Call my office. Get a hold of my assistant through the emergency line and have her call my lawyer."

He walks up to me, "What's going on?"

"I have no clue. I know I'm innocent though. Call my assistant. Please!"

"You got it man."

They tuck my head into the back of the cop car and drive away as I drop my head down to the headrest.

This cannot be happening.

I'm placed in a room with a table in the middle and chairs on either side where I sit in silence, waiting for a detective to come in.

"Well, well, well," I hear a man enter the room from behind me. "Did you really think you would get away with it?"

"Look, there has been some kind of mistake. Why am I here and what has happened to Becca?"

"Well, why don't you tell me what happened to *Becca*?"

"I have no clue. Someone said murder. Please don't tell me something has happened to her."

"Look, drop the shit. You're screwed. We have your fingerprints all over the room and I bet once we get a sample from you we'll find that it's your semen we found with the rape kit, too."

"Rape kit? Fingerprints? What are you talking about? I have no clue what's going on. And where is my attorney?"

"Fine. We'll wait for your attorney to show up but your ass is mine. Evidence is evidence buddy. Facts are facts."

He gets up and walks out of the room, leaving me alone again with my thoughts. *How can Becca be dead? What happened? And how am I being blamed for this?*

An hour later my attorney walks through the door, sitting in front of me with a sad look on his face.

"Frank, lay it out straight to me, what's going on?" I ask.

"Preston, it's not looking good. Don't say anything until I get you out of here."

"But that's the thing, Frank. I didn't do anything. I don't know what's going on."

"Just keep quiet. I posted your bail and they should be coming in here soon to let you go. We will talk once we get back to my office."

I sigh heavily. *Why doesn't anybody want to listen to me? I'm innocent!*

I spent all day and night in jail and was finally released this morning. Thankfully, my attorney, Frank, is a friend of mine for the last 20 years so, even though it's Sunday, we're sitting at his desk going over everything.

He shuts the door behind him as he walks into his office, handing me a glass with dark liquid and one ice cube. "Here, I think you need this."

"No, I don't need shit. I need you to believe me that I'm innocent."

"Preston, how long have we been friends? I need for you to be real honest with me right now. Who is Rebecca Anderson and how do you know her?"

"She's someone I care about. Tell me Frank, is she really dead? How come no one will tell me what happened?"

"Yes, Preston, she's dead. I've seen the evidence and it's not looking good. She was stabbed and raped."

"No... no way..." I shake my head in disbelief, "How could this have happened?"

"Preston, they have your fingerprints at the scene, with a few smears of dried blood. They are demanding you to give a DNA test to compare with the semen they found."

I stand up, pounding my hands on the desk, "Frank, you have to believe me. I did NOT do this. I'm being set up. I promise you."

"Look, I want to believe you but as I said, it's not looking good. Who would want to frame you? Do you have any enemies I don't know about?"

I look down, racking my brain for anything but coming up with nothing, "Fuck Frank, I don't know. I can't think of anything but I can promise you I didn't do it."

"Ok, well, let's start with where were you Thursday night around midnight?"

"Um, I can't tell you," I say looking down.

Frank sits back in his seat, "Well, that's not going to work. Preston, you have to tell me everything. If you want me to get you out of this, shit, if you want me to believe you, you have to tell me where you were."

I shake my head, "Fuck! Ok, this is strictly to stay in this room."

"Agreed. You have client/attorney privilege so I can't say anything, and come on, you're one of my oldest friends."

I tell him everything. Everything about my private club, how there are no names, no faces, how Becca was someone who helped me start it, and how I stayed there all night till early Friday morning.

"Damn Preston. First, how come I didn't know about this?" he tries to joke but knows this is not the time. "But more seriously, if you have an alibi then we're all good. We will still have to figure out how your fingerprints are at the scene but at least it's a start to create a shadow of a doubt. So who will vouch for you that you were at this club all night?"

I shake my head, looking down again, "Were you not listening? It's a secret club. I can't bring anyone into this without bringing the entire place down. Besides, no names, no identities, remember?"

"Well, how much are you willing to risk to keep this secret? You could be looking at life my friend. You may not have a choice. Obviously, you have to know someone there who knows who you are who could vouch for you."

"Shit," I shake my head, looking down, "There is one person. But she doesn't know who I am. I'd have to reveal my identity to her but she's who I was with. But fuck, it's not as easy as that. She might not be willing to share this secret and who knows what's going through her mind right now, she's Becca's best friend."

"Ok, who is this woman?"

"Her name is Kamii, she's an attorney as well..." I say, rubbing my hands down my face, "A criminal defense attorney."

"Even better. I'm in business law; we'll need a criminal defense attorney. But wait, you know who she is but she doesn't know who you are?"

"No. She doesn't. Remember, I own the place so I have everyone's applications. Let's figure this thing out before we bring her into the mix. There's got to be a way we can do this without involving her."

Frank lays out all the evidence that was given to him at the police station. I'm totally baffled by this whole thing. Everything points to me. How in the hell are my fingerprints there, in dried blood at that? They also have footprints of the same shoes that I own and searched my apartment where they found them with dried blood in the creases and sole but something is not right with them.

I'm being set up but I have no clue by whom.

I'm searching my brain, trying to figure out who could possibly have done this. How did they get my fingerprints? And those shoes?

But most of all, I can't forget the fact that I've lost a dear friend and now I have to go to Kamii to help clear my name.

I haven't spoken to her since she walked out of the room Friday morning. The one thing that is keeping me sane is the fact that she honestly knows I'm innocent. I was wrapped around her all night, and made love to her the next morning. I know she will believe me. But will she vouch for me is a different story.

To do so, she'd be outing her entire experience at my club. Is she willing to do that? Put herself on display like that, for me? I just don't know.

After working on a game plan, I head back to my apartment knowing the only thing I can do now is wait, which sucks.

Looking around my house I sense it, something's different. I was only home for a little while before I was arrested and this was the first time I've come back.

I can tell they searched the place, and not carefully I might add, but that's not it. I can't put my finger on it but something just feels different. It's a smell, it's the air, it's a feeling I can't describe. It feels familiar but at the same time that makes no sense at all. My head spins as I walk further in, turning on every light and checking for signs of someone being there.

The place is empty but the feeling doesn't go away. Exhausted from the day, I just want to ignore the mess the police made and go to bed. The only thing I pick up is my wedding photo that's sitting facedown where I have it placed on my dresser. I'm not even sure why they touched it at all since it's the only thing moved there but it's all I care about.

Now that I look at it though, all I can think about is Kamii, which I know isn't right but I can't help it. *Why can't I get her out of my mind?*

I've already given my heart to Kim and, even though she's dead, I still feel awful that my heart aches at the thought of never having Kamii again.

Sex at any club I went to was always just sex for me but with Kamii, it's been different. Since the first time I laid eyes on her, I've been drawn in a way that I can't explain. I don't want to have these feelings but no matter how hard I fight it, they won't go away.

The next day I met with Frank again to try to figure things out some more. I want to be absolutely positive that we have looked at every angle we could before we involve Kamii. Whoever is trying to frame me has done a good job. It will take a miracle to clear my name and I'm praying that miracle's name is Kamii.

Now that the story has gotten out, the media has been all over my building and work to try to get some information. I've always been proud of the fact that I've made a name for myself here in San Francisco but I guess being known also has its drawbacks, too, like when you're being framed for murder and it makes the top story of the nightly news...

Frank set up a meeting between him and Kamii for later in the day. I wanted Frank to go over everything with her without names or incriminating details before she knew what was actually going on. I didn't want her to know she was going to be defending the person who supposedly killed her best friend until she knew all the facts. Since Frank is not a criminal defense attorney, he met with her under the pretense that he wanted to hire her for a case he was working on but because of client/attorney privilege all names and strict details are being left out.

I'm standing outside her door, listening to see what she thinks before I enter the room.

After she goes over everything Frank gave her, I hear her say, "Mr. Austin."

"Please, call me Frank."

"Frank, I'd love to help you out here but I'm going to need more. This looks like a pretty open/shut case. Everything points to your client being guilty. You will have to give me more to work with. What is this iron clad alibi you talk about?"

That's my cue. I walk in, looking her straight in the eyes. Those same eyes that did me in the first time I ever saw her and have died to see like this again but now all I see is the pain she's had the last couple of days. No, these aren't the same eyes I've been dreaming of. I know because, even with her mask on, her eyes lit up behind the dark colors. Now her eyes look dead inside.

I stop when I'm directly in front of her desk, standing tall, leaning on the desk slightly, looking her dead in the face, saying, "You. You're my alibi."

Kamii

I'm what? Did I just hear this guy correctly? I stand up, placing my hands on my desk like he is, "Look, what's going on here? Who are you?"

"Look at me. You know who I am. I was with you that night. All night. You slept with my arms wrapped around you while someone we both love was murdered. I'm being framed and you need to help me."

He reaches his hand out to me and I'm frozen, a complete statue staring at him, then staring at his hand that's still outstretched. Completely losing it, I fall to my chair, tears following down my face as I cover them with my hands.

"No, no, no, this can't be happening," I say through my hands that are still covering my face as I shake my head side to side.

"Believe me, I'm just as shocked as you are. But this is happening. Becca is dead and I'm just as torn up about it as you are."

I stand up, outraged. "You killed her! You did it! You had to have. All the evidence is here."

"No, I didn't. Please believe me. I'm being framed. I promise you."

"Why should I believe you? She was my best friend. And she's gone. You hear me? She's gone! And I don't even know you!"

"You do know me. What we shared that morning was more than what my club offers. I know you felt it, too. And now this… I need you. Someone is framing me for the murder of someone I cared for deeply. Please, you're my only hope. I was with you all night. There is no way I could have done this."

"I need a minute," I say, running out of my office and down the hall to the ladies room.

How did my life turn into this? How am I having to deal with all of this again? Could this really be Eros? The more I thought about his voice right now, the build of his body and more importantly, the way *my* body reacted to the look in his eyes. Those crystal clear blue eyes that always looked back at me. I know deep down that it's him.

I've cried all weekend, making myself sick to my stomach and now this? There is nothing left to do so I scream at the top of my lungs, not caring who can hear me.

The bathroom door opens and I watch as Eros walks in. He keeps his distance, standing by the door, quietly watching me.

"My name is Preston Babcock. I'm 36 years old and I'm also the owner of Bridge. That's how I knew who you were and that you were a lawyer. I can tell you anything you need to know about me, especially the fact that I'm innocent. But you know that I am, because I was with you that entire night."

I look at him in the mirror through my blurry tears. "How do I know that for a fact? I was asleep. You could have gotten up without me knowing."

He walks up behind me, turning me around so we're face to face. "Don't say that. I was there all night. I never left your side and when you woke up, you were still wrapped in my arms. I didn't do this. I promise you. I'm being framed. You're the best defense attorney around and there's a reason you were brought to me. You can help me."

Even though I was asleep, I know deep down he never left me. Every time I'm near him I can feel his presence deep in my soul. I've had this emptiness inside me since I walked out of the club that morning, before I even knew about Becca. And now that he's here, standing with me, I feel whole again.

This case is too much, every sign points to him, and even if I do believe him, I'm not sure if I can help.

"I don't know. All of the evidence is there. And she was my best friend. I still can't believe she's gone."

Tears start to fall down my face and Eros, I mean, Preston wipes them away with the tip of his thumb.

"Becca and I were friends. I cared for her. She was one of the only people who knew that I owned the club. That's how close we were. Believe me, I'm devastated over losing her, too. But something else is going on here and I need your help figuring it out."

"How can we prove all of this evidence wrong? How can we prove that you didn't do it? Even if I am your alibi. We will need much more than just my word to prove your innocence."

"I know, but just having someone on my side who truly believes me and is willing to fight for me is all I need right now. The truth will come out, as long as I have you on my team. Please say you'll help me."

"I'll help you," I say quietly, still in shock that all of this is happening.

He leans down, lightly brushing his lips to mine before whispering, "Thank you. I don't want to bring you or the club into this. I'd like to keep that a secret. I know you don't want the world to know either. We have to find out the truth and hopefully we will never have to use you as my alibi because we will know who is truly behind this. For Becca we will figure this out."

I watch as Preston turns around, leaving me alone in the bathroom as he walks out the door. I can't believe any of this is happening. Right when I finally get out of my funk from losing Nick, this happens. I was happy, now I feel like I've died all over again.

Chapter FOURTEEN

Kamii

Every report, evidence tagging and pictures I could get of Becca's murder cover my coffee table. There has got to be something that I'm missing. I haven't brought myself to look at the actual photos of her. I know I'll have to eventually but that will take more time and a lot more wine.

The report reads that she was murdered sometime between midnight and two in the morning so that has to mean it was right when she got home. Could someone have been waiting for her? Was she followed? There are so many questions I have and I can't help but think that if I didn't stay with Preston, and she came to my place like she should have, then she would still be alive.

Guilt rips through my body for the hundredth time today as I try to swallow down my pain.

I start reading a report for the third time when there's a knock on my door making me jump in surprise. Tip-toeing to the door, I look through the peephole, trying not to make a sound incase I don't want to talk to whoever is here.

My breath catches when I see Preston. He's standing tall, both hands nervously placed in his pockets, pushing down as far as he can and rocking slightly on the heels of his shoes. I watch as he looks around, pulling his hand up to the door again but stopping before he knocks. His hand falls to his side again, his face looking down as he starts to turn and leave.

Before I can even think, I yank the door open, "Preston."

We stand, staring at each other, both not saying a word. I don't know what else to do. I wasn't even sure I wanted to open the door, but when he started to leave my body stopped him before my brain could think.

He looks down, breaking our eye contact as he whispers, "I'm sorry to come here. I… It's just… Fuck, never mind."

Slamming his hands back into his pockets, he turns on his heels to leave and once again, my body reacts without my brain and reaches out to stop him. "Wait. How did you know where I live?"

He turns but won't look me in the eye. "I know everything about you. Not only do I own Bridge, so I have all of your paperwork, but I've done my fair share of research about you as well. I guess I'm just lost at who I can trust now."

"Then why are you here?"

"I can't sit home knowing my life is holding on by a thread and I have no clue why."

His confession breaks my heart; the poor guy looks so lost. I step toward him, holding my hand out to his. "Here, come in. I was actually just looking over the evidence I got from the police today."

We walk into my apartment and he stands by the door. I know I haven't known him for that long but he seems different standing here, in my apartment, looking nervous as hell. *What happen to my strong, dominant Eros? Oh yeah, murder.*

I guess murder charges will bring even the strongest person down. Especially when it's someone you were very close to.

"Here, have a seat." I point to the chair next to me. "Can I get you a glass of wine?"

"Wine. Yes. Please." He rubs his hands on his jeans, fidgeting as he walks toward the chair.

As I pour his wine in the kitchen, I glance in the living room to see him staring off into space with a look of lost torture across his face.

Who could be doing this? Why would someone want to set him up?

I walk into the living room, pulling him out of his trance. "If we're going to solve this it's my turn to know all about you."

Our hands briefly touch, sending chills everywhere as I hand him his wine. His lips form a hint of a smile as our eyes catch and we stare for a brief moment before I nervously look away.

"I really know nothing about you. First, why did you want the club to be so secretive? Are all, um, sex clubs like this?" My body flushes as I say sex and

I feel my cheeks flame with heat. How come this feels so different without my mask on? I feel like my shield is completely gone and the nervous, shy girl has re-emerged.

I stare at his lips as he slowly opens them, releasing a long breath before answering, "I didn't want my personal life to intertwine with my needs."

"What do you mean? How long have you lived this lifestyle?"

"About a year."

"But this club just opened right? Where did you go before?"

"I went to a few different places. Checking them out, seeing which one fit my needs."

"So what are you needs, Preston?"

He looks me dead in the eye, not wavering an ounce, "You."

My heart flutters and I start to pulse with my own need. Trying to stop the sudden ache consuming my body, I close my legs, crossing them slightly to apply pressure where it's needed most.

I watch as his eyes change right before me. They turn darker, sharper and more open than the eyes I met at the door. I'm frozen, stuck to my seat, holding my drink to my lips, mid-drink but not finishing the actual sip.

No, I have to stop this. I'm his lawyer.

I look down, breaking away from his spell, setting my drink down and whispering, "Things have changed, Preston. We aren't in the club. I'm your lawyer. If we're going to find out who is framing you then we need to stay focused," as my fingers instantly go back to their old habit of nervously pulling at my bottom lip.

I glance up and he's shaking his head, rubbing his eyes before running both hands through his hair. "Shit. I'm sorry. I know and I couldn't agree with you more. I don't know what came over me."

"It's ok, but I need to know more. I need to know everything about you. Even things you don't think are significant. They might be so spill it." I glance up, giving him a playful smile, trying to change the sudden mood filling the room.

"It all started about a year ago. My wife and I originally went together."

"Wait, what? You're married?" A sickness comes over me and I have to swallow the bile coming up in my throat.

He looks down again, "No. I'm not anymore."

Thankful to hear he's not married, I swallow my stomach down trying to calm my nerves, "Ok, so you're divorced. Where is she now?"

"I'm not divorced. She's dead."

"Oh Preston, I'm so sorry. What happened?" *I can't believe I just said that. I hate when people say that to me yet that was my immediate response.*

He shakes his head, looking down, barely whispering, "She committed suicide." I sit silently, not sure what to say so he continues. "I tried to stop her. But I couldn't."

I can tell this is still a very sore subject for him so I don't press the issue. "Is this why you wanted to keep your personal life separate?"

He shakes his head *yes* as he picks up his wine taking a big sip. I wait for him to finish, hoping he will elaborate some more. When I stay silent and open my eyes slightly, tilting my head to the side, silently persuading him to go on, he finally does.

"I have needs, as I've said before. These were needs that I hoped my wife and I could accomplish together. Once she proved me wrong, I didn't want to make any personal connections with the people that fulfilled my… needs."

Wow. That felt like a sting in the chest to hear. All I was, was someone to fulfill his *need*?

I pick up my glass, contemplating why it hurt to hear him say that before it hits me.

I'm such a hypocrite.

That's exactly why I asked him to keep our masks on the last time we had sex. I have needs, too. And same as him, I didn't want the personal connections. Been there and I will never do that again.

So how did we end up here?

He goes on to explain the few months after her death. How he tried other clubs but was having trouble fulfilling his needs without intertwining personal feelings or feeling like he was betraying his wife.

I ask before I even think, "Why are you so against personal feelings?"

He looks at me, pain in his eyes showing me that I clearly hit a sore spot. "I know it doesn't make sense that I wanted to fuck other people but I loved my wife. I have mourned her death every day, especially knowing it was my fault. Sex is sex. It's a human need, love on the other hand is something that you only have," he pauses, looking at me, not finishing his sentence.

I pry him to finish, "You only have…?"

His lips part, looking as lost as ever before he continues, "I thought you only found once."

We meet eye to eye, both of us staring, not giving anything away to one another, yet not smiling, smirking or even breathing. I feel my body heat up from my toes to my fingertips and I finally break away, looking down to my notepad as I try to think of something to write down.

My mind is blank of anything I could write down so I continue with the questions, "Is this why you started your own club?"

"Yes, this way I could control the rules and keep everything separate. I met Becca at another club that I tried after my wife passed away and we bonded in a purely friendship way. I never had any personal feelings for her beyond that friendship. And she truly was one of my closest friends."

Tears fill my eyes as I think of Becca, my closest friend, too.

Gone.

Everyone important in my life ends up dead. Am I cursed? Is this God's way of getting back at me for being a criminal defense attorney? I shake my head at the thought.

"Beyond the club, what else do you do?"

Instead of answering me, he reaches into his back pocket, grabbing something out and handing it to me. I look down to see a business card reading Babcock Construction.

"Wait, you own Babcock Construction?"

"Yes, I do," he looks down.

"Ok, hold on…" I pause as I remember everything from my date with Kevin. "So that's why he kept saying your name... He knew you were the owner of Bridge and he was trying to see if I knew as well."

He squints his eyes, "I don't follow."

"I met a guy a few weeks ago. We went out for drinks and he was acting really weird but he kept saying your name and actually recommended you to me since I'm looking to remodel a house to live in."

He takes a deep breath in, releasing it slowly. "Yes, Kevin... I'm sorry he did that to you."

I pause as tingles creep up my spine, remembering the feeling when he said my name. "But wait, could he have done this…?"

"Done what?"

"This. Becca. The whole framing thing?"

"No way."

"No, you don't understand. He stopped me after work and was really pissed off at you. He said, 'He'll pay for cancelling my membership.'"

"There is no way he would kill someone over cancelling his membership. No one is that crazy."

If only that were true. Unfortunately, I've seen first hand the evil that lives within people. "I wouldn't be so sure."

"No, Kamii, I may not know him that well but he's not a killer."

"But someone is. And believe me, you never know what someone is capable of, especially when they feel jaded. Did he know that Becca was a member as well?"

"I don't know if they knew each other, actually. I handled his application where normally she processed them."

I write his name on my notepad as a possible suspect, even if he thinks so or not, as of right now he's our only lead and he even has a motive to try to frame Preston. "Who else would have known you even knew Becca? I need a list of all the members of the club."

"No can do."

I look up shocked. "You're kidding me right? I need to investigate everything and since members of the club are the only people who knew both you and Becca, there is a good chance this person is from the club. I know you think it's all anonymous but Kevin proved that some people just can't keep their mouths shut."

"No, there's no way it's someone from the club."

"How can you honestly say that?"

"Because I just know. People who I let into my club hold a higher standard of persona. They would not kill anyone like this. Especially someone from within the club."

"You can think that all you want but I still need to rule them out for sure. Or what about that woman I saw trying to talk to you a few times. Who was she?"

His face turns a slight shade of red as he clenches his jaw tightly before saying, "I told you, no. I promised secrecy at my club and I will go down for this murder before I break that secrecy. I would hope as a member yourself you would understand that. And I don't know what woman you're talking about anyway."

I have to be thankful he wants to keep his promise but at the same time I don't understand why he would rather go to jail than give me that list if it ever came down to it.

"Well, how can you explain the link between you and Becca? Who else knew you were even friends?"

"No one really, but that doesn't mean people didn't see us together. She is the only person I have had any type of outing with since my wife died. I mean, we would go to lunch or dinner together sometimes. Especially when we were setting up the club. She was my right hand man, per se."

"Which proves my point even more. It has to be someone from the club."

He looks me dead in the eye, stern as hell, slowly stating his point, "I. Said. No."

"Ok, fine. No list. Tell me of any enemies then. Any business deals gone bad?"

"None that I can think of. Customers are pretty happy with our service."

"Well, you need to think hard. Whoever this is," I pause, looking down to the evidence, "knew things. Personal things, beyond just that you were close with Becca. They knew your shoe size, and the brand of shoes you wear. Come on, how many people wear size 13 Salvatore Ferragamo shoes? Those are what, $800- $900 a pair? Look," I grab a photo from the pile, "they found bloody footprints at the scene and they found the same shoes at your house with blood residue still on them. How did the shoes get in your house?"

"But that's the thing. Those aren't my shoes anymore. I had a pair like that but got rid of them a few weeks ago."

"What did you do with them?"

"Donated them. Every six months I get a new pair and donate my old ones to the Veteran's home for people who need nice shoes to go on interviews for jobs. Look, those are last years model." He takes off a shoe he has on, showing me the bottom, "See the bottoms are different. If those are truly mine then those are my old pair and I was wearing this pair at the club that night."

I interrupt him, "But Preston, how is that even possible? And how in the world do they even have your fingerprints at the scene? Someone went through a lot of trouble, methodically planning this out and being very high tech about it. I know there are ways to duplicate fingerprints but we're talking some 007 stuff here. When I first saw this evidence, I told your lawyer it was an open/shut case."

"But you know I didn't do it," he stands up, pleading to me.

"Yes, you're lucky that I do know that. But knowing and proving are two completely different things. I need to prove, without a doubt that it wasn't you."

"What about your wife? Where is her family? Do they know why she killed herself? Could they be trying to get back at you for something?"

He sits back down, shaking his head as he runs his fingers through his hair. "Her parents have kept in touch with me and no, they don't know why. She has a brother, Trevor. He's kind of a mess. In and out of jail, I have no idea where he is now. They were close and whenever he did come around it was only to ask for money."

"Would she give him some?"

"She always would. I'd get so pissed for her enabling him."

"Ok, now we have a motive. He was probably upset that she couldn't give him money anymore. How can I find him?"

"I'd have to go through Kim's stuff. I have no clue where he is. Last I heard he was living in Oakland somewhere."

I write down on my note with a big red pen circling his and Kevin's name, satisfied with the progress we made here tonight, even though I still need to get the names of the members or figure out who that woman was at least?

Chapter FIFTEEN

Preston

Even though I didn't want to leave, Kamii made it pretty clear it was time for me to go. It's past midnight and I'm happy to see the media has taken off for the night so I'm clear to head up to my apartment without being harassed.

After parking my car in the underground garage, I walk into the elevator only to be stopped as someone jams their hand into the door, stopping it right before it closed completely. With my nerves completely on edge, and the fact that I thought I was alone, I tighten my fists, mentally preparing for anything as the door opens back up, revealing a man, staring at me with a blank stare.

"Are you getting in?" I ask sternly.

"Depends?"

"Excuse me?"

"You're Preston Babcock right?"

Aw shit... "Who's asking?"

"Becca meant a lot to me. I'm here to defend her, since she obviously couldn't defend herself against you."

I hold up my hands, "Look man. She meant a lot to me, too. I promise, I didn't do anything to harm her."

"Bullshit! You killed her. And I promise you this, you will go down for her murder. You will rot in prison for what you did to her. All the evidence is there. You killed her. And if I wasn't who I am, I would kill you myself right here, right now."

With that, the man turns and walks away, not saying another word as the elevator doors close again, for good this time. I fall up against the wall as nerves fill my body, making my chest pound and my hands tremble. *What the hell is going on?*

As I pass by my hall closet once inside my place, I notice the light is turned on inside with the door still closed. I must not have noticed it on in the daylight when I picked up my house from the police search. A heavy sigh escapes my lips as I open it up to shut it off. I try to stay out of this closet because it has some of Kim's old things and just brings back too many memories.

I look up at the box I had put there almost a year ago, after Kim passed away that's full of her belongings. Emptiness runs through my body, making my stomach turn and my nerves stand on end. I promised I would never touch the box again. It's just too hard but I know now I have no choice and since I already opened the closet door, I might as well go all the way into my memories of hell.

I know the info I need to find Kim's brother, Trevor, is in that box. He was a crazy son-of-a-bitch and as of right now he's our only lead. I have to find him.

Swallowing my gut down, I pull the box off the shelf and start to go through it. The pictures, a few of her favorite clothes and her jewelry lay on top making my chest clinch at the sight. *This is just too much.*

I need a drink.

I leave the box open on the floor and walk into the kitchen. After taking a swig of Jack Daniels, straight from the bottle, a faint sound catches my attention but I ignore it and head back to the box.

Kneeling down, looking at the contents again makes my chest burn with hatred for myself. *Yeah, I need another shot.*

After quickly taking another shot, I sit back down and start to remove some things. Under her favorite blanket, that she was so proud she made herself, are pictures of us at Lake Tahoe, wine tasting in Napa and the one taken the day we found out she was pregnant. Too bad like everything else in my life, we lost that baby two months after the photo was taken.

Getting up to take another shot, I head back to the box and find her address book which does indeed have Trevor's address in it. As I place the address book to the side to start putting things back in, the sight of a caricature we had done of us on Pier 39 catches my attention. We had it made right after I proposed at the same spot I first met her. She said it would be a great reminder to always be silly and never take life too seriously. Why she didn't believe her own words I will never understand.

Needing another shot, I head back to the kitchen when I hear the sound again but only louder. I listen more intently to try to figure out where it's coming from. It's a fast beat, a song, but I have no clue what. I can't pin the instrument but it reminds me of a Jamaican steel drum with the high, shallow beat.

After taking another swig, I put the bottle down, going to investigate the sound further. It sounds like it's coming from my bedroom but when I get there it feels like the sound is coming from the kitchen, where I just was.

Storming back in there, I grab the bottle, taking yet another shot before stumbling back, closing my eyes and listening carefully to the beat that sounds like it's on repeat.

This time, I take the bottle with me as I roam the house again. Looking in every room, following the sound everywhere yet nowhere. I'm losing my fucking mind and, since I never ate dinner, my consciousness too from the six shots I took in the past ten minutes.

Holding the bottle up, I go for one more shot before I realize it's empty and, without thinking twice, I throw the bottle against the wall. Happy to hear that the blast of the bottle stopped the tune playing over and over in my head as I fall down on my bed, my face smashed into the blankets and pass out.

My head spins as I open my eyes, trying to move my body but the stiffness from sleeping sideways, half on and half off my bed hurts more than I like to admit. I've never been a big drinker and this is exactly why.

After trying and failing to lift my head, I plop it down where it landed last night only to feel the drool that slipped from my mouth throughout the night. Sighing, I pull my body up further on the bed to a more comfortable position and pass right back out.

If it's not the sun shinning through the window hours later that wakes me up then it's that damn beat again. I must be losing my mind. I grab my head, letting out a deep groan trying to rid the sound. But I can't. I hear it, over and over. The same beat and it's driving me fucking nuts.

Dragging my sorry, stiff ass out of bed, I blindly reach for the remote that always sits on my dresser. But it's not there.

I look around the room, confused that it's not where I *always* put it. I'm anal about things like that. There is nothing more irritating to me than a missing remote. Grabbing my head from the pain and annoyance that's running through it now, I look up to see the remote sitting inside my shoe by my bedroom door.

I know I was drunk last night but why in the hell did I put my remote there? Leaning over to pick it up, I turn on my sound system that's linked to my Pandora station as *Blow Me Wide Open* by Saint Asonia begins.

The deep guitar strings play hard against my ears but the sound drowns the drum beat out so I could care less that my head is pounding as I strip to take a hot shower, trying to rid my body of this pain I'm in.

Chapter SIXTEEN

Kamii

I don't waste any time and go straight to Kevin's office the next morning. Do I think he did it? I don't know. If there's anything I've learned, it's that people are capable of unbelievable things and to never be surprised by what someone can actually do, especially when it comes to revenge.

As the elevator doors open, I'm greeted by a receptionist giving me a warm smile, "Good morning, can I help you ma'am?"

"Good morning. I'm here to meet with Kevin Foster."

"Of course, is he expecting you?"

"No, actually, if you could just tell him his friend is here, and please emphasize the *friend* part, to visit him, I'd appreciate it."

She gives me a weird look as she picks up the phone doing exactly as I asked while looking down and not at me. Within seconds Kevin is walking down the hall with a smirk on his face as his eyes meet mine.

"Well, well, well. Hello *friend*. I kind of hoped it'd be you. To what do I owe this surprise visit?" he smirks walking up to wrap me in a hug.

I shrug out of his embrace immediately, "Can we talk?"

"Sure, come on back." His hand lies softly on the small of my back as he leans to his receptionist, "Thanks, Lynn."

Once in his office, he closes the door behind us and walks to where I'm standing with a look of lust on his face as he reaches to place his hands on my hips. "So… here we are. Did you miss me?"

I push him off and walk across the entire room. "Drop the shit, Kevin. You know why I'm here."

"Well, I have hopes of why you're here but since you just walked out of my embrace, I'm starting to think I'm wrong. So why are you here, Kamii?"

"Did you do it?" I ask bluntly.

"Did I fuck you? Yes. And damn was it good," he smirks as he rubs his finger along his lower lip.

"No. Becca… Did you do it?" I ask, trying to push through his bullshit.

"Becca? Is that the girl I fucked at Passage last night? Hmmm, do I sense some jealousy from you?"

"Stop playing dumb. I'm the best criminal defense attorney in the City, if you did it, I'll find out so you might as well admit to it now. You said you would make Preston pay. How could you?"

"What? Look, I have no idea what you're talking about," his hands go up, slowly waving back and forth like he's holding a white flag and giving in.

"Answer me, did you murder Becca?"

"Did I WHAT?" he yells in shock.

"You heard me. Preston Babcock is being framed for the murder of Rebecca Anderson and you're the only person who knew them both *and* you said that Preston would pay."

"Look, whoa, stop right now. I DID NOT murder anyone. Yes, I was pissed at Preston for yanking my membership but I would NEVER murder anyone. When I said he would pay I was just talking out of my ass. I never planned on actually doing anything."

"How am I supposed to believe that?" I walk up close to him, trying to change his mood by throwing him off by being seductive with him. "You sure were pretty believable when you had me pressed up against that wall downstairs."

He doesn't fall for it and puts up his hands between us, "Look. I don't even know who Becca is and I can promise you, I *did not* murder anyone."

"You do know who she is. Becca was the other woman with me when we all had sex at the club together."

He sits down in his chair, the look on his face unmistakable. He didn't do it. I can tell by the expression on his face. The thought that someone he just had sex with being murdered hit him hard enough to prove to me that he's innocent. That's a look that no one can fake because you truly never know how you'll act until the moment happens. Believe me, I know.

Everyone thinks you'd be surprised, over emotional but that's not it at all. It's more of a dead silence of emotion and expression as every thought flashes through your mind in realization of what really just happen. You're mind and body go into shock more than anything else.

He runs his hands slowly down his face, like he's trying to wipe the memories from his mind. "Look, I never knew her name. Just like you, she never gave me her *name* and I first met her that night. I promise you, I didn't do this."

I place my hands on the desk that sits between us. "I'm going to need an iron clad alibi or believe me, I'm giving your name to the head detective on the case as someone who we believe is the main suspect. So far, you're the only person who both knew Becca and Preston, you were also the only other person, besides Becca, that knew who Preston was and that he was the owner, *and* you *did* threaten Preston to me, personally." I turn around to leave but before I reach the door I turn and taunt, "You know where to find me."

Even though I could tell he didn't do it, I still wanted to scare him a little and the look on his face was priceless. That's what he gets for messing with me like he did.

As I walk into my office, Stefanie hands me a message saying the Detective has some news for me. My stomach twists when I hear him on the other end of the phone line explaining to me that the tests came back positive. The semen they found inside of Becca was positively identified as Preston's.

"Stop the shit, Kamii. You and I know he's guilty. This is a low, even for you. Please don't waste my time, dragging this out to trial just to prove to you over and over again that this guy did it," the detective scolds me through the phone.

I've built quite the reputation within the police department over the last few years. I'd love to say I'm their favorite person to work with, but, by the tone of his voice, I know deep down they dread when they see my name attached to a case. I'm a hard ass, the best in the city, and this case will be no different.

Without giving away anything, I calmly reply, "He's innocent and I'll prove it to you. Thanks for the phone call but if that's all, I need to get back to proving you wrong."

"Fuck, Kamii. Really? I hope he's paying you good for this shit. Looks like your good name is about to go down. Have fun with that."

He slams the phone down making me wince in pain as I remove the earpiece attached to my ear. I've never let the detectives get under my skin but this took me for a loop. Whoever is framing Preston planned this out thoroughly, trying to make it an open/shut case.

They just didn't plan on me.

I send a text to Preston telling him to meet me at my office and wait for him to arrive.

He walks in twenty minutes later wearing an old 49er baseball cap, looking down to the ground as he whispers hello. In that moment, everything hits me about how hard he is really taking all of this.

He finally looks up from the brim of his hat and the look on his face pulls at my heartstrings. The bags under his eyes are so dark, I wonder if they're black eyes from a fight he's gotten in rather than just lack of sleep. His normal straight, demanding posture is lacking and his hands are stuffed in the front of his worn-out jeans.

"Hi," I whisper, afraid if I talk too loud he might crumble.

He smirks. Not saying a word and looking at the notes on my desk.

"I have news that you aren't going to like," I say as calmly as possible.

"I figured that's why you called me here." He stands up straighter, taking a deep breath, "Give it to me."

"The semen they found was a positive match to you."

"What the fuck? How is that even possible?" he throws his hands in the air while turning away from me.

"Well. Did you have sex with Becca that night?"

He walks up, placing his hands on my desk, leaning over and looking me straight in the eye. "Fuck not telling you everything. I'm all in. Kamii, I have not been with anyone since the day I first saw you at Rickhouse, that night when you first met Becca over a month ago. I talked to you briefly then left. Something about you knocked me out from that moment I first saw you and I walked away knowing I was going to get myself into some shit if you joined Bridge, and I was right. Even when you wanted to be with the other members, I would just watch. Making sure you were ok and waiting until it was my turn to have you again. So when you ask if I had sex with Becca that night, the answer is absolutely, positively, no. I have not had sex with anyone but you for the past month. I told you. I need you."

"I… I had no idea. But, you, you didn't want…" I can't believe what I'm hearing. He's felt this way this whole time?

"I know. I told you I didn't want any connections and I tried really hard to keep my distance from you but I just couldn't. And I still can't, Kamii. I'm a wreck. My life is over and all I can think about is losing you. Tomorrow is Thursday and I'm terrified to go back to the club but only because I am afraid you won't be there."

"And I won't. I can't go back there. Acting like nothing's wrong. Does anyone else know? Would they even know that one of the founding members is dead, rather than just not showing up anymore?"

"No, they won't. She helped me recruit other members but it was always done in secrecy and she wore her mask when she recruited from other clubs."

"I can't, no way." I look away as tears fill my eyes.

"But I need you," he pleads, holding out his hand to me.

I look him dead in the eye. "I can't go there acting like my best friend is alive and well with people who know who she is but yet have no clue that the real her is dead. Murdered. By who we still don't know. And besides that, we still don't know if it was someone from the club."

"It wasn't. I told you that."

"Yes, I heard that's what you believe but I don't share that same belief, especially after this positive semen test. Preston, it has to be someone from a club you have at least been a member of in the past. How else does someone have a sample of your semen?"

"A sample? What the fuck are you talking about?"

"Well, I thought about how this is even possible. If you didn't have sex with Becca that night, and you say you haven't had sex with anyone since me, then someone had to have been planning this for a long time. You had to have sex with this person at some point and they saved it. If you freeze it at a certain temperature then it keeps for however long you want it to. This is how they do artificial insemination. Nick and I froze some of his semen before he died because he was so much older than I but I wasn't ready for kids right then. I unfortunately know more than I wish to share about the process."

"Who's Nick?" The anger in his eyes as he says Nick's name sends a chill through my body.

"My husband, who passed away five years ago," I say matter-of-factly and not backing down from the anger I saw cross his face.

He stares at me, not saying a word. Reaching for my hand, he caresses it softly, completely changing his tone, "Kamii…"

"Don't. Stop. We're not doing this." I pull my hand from under his. "I need a list of all the women you have had sex with. They have to be involved somehow."

He shakes his head. "Kamii, I have no clue. At the public clubs you don't really exchange names. Just a glance, a smile and a fuck," he shrugs, unapologetic.

"Well, did anyone know who you were? Business wise at any of these clubs?"

"I have no clue. I didn't wear a mask when I went to those clubs so I don't know if they would have recognized me but at the same time I didn't walk in saying exactly who I was. If I could get away with it, I never even gave them my name."

"Preston, I'm trying to help you but I'm going to need more input from you. Were there women at Bridge who you had slept with in the past?"

"Yes."

"Then I need those names?"

His jaw tightens as he bites out through his teeth, "I said no."

"Then fine, rot in jail. I can't help you," I flippantly say as I turn around to sit back at my desk.

"There has got to be another way. What about Kim's brother? I found his info last night. He's in Oakland, here."

He hands me a piece of paper with his name and address on it. I pause, trying to think of any possibilities that could lead to him.

"Ok, so you said that Kim committed suicide after you went to a few clubs together?"

"Yes. She went more than a few times. And I thought she was enjoying it until the day she jumped from the bridge."

"Wait, she jumped from the bridge? What bridge?"

He looks down, ashamed as he whispers, "The Golden Gate."

"And you named your club Bridge? I don't find that a coincidence. Why would you do that?"

"There's no such thing as coincidences," he says quietly, with no emotion.

Wow, this is a little much. Talk about self-torture. He must have been really screwed up over her death. Why else would he name his club that? I don't want to ask more questions about his wife's death so I move on, "Was she close to her brother? Was it possible that she told her brother what you guys were doing?"

"I guess it's possible. He actually did come over to the house a few times before she died now that I think about it."

"Have you heard from him since?"

"No. I haven't. He didn't even come to her funeral. Everyone else in her family did but he was a no-show."

"Ok, so it's possible that he knew the true reason that his sister committed suicide. That definitely gives him a motive to frame you. I'll go research it more."

I stand up to escort him out of the room. He takes my hint and reaches the door before I do, opening it up but slamming it shut and turning to me.

"I can't leave Kamii. I told you. I need you." He weaves his hand through my hair, pulling me toward him.

I go without hesitation, not knowing how much I needed to feel his hard body against mine until we were pressed together.

"Please, let me have you." His lips land on mine before I have a chance to say anything.

I can't help it. His mouth molds to mine and I open up, allowing him access and giving him permission to take me however he wants me. I hear his low groan as he kisses me deeper, realizing what I just gave him.

Before I can realize what I've done, I'm pushed up against the wall with my back to him and my skirt pushed up around my waist. His fingers find my heavenly spot, pushing any thoughts of stopping him completely away and falling deep into his spell. When his fingers roll around my clit, all of the tension from the past few days floats away like a little kid blowing on a Dandelion.

His breath warms my shoulder, as he whispers, "You make everything better. Since the day I met you, you've taken my pain away and right now proves it even more."

I completely agree. I've been a mess since Becca's death and the moment he touched me I felt like I could finally breathe.

His fingers tease my entrance before pushing inside, once, twice, on the third time adding another finger to stretch me out more.

"Already wet for me. I'm going to take you. Can you be quiet? Your assistant is right on the other side of this wall."

Any words completely escape the ability to form from my lips, leaving me to just shake my head up and down. The word *yes* is screaming in my head but I'm not able to actually say it out loud. The thought of someone sitting right on the other side of this wall not knowing that I'm getting fucked from behind soaks me even more.

I feel Preston's smile against my shoulder. "You like that don't you? Knowing that someone could hear you getting fucked in here. Sneaking around like a bad girl."

I shake my head up and down *yes* and before I can respond he thrusts in me roughly, standing still, holding me tightly while filling me deeply.

"I'm going to move and it's going to be rough. I want to tempt you to scream my name and watch you fight not being able to."

Biting my bottom lip, I nod my head *yes* again, giving him full approval for his sexual attack against my body, knowing I am going to love every second.

His body starts to pound, pushing me against the wall and I have to close my eyes to focus on not making a sound. Both of his hands grab both of mine and he holds them up against the wall, confining me even more as he completely stops his movement. Having his cock inside me, teasing me by not moving is driving me wild.

I wiggle my ass as much as I can to try to get some friction between us when he whispers again, "Oh, no you don't. You can't move. You like this don't you? You like my cock buried so deep inside you, driving you wild, knowing that I only have to move an inch to make you cum?"

A low moan slips from my lips and he moves both my hands under the hold of one of his and covers my mouth with the other. "You have to be quiet. I'll give you want you want. What you need. I always will. Remember that."

And he does. He moves just an inch and after so much buildup from him being inside me but not moving, just teasing, he was right. An inch was all I needed and I explode all around him, my pussy twitching tightly around his cock in waves of my release. His hand wraps more firmly around my mouth, capturing my moan as I lose control and he follows right behind me. Grunting as he thrusts harder inside me.

Holding me tightly, he whispers in my ear again, "You need me just like I need you. Please don't ever push me away."

Chapter SEVENTEEN

Kamii

I drive into Oakland, following my GPS to the address that Preston gave me for Trevor. Oakland has some really nice neighborhoods and some really bad neighborhoods. Unfortunately for me, Trevor lives in one of the worst areas in the city.

I know I shouldn't be surprised when I pull up to his run down house with the front porch looking unsafe to even walk on. I can see places where the wood is almost completely rotted away and forget about any reminiscence of paint on the trim. Thankfully there is no one out front or at any of the other surrounding houses.

When I told Preston I was coming here he demanded that I have one of our male paralegals go but there was no way. I'm the best because I do all the research myself. There are little things that people may think are insignificant but they are always the turning point of evidence that I need to break the case.

As I approach the door, I notice the doorbell is not only broken but literally has bare wires sticking out, so I swing open the screen door, that is only hanging on by one hinge, and knock on the door.

I hear someone stir but no one answers the door so I pound harder, letting them know that I am not going away.

After a minute, a tall woman, with dark long hair and crystal clear blue eyes opens the door. Her appearance catches me off guard. Not because she's beautiful, or because she's giving a look of death, but because she doesn't fit.

Something is off.

I squint my eyes to try to envision what a mask would look like on her face. Her hair and height definitely match the look of the woman I saw trying to get Preston's attention at the club. *God, I wish I had paid more attention to her.*

"What do you want?" she spits out with a stare that says I'm a total bitch and don't you dare fuck with me. Ok, maybe not everything is off. Her attitude definitely fits in this neighborhood.

I give it right back though, "I'm not here for you. I need to talk to Trevor."

"Yeah, good luck with that," she taunts instantly.

"Where is he?"

"Jail," she states very matter-of-factly with no emotion.

"Who are you then?"

"Look bitch, I don't know who you are or why you're here but since you didn't even know he was in jail, I would say who I am is none of your business. Now get off my front porch before I grab my gun."

Without a word, I turn around and walk to my car. I've been doing this long enough to know when I'm fighting a losing battle and I wasn't going to get anywhere with her, no matter how creative I got.

As I drive home I call my assistant, "Angie, I need you to do a court records search for a Trevor Pierson. He's in jail and I need to know for what and when he went in?"

She gives me a simple, "On it," and I can hear her typing away on the computer in front of her. "I see here that he's in jail awaiting trial for a home invasion in San Francisco."

"When?"

"Date of offense is September 3."

Becca was killed on September 10. *Damn.* "Ok, thank you."

I hang up and call Preston. "Trevor's a no go," I state after he answers.

"Well, hello to you to," he laughs as he responds.

"Sorry, work mode. Just facts. Trevor was in jail the night Becca was killed."

"Fuck. Well, not surprised there. For what?"

"Home invasion. He's awaiting trial now."

"Ok, so now what?"

"We keep digging. Try to find someone else who would want to frame you. I want you to make a list of anyone who you might have pissed off anytime in your life. Also, did you deny a Bridge membership to anyone?"

"Yes, one guy. There was something about his membership application that didn't seem true. I just had a feeling and when Becca couldn't track anything else about him we denied it."

"Didn't you think this was important enough to tell me?" I say not trying to hide my irritation with him.

"Sorry, yes, I guess I should have. My mind isn't thinking clearly these days."

"Well, it needs to be. Preston, I can't help you if you don't tell me everything. Find that application and email it to me."

"How about you come to my house for dinner?"

"Preston, I…"

"I told you. Don't push me away. I'm not going to Bridge tonight but I still need you."

I pause for longer than I would like to admit, knowing that my silence is only admitting to him that I want him, too, or I would have come back with a fast no.

"I'll text you my address and see you at six," he says, hanging up before I even respond to his first question.

Preston

Fuck me.

I'm in so deep but it's too late to do anything about it. I knew from the second I saw her she would do this to me, and here I stand, in my kitchen, making her dinner instead of heading out to the club that I thought was everything I needed.

Now all I want is her.

And my freedom.

Funny how in order to get one I also get the other.

Hopefully.

I walk to my living room to turn on some music when I see the light from below the closet door shining bright. *How the hell is that on again?* I walk over, opening the door just enough to reach the switch and turn it off, shaking my head when I can't figure out why it was on in the first place.

As I walk back into the kitchen, I look at the clock showing it's past six. She should be here any minute so I open up the bottle of wine and reach for two wine glasses only to notice that two are sitting right-side-up instead of hanging upside-down on the under cabinet holders I have mounted.

Trying to think when was the last time I had wine, let alone two glasses racks my brain. It had to have been months ago when Becca came over and we first discussed the club. *There is no way these glasses have been sitting here this long instead of hanging where they belong...*

My thoughts are scattered when the faint drumbeat starts again. Fuck, I swear I'm not losing my mind but I keep hearing this same beat, over and over again at random parts of the day. I have searched all over my house but I can't pinpoint where it's coming from. It seems to bounce around, if that makes any sense at all.

I hear it coming from the bedroom then when I get there it seems to have moved to the living room.

Just as I start to really get pissed off, I hear a knock on the door and the faint beat stops abruptly. I walk from room to room, listening intently and it's gone.

What. The. Fuck?

I answer the door with an obvious look of confusion.

Kamii tilts her head squinting her eyes, "You ok?"

"Yeah. No. Here, come in," I say shaking my head.

She sets her things down on the entry room table before moving into the kitchen. "What's wrong?"

"I know this sounds crazy but I keep hearing this very faint beat, like from a Jamaican steel drum that plays over and over again. It just started again before you knocked on the door, then it stopped abruptly."

She pauses, looking around like she's searching for something in the air, "I don't hear it. Are you feeling ok? Are you getting enough sleep? Maybe it's just your ears ringing?"

I wave off the idea, trying to change the subject. It's bad enough I think I'm losing my mind; I don't want her to think I'm crazy, too.

"So what do you have for me?" Kamii asks sitting at one of my barstools.

"Here is his application. I'm not sure what it was but something just seemed fake. Becca handled all of the new applicants and this one stood out to her so I looked into it. When we researched potential members, we would look at things that hopefully people wouldn't think of. Of course, we did the common background check, Facebook and all other social media things, but something about him didn't add up. His photo, his address, his job, and even what he posted on social media, they all seemed like different people. I only wanted people I was 100% sure of so I just passed over it, not thinking much and moved to the next. This is why I wanted it so secure. There are some crazy people out there and since we're a sex club, I only wanted honest, true people looking for a good time."

"Ok, I'll look into him. And what about anyone else who might be upset with you?"

"I truly can't think of anyone, at least no one that would try to frame me for murder, but, the other day, someone approached me in the garage of my building. The garage is a secure place so I'm not sure how he got there. He threatened me saying he was defending Becca and I was going to rot in jail. It seemed different though. I got the feeling he didn't kill Becca but he's definitely looking forward to me going to jail for it."

"Can you explain what he looked like?"

I shake my head, trying to remember, "I'm horrible at this and it was dark. He was my height, pretty good build, white guy with a short haircut. Probably in his mid thirties."

"Wow, yeah, you are bad at that. Ok, I'll add him to the notes and let me know if he comes around again."

"Ok, can we be done with this investigation for tonight?"

"Preston, we can't stop until we prove you're innocent. Did you forget what's on the line?"

I turn her chair so I can step up in between her legs, looking straight into her eyes. "How can I forget? This is my life. My nightmare I'm living in. But with you here, I only have one thing on my mind. Please, let me have what I need."

I watch her pulse point start to thump and I know she's just as affected by me as I am by her.

"What do you need tonight?" she finally replies.

"You," I say as I lean in, locking my lips to hers, pulling her body into mine.

Murderer

can't watch this shit. I flip off the video, disgusted at the thought of watching these two have sex.

Who is this chick? It looked like they were all business at first, going over a piece of paper that I couldn't see from this far away. I figured it was his lawyer but now I'm not sure. Becca was the only woman he ever had over.

Until now.

What, I get rid of one and he moves just as quickly to the next?

I was having so much fun messing with him, playing music through the tiny speakers I installed in his ceiling. I would switch which speaker I used, changing from room to room and I loved watching him go crazy trying to figure it out. When she showed up though I stopped my game, Preston is the only pawn I want. If she wants to play I'll have to take her out, too.

Chapter EIGHTEEN

Preston

I have to clear my head. I swear all this stress is making me lose my mind. Somehow I even set my alarm for 3 am instead of 8 am. How does that even happen? Then of course the music I've been hearing started right up again, so faint that I could barely sleep the rest of the night. I've never even heard this beat yet it's stuck in my brain like the most annoying song lyrics you can think of.

The media is still swarming outside of my building and my work. I've already lost a few contracts I was working on claiming they decided to go with another company but I know it's bullshit. My face is plastered all over the news. When a high roller in town is framed for murder, believe me, the media does its own job of making sure everyone thinks I killed her.

I sneak out of my building through the service elevator with a hoodie pulled up and sunglasses on. I have a ton of steam built up and need to go for a run. There's nothing like the crisp salty air of San Francisco to clear your mind.

I head down to the pier, which is only a few blocks from my apartment that's on the edge of the Russian Hill district. It's always crazy crowded with people but I love the long, flat run from Pier 39 down to AT&T park. They are a little more than three miles apart so it's a good six-mile run roundtrip.

I'm almost back to my place when someone comes up behind me, pushing me, making me stumble and almost fall to the ground.

After gaining my footing, I turn around, "What the fuck was that for?"

"You know exactly what that was for!" the man screams back at me.

Sweat drips down my forehead as I raise my arm to wipe it away, noticing the same man from the elevator door in my garage a few days ago. "Look," I walk straight up to him, not backing down and getting right in his face, "I don't know who you are but you need to back the fuck off!"

He returns my stature, pumping his chest right back at mine, "I will not back off until you rot in hell."

I grit my teeth, opening my eyes as wide as I can, "I did not kill her."

"I know you killed her. I've seen all the evidence. And I know about your little club."

My eyes widen for a second before I bring my anger back in, denying anything he has to say. "What club?"

"You know exactly what club. I know all about Bridge. And you're going down. I promise you that. Anyone disgusting enough to not only attend a club like that, but actually own it, is only going to hell. I'm happy to say you will be going to hell now on this world before you enter hell on the other side as well. For eternity," he spits out.

I have to laugh. I've never been a religious man but I can tell this guy is very religious and believes just because I was having sex with whoever I wanted, in a safe environment, then I'm a horrible guy who's going to hell.

I'm over denying that the club exists to him and so I try another tactic to get this guy off my back. "Yeah, well if you truly believe that then you must also believe that Becca is already in hell, waiting for me, because she not only was a member of my club, she helped me start it and loved it as much as I did."

"No, she didn't! You brainwashed her. This was all your fault. She was a good, sweet, Christian girl until she met you."

I go for the kill. I have no clue who this guy is but he's fucking with me on the wrong day. "Yes, she was an amazing girl. Someone I cared for very deeply. And believe me, she loved that club and especially fucking me and any other guy at the same time. She loved having two cocks buried deep…"

I don't get to finish my thought as the guy takes a swing, landing his fist right across my jaw. I see nothing but rage as his other hand reaches up to take another shot but I block his punch and sock him in the gut with my other fist.

The guy can fight; I'll give him that. We go a few blows before he traps me in a wrestling move, making me feel like he's going to break my arm.

He leans down, whispering in my ear, "As I said before, if I were anyone else I would kill you myself right now, so feel lucky that I'm not but I'm done with this shit. I'm breaking your little secret wide open. I'm sure the press would love to know all the ins and outs of Bridge."

I clench my jaw, helpless in this man's grip. "Fine. Go ahead. Just know, it will prove that Becca was a member and if you're truly so against it then you'll be the one smearing her name, not me. Believe what you want about her but hear me now, she loved that place."

The guy spits in my face and releases his grip, walking away without saying another word.

Kamii

"I have that background check you requested," Angie states as I walk in the office. Lord knows what I would do without her. She's my right hand man, or woman I guess, and always comes through without fail. "Great. Let me see."

"You were right. This is full of lies. Everything from his address, social media to his photo is fake."

"Yeah, I'm not surprised to hear that. Any clue who it could be for real?"

"Unfortunately, no. They covered their tracks pretty well. None of it's joined together. I actually went to the address but when I asked if Travis Peacock lived there they, of course, said no. It was the sweetest older lady so I dug further, only to learn that they've lived there the past 50 years and never had kids."

"Angie, I appreciate you going above and beyond for this but I wish you didn't go to this address by yourself. You never know what you could have walked in on."

"Oh, don't worry. I took Anthony," she winks at me with a smirk. "It was 100% worth the, um, outing."

I have to laugh; she's never been shy about her and Anthony, the paralegal from the 5th floor. I wonder if she would be open to a place like Bridge. Then it hits me. This place will never be the same for me and I don't see myself ever going back. The thought stings somewhere deep in my chest.

Thankfully, Angie continues, pulling me out of my instant funk. "The phone numbers just ring and ring. I called the phone company and were able to track down that they are numbers attached to those pre-paid cellular plans that don't have names attached to them."

"Ok, what about the social media accounts that Preston found?"

"That's the thing. Someone went through a lot of trouble to set this up. The account was set up almost a year ago. With random posts here and there of the same guy, going places, discussing things and showing shots with friends. But a little over a month ago the posts stop, actually, a few weeks after the date on this application. Though the account still exists, it's been completely inactive."

"Ok, I guess that's a little odd but not totally out of the normal."

"No, so I started doing searches on the pictures. Running it through the facial recognition software we just got and I got a hit. But get this, from a royalty free photography site. I clicked on the photographer's folder and there they were. All the photos that were posted on this Facebook page were downloaded from this site."

"So we definitely know it was a fake account but why go through all the trouble of creating a persona, posting over a year of stuff?"

"Hey, that's why you get paid the big bucks. I just do the research," she laughs. "What's this an application for anyway?"

"That's confidential," I deadpan.

She gives me a smart-ass look that I give her right back. I love that she is like this with me now. She's been my assistant since I started here but just recently she's opened up to me more and become more of a friend.

I guess it's really me opening more up to her. I hope I don't lose this side of me and sink back into my hopeless, workaholic ways after I'm done with this case and I have nothing else left of Preston or Bridge.

Trying to stay on track, I smile back at her, "Ok, thanks. Keep me posted if you find anything else."

"You betcha," she sings as she turns back to her computer, waving me into my office.

After dropping my bag on my desk, I look over all the information again that Angie just gave me. When people make a fake profile they often use similarities from their personal life. You can call it not being original but I call it just plain stupid.

After staring at the paper for a few minutes two things stick out to me. First the address number, 350. That is the same number as Trevor's place in Oakland. And of course, there's the name on the application, Travis Peacock. Trevor's last name is Pierson, and I don't miss that fact of how close Peacock is to Babcock.

A knock at the door takes me from my ah-ha moment and I'm greeted with an extremely good-looking man standing in my doorway. I feel my face flush as I close the folder with the application and smile at the gorgeous man.

I'm still amazed at how much me being a member of Bridge has changed my personality and how comfortable I am with good-looking men who are strangers to me. I used to be extremely shy, never thinking I had a chance with any of them and now all I can think about is what they would look like naked, how long it would take me to get them that way and what sound they made when they came.

"Ms. Schafer, do you have a minute?"

"Yes, but please, call me Kamii. How can I help you?" I stand up, pointing him to the chair in front of me to have a seat.

"Yes, Kamii. I've heard a lot about you. A lot of… good things," he says in a sweet manner.

"Well, thank you. And whom can I thank for sending you my way?"

"Becca," he says with an instant frown on his face.

My heart instantly sinks. "I'm sorry. What did you say?"

"No, I'm sorry. I should have introduced myself first. I'm Nicholas Anderson. Becca was my little sister."

Oh shit. I didn't know Becca had a brother. Let alone such a gorgeous brother, but of course, his name is Nicholas. Life just wants to punish me that way.

He continues when I don't say anything in return, "She spoke of you constantly. Said you two had gotten pretty close, pretty fast."

"Yes, we were very close and spent a lot of time together. I'm devastated by what has happened to her."

His demeanor changes instantly as his jaw clenches tightly before he responds, "Then can you explain to me why you're defending the man who obviously killed her?"

"Everyone is innocent until proven guilty. It's my job to find who murdered her and I promise you, I will."

"We already have. It's Preston Babcock. Every piece of evidence found at the scene points directly to him. Case closed. Let us put this guy in jail so he can rot in hell before he spends eternity in hell."

"What do you mean we? How have you seen all of the evidence? Nothing should be public record until the trial."

He sits up straight, looking me directly in the eye. "I'm SFPD. I was on the scene when you called police after you found her. I heard her address over the radio and got there as soon as I could. I've seen everything there is to see and I have to admit, I'm disgusted with you right now. I can't believe that you would defend the murderer of your best friend."

Oh my God, yes, this is the guy she spoke to at her building the day there was a break in. Why didn't Becca want to introduce me to her brother? Because he's a cop?

I stand, walking slowly to the other side of my desk to try to get through to him the best way I can. "That's exactly it. She was my best friend and I want nothing more than to find the person that killed her. And the only thing I know for absolute certain is that Preston Babcock is innocent. Someone is framing him and I promise you I will find out who is responsible for this."

He stands up, standing a good foot taller than me, and moving closely, looking down into my eyes as he fights back, "How can you even say that? It was him."

"I promise you, it wasn't. He has an iron clad alibi."

"What could be so iron clad that you would honestly say he is being framed? His fingerprints were found with her blood on the doorsill, and even his sperm is positive. He. Killed. My. Sister."

I put my hand on his chest, trying to calm him down. "I've seen all of the evidence. I know how crazy it sounds but I promise you, he's innocent."

"Then what's his alibi?"

"That's attorney/client privilege. I can't share that with you."

"Bullshit!" he turns to walk toward the window looking out like he's contemplating saying something else.

He looks down, rubbing his eyes before he whispers, "How much did you know about my sisters, um, activities?"

Oh shit, I don't like where this is going. I play dumb. "What do you mean, activities?"

"I didn't want to believe it was true. She was raised better than that. She knows that sex is something to be shared between husband and wife."

My heart races out of control. How does he know?

He's quiet before looking at me with sadder eyes than when he first walked in. "I heard this might have been going on. I shot down the idea and steered the other officers away from the thought only to look into it more myself. I just can't believe it's true."

"You have to fill me in here. I don't know what you're trying to get at."

"She belonged to one of those underground sex clubs."

Oh shit! "Wha, um, what do you mean, underground?" I try to say with nothing but pure shock in my voice, hoping he believes me.

"I didn't want to believe it either. But Babcock confirmed it himself. I know it was wrong but I had to confront him about it. I stopped him on a run this morning," he looks back to the window before he continues, "he not only confirmed that the club does exist but said she helped him start it."

Why in the hell would Preston do that? Has he lost his mind? I'm silent, trying to tread water as I figure out what my next move is.

Nicholas turns around, "Please tell me you didn't know and you aren't a member, too?"

Deny. Deny until I die is all that goes through my head. "No. I had no clue she was a, um, member of a, um, sex club." I get an idea, "This could help with my investigation though. How did you find out about this club? Where is it? Can I get a list of names that belong? Maybe someone within the club is framing Preston."

He shakes his head slightly, "I don't know who the members are. I just know it exists. It's even located behind his showroom, that crazy bastard thought he was being secretive."

"Ok, so how did you find out?"

"I knew my sister was up to something. Another police officer saw a picture of her on my desk and said he recognized her from a club and got all hot and heavy about their time together before he knew she was my sister. I could have beaten him up that day. How dare he say those things about my baby sister."

I walk up to him, trying to comfort him so he'll continue to talk.

"He said it had been a few months since he saw her at another club he frequents so one night I followed her."

My chest tightens and I have to hold my breath to keep him from hearing my fear.

"I watched her walk into a dark alley, then I watched as other people followed, all staying for a few hours before leaving. The place was obviously secretive and not many people knew about it. I went back the next day to see it in the daylight and it was nothing more than a warehouse door. I was sick to my stomach; I can't even imagine what was happening behind those doors. I don't even want to know, actually."

I try to comfort him again by placing my hand on his arm and rubbing it slightly, trying to get more info, "When you saw her, was she alone?"

"Yes, the first night she was."

Oh, thank God! It was odd for us not to go together but there were times I went straight from work alone and met her there. But then what he said hits me. "The first night?"

"Yes, she went back on Saturday, again alone. I went back every night that week with no sign of anyone until Wednesday night when she walked down the alley with Preston's arm wrapped around her as they walked in. I sat and watched but no one else ever came. Just the two of them. They stayed for over two hours then left, going their separate ways."

Whoa, what the hell? Why were they together, there, on a night it was closed? Preston said he hadn't slept with anyone but me. Is he lying? What else could he be lying about?

Nicholas turns to me, tears filling his eyes, "I wanted to talk to her. I was just trying to figure out how and when, and now, I can't."

I wrap my arms around him, bringing him close to me as he starts to cry over the death of his baby sister.

Chapter NINETEEN

Kamii

Me: We need to talk.

Preston: What's up? Everything ok?

Me: I just have some questions. Meet me at Starbucks next to my office. Say half hour?

Preston: It's late. How about I come over or you can come over here?

Me: I don't trust myself and I need answers.

Preston: See you there.

    I look at my clock realizing it's past ten at night. It's late but since the Starbucks is open 24 hours I knew it was a good place to meet. I can't tell you how many times it saved me working way too late into the night, really just not wanting to go home over the years. And here I am again. Not wanting to be home and nowhere near wanting to go to sleep. My mind is going crazy over knowing that Preston and Becca were there, alone, on Wednesday night before she died.

Preston shows up right on time, dressed as casual as I've ever seen him in a hoodie and jeans. He still makes my insides ache just seeing him, even like this. Which reminds me why we're meeting here, in public.

My hot tea warms my freezing hands as I wrap them around the cup. It may be summer but San Francisco doesn't know seasons and it's always cold here. His eyes meet mine and his warm smile welcomes me in as he approaches my table.

"Hi," he says in an almost whisper after he sits down, keeping silent for a few beats as we stare at each other.

"Hi," I finally reply.

"So what did you want to talk to me about?"

"I need to make sure you're telling me the absolute truth."

"You know I am. Are you really starting to doubt me? Please Kamii, I need you, more than anyone else, to believe me and my innocence in this matter."

"I know that but there are things you're keeping from me."

He cuts me off, "No, I'm not. I'm 100% open and honest with you."

"No, you aren't because you won't give me the list of members," I plead.

"We've been over this," his jaw tenses.

"I know we have but that's just one thing. I also need you to be honest with me about your relationship with Becca."

"I have been. Why are you questioning me?"

"I had a visitor today, Becca's brother."

"I didn't even know she had a brother."

"He knows Preston. He knows about the club. He figured it out before Becca was killed. He was staking out your place the week she was killed."

"Wait, holy shit. That has to be the guy who just attacked me while I was on my run today. He said he knew about it."

"Yes, that was him, he's SFPD, Preston."

"So. I don't think he'll go public with it. He threatened but when I told him the only good it would do would be smearing his sister's name in the press, he seemed to back off."

"Yeah, I agree, I think he'll keep it a secret."

"Ok, so then why are we here?"

"Preston, you said you hadn't had sex with Becca for more than a month."

"And I was completely honest."

"Then why were you both at the club on Wednesday night, by yourselves? He said he saw you enter together and leave a few hours later."

"We were just going over paperwork and setting things up with the place.

There were a few things that needed to be done to the bar and the wall in one of the rooms. She came to help and just hang out."

I look down, ashamed that I'm even asking him these questions. It's not like we're dating. Hell, I didn't even know his real name until the other day, and he literally watched me have sex with two other guys. But why was I so jealous to hear he spent time alone with Becca?

When I look up he has a slight smirk covering his gorgeous face. "You were jealous."

"No, I wasn't jealous," I bite back. "I'm trying to get you off the hook for murder. I just need to know everything. Don't you remember, your semen was found in her? I thought you were lying about the last time you had sex with her."

"I already told you it had been awhile. Not since I met you and besides, I was with you that entire night. My dick has only been inside you for the last month," he smirks.

The way he said that made me start to ache in need. My legs involuntarily clench and he grins when he notices.

"You liked that thought didn't you?" he smirks.

I close my eyes, taking a deep breath before opening them again. "Preston. I'm your attorney. We need to keep a distance between us. I can't stay focused when you are constantly making me feel this way."

He reaches for my hand, "But you do feel it?"

I pull away, not answering him. "Like I said, I need to stay focused. I found something on the application today."

He sits back, the smirk not leaving his face but thankfully respects my words. "Ok, hit me with it."

"I think the application was Trevor filling it out with fake information. There were a few things that related to him personally that I don't think are just a coincidence."

"There are no such things as coincidences," he cuts me off stating very matter-of-factly.

"Wow, and here I thought I was the skeptical attorney," I smirk. "So yeah, I think it was him."

"Ok, but we already know he was in jail when Becca was killed so that doesn't really help us."

"I know but there has to be a tie somehow. Like you said, there's no such thing as coincidences. He obliviously knew about the club and that you owned it or he would have used his real name."

"There's no way it could be him. One, why would he be trying to get in my club, I mean, how would he even know about it? Believe me, he's not one who hangs out with the caliber of people who are members, so a recommendation would have never happened, and that is the only way people knew about it. Two, Trevor is a piece of shit who has fried all of his brain cells using drugs. He would never be smart enough to put an application together like that. Putting in all that leg work with the Facebook account and such."

"Ok, so then maybe he really is involved and he has someone working with him. Or I guess this other person is who actually murdered Becca since he was in jail."

"But wait, how far back did this Facebook page go? I always scrolled a ways back to see what was truly going on. I'd have to look again but I'm almost positive it went back ten months or so, almost a year. There is no way he could have been planning something like this. I didn't even own the club then. It can't be him."

I sigh, trying to think. It doesn't make sense. None of this makes sense.

Chapter TWENTY

Kamii

I've been racking my brain and still things just don't add up. There has got to be something I'm missing. No one is that good at hiding things. There is always someway to prove it.

Fingerprints can be easy to lift if you know what you're doing and they can be found on anything a person touches so say he sets down a glass at a job site and someone takes it before he even notices then boom – there are his prints, stuck to the glass, ready for someone to do with as they wish.

The process to lift those prints, then turn around to make them a mold and into useable prints is a completely different story. It takes some very high tech pieces of equipment and material and over all that, time. And this is what I can't understand. Who would hate Preston that much that they would spend all this time setting him up for murder?

And why? What would they get out of it?

I've looked into his past business dealings, his past relationships before his wife and even spoke to other clubs he would frequent before starting his own and I can't find one person to say anything bad about the guy. It's kind of sickening really. He can't be that perfect. Is it all just for show? Did someone find a dirty secret he's been hiding, well, besides the whole sex club thing?

There has got to be a reason someone would hate another person so much that they would kill an innocent person just to bring the other person down.

I still believe it has to be someone within Bridge. How else would they get his semen?

Since I was coming up with dead-ends, I hired my own forensic team to do an autopsy and examination of everything that night and her body. The cops still think this is an open/shut case so I know they didn't look at the body or surrounding things as well as I would have.

My team found something and I'm sitting here waiting, not so patiently I might add, for my phone to ring. When it finally does, I answer on the first ring, "Give it to me."

"Yes, we found two things. First. We found two long dark hairs on her clothing."

Hmm, she was a hairdresser but at the same time, I can't imagine her wearing the same clothes she wore to work to the club. "Ok, can we get a DNA sample off of it?"

"Yes, we can. These hairs were yanked out so there are still some samples we can draw from. And next, we found cells under her fingernails."

"Yes! Oh, this could be good. You can fake fingerprints, you can even plant the semen but you can't fake cells."

"Exactly. Those are only there if you grab someone real hard and scrape them off yourself."

"Great. Good job. Go run those tests. If we can prove that this hair and these cells came from the same person then we have a much bigger leg to stand on and can at least start to prove there is a shadow of a doubt. Thank you."

"You bet ya. I'll run the tests as soon as I get back to the lab."

We hang up and I smile from ear to ear as I text Preston.

> **Me: We got something. Not positive yet, but I have a good feeling.**
>
> **Preston: Finally. Can we meet?**
>
> **Me: I can't. Sorry. I have plans.**
>
> **Preston: Plans? With who?**

I don't respond. I'm not really sure what to say. I've been trying to keep my distance, no matter how hard I don't want to, and being away from him is killing me inside, but we can't be together. I'm his attorney and all we had was sex.

The most amazing sex ever – but it was just sex.

Becca's brother called and asked if I wanted to get together to have dinner tonight. His voice was so sweet, I couldn't say no. Poor guy is torn apart by losing his sister.

I'm back to my working late and going to the gym routine so dinner out with him sounded like a good plan at the time. Though now, I'm regretting saying yes.

I'm still heartbroken over losing Becca and I'm not sure if sitting across from her brother will be the right thing to mend it. What if all he wants to do is talk about her? I will seriously break down. I don't deal with my emotions that way. I tuck them in, keep to myself while I slowly die each day.

That's the real me.

I asked that we meet at my work so it felt like less of a date, since I have no clue what this really is, and before I know it, there's a knock at the door.

He smiles almost shyly as he opens the door, "Hello again, Kamii."

"Hi there, Nicholas. How was your day?"

"Good. Long. I'm ready for some food. Any suggestions of where you wanted to go tonight?"

We discuss some options and settle for a quaint little Italian place up the road that we can walk to. Little is discussed on the way to the restaurant, which is totally fine by me. It wasn't uncomfortable in any way, just quiet.

After we're sat at a corner table for two, he breaks the silent by blurting out, "Look, I really would like to just forget about Becca for one night."

I let out a sigh of relief before he continues, "Oh lord, that came out all wrong. I'm sorry. I just. This has all been too much. And I know you were really close. And I'm sure you thought that's why I invited you here, to talk about her, but it really wasn't. I just needed a night off from thinking that my family has completely collapsed."

"No, I'm really glad to hear you say that and I can't agree with you more. I know she was only in my life for a short while but I'm seriously lost without her and I need a distraction just as much as you do."

"Thank goodness. I mean, don't get my wrong, I love my sister."

I hold up my hands stopping him there, "No, no worries here."

"I just, I mean, I know she loved you. She talked about you constantly. So I guess deep down I wanted to get to know you as well."

A smile fills my face, "Well, I'm flattered."

"I also wanted to thank you. I take it you were the one who was trying to get her away from this horrible place she was going to with that Preston guy."

I almost choke on the bread I just stuck in my mouth. Is this guy serious? He really has no clue that she's the one that actually introduced me to Bridge. I guess I should be thankful but I'm still shocked.

I play dumb, "I'm sorry...?"

"Preston brain washed her, believe me, she was not raised that way. We come from a very religious family who believes in no sex before marriage."

Wow, I have to hide my shock again. Not only because this is so far from the truth of who Becca really was but because I know this guy is not married and I don't even want to think that he could possibly still be a virgin.

"I still can't believe you're defending that bastard. All the evidence is there."

"You know I can't discuss the case but believe me, I have one rule now, to never defend someone if I don't honestly think they're innocent."

"I'm sorry, you're right. Ok, no Becca, no case. Tell me about yourself?"

I tell him a very abbreviated story of myself, leaving out anything about my marriage, my family; because really there's nothing to discuss, and my friendship with Becca. So really, it's a very short story.

He tells me about being a police officer, how he was raised in a loving, still married, family and how his faith is very important to him and helps him get through the day with all the horrible things he sees first hand.

By the end of dinner I'm truly enjoying myself. He's a great guy, has a wonderful personality and seems to want to settle down with a wife and kids of his own. He should be every girl's fantasy. A gorgeous guy, more than willing to fall in love and sweep a girl off her feet but it's just not for me.

I've been there. Married the guy of my dreams and he was taken away in an instant. My chance has come and gone.

Preston

Kamii has plans and she won't tell me what. It has to be with a man. Could she really be going out on a date? Why is this silently killing me inside? Never mind, I know exactly why and this proves that it will never happen and I need to get my mind off of her.

It's Thursday so the club is open and I'm not sure what's worse, heading to the club alone, knowing both Kamii and Becca won't be there, or sitting here by myself while my thoughts gnaw on my brain along with my heart.

Trying to heal my heart wins so I grab my keys and head down to the garage.

Now, I know my brain has been somewhere else lately but when I walk to my assigned parking spot I can't help but stop and stare at the empty space that I've always parked my car in and then at the occupied spot next to it. Each apartment building gets two spots and I've always parked in the spot on the right but yet my car is parked in the one on the left.

You would think something like this is muscle memory since I've parked in this same spot for the past seven years, so I'm completely baffled that I pulled my car into the wrong spot.

Shaking my head, feeling like I've officially lost my mind, I know a good release with a complete stranger is exactly what I need to rid my mind of both this case and, more importantly, Kamii.

I drive straight to the club, grabbing my mask from the center console, anxious to have something in my life back to normal with this one act.

Thankfully, the place is busy and people are already starting to scene. The normal twitch I feel in my cock when I watch people fucking doesn't happen so I turn away and walk to the bar, asking for a shot of Jack Daniels and taking it back before slamming it down on the bar a little harder than I should.

Two arms wrap around my waist, leaning in, whispering, "You look like you're in need of a release tonight."

Her voice is familiar and for a brief second I think it's too good to be true and Kamii is behind me, here in the club, ready for me. Needing me like I need her.

As I wrap my hands around hers, ready to greet her, I turn around only to see a woman who's tall with long brown hair who definitely is not Kamii.

I'd like to say it's just disappointment I feel but it's not. Utter, soul-shattering sadness is what comes over me in that second that I realize it's not her and I'm done for. Without a word, I let go of her hand, turn away from her and walk out of the club, heading straight to Kamii's place.

Kamii

My home isn't far from the restaurant so Nicholas walks me home, talking like old friends along the way.

At my apartment complex door he grabs my hand, pulling it up to his mouth, kissing it gently. "I can see why Becca liked you so much. I'd love to see you again," he says sweetly as he kisses my hand one more time before dropping it down but not letting go.

He's so charming and polite, I almost have to laugh. I have gotten so used to guys being more forward, knowing they only want one thing and, if I'm honest with myself, me, too.

I really like this guy, and I'd love to see him again as a friend but that's all this will ever be. I'm not sure how to let him down so I just smile saying, "That would be nice." Because it will be, just not in the way he thinks.

"Great. Have a good night. Thank you again for accompanying me to dinner."

"Thank you," I turn around, walking into my building and waving goodbye as I close the door.

"You have got to be kidding me?" A man's voice appears to my left, startling me before I see Preston come out of the shadows.

I slap his arm, "Don't do that. You scared me!"

"You went on a date with that guy? Becca's brother? What are you thinking?"

I try to blow him off, walking down the hall to my door, trying to act like I'm not affected by his presence. "He's a nice guy. Why are you here anyway?"

"Nice guy?" He puts one arm on my door, pushing his body against mine while leaning down to whisper in my ear. "You don't do nice guys. You can't fuck *nice*."

"What are you, jealous?"

"What if I am? I told you, Kamii. I need you. But you need me, too. Do you really think he can make you happy like I can? I saw you with him. Your body language said it all. You were completely closed off. Not welcoming him toward you. Not like you are with me."

I turn to face him, our mouths only inches apart, I whisper, "Really, how am I with you?"

He puts his hands on my hips, pulling me even closer to him. "Your eyes darken when you're around me. Your lips part, dying for me to kiss them. Your breathing quickens and your body opens up to me, allowing me to do whatever I want. Like your body is mine."

And just like he explained, I stand there helpless. Waiting for him to kiss me, take me as his own and do as he wishes with my body.

A sexy smirk fills his face as he leans down to whisper again, "Why don't you unlock the door so I can take you inside before I fuck you on your doorstep?"

I turn to unlock my door, opening it up only to be picked up, swung around so he's holding me up high as his lips crash into mine.

Just as quick as he picked me up, he sets me down on a stool at my kitchen counter. Wrapping his hands around me from behind, he whispers in my ear, "You're mine Kamii. I want nothing but you and I'll do anything to make sure I have you. You take my pain away. Let me do the same for you."

A chill falls from my shoulders, down my arms and tingles to my toes while a need fills my body that I can't deny any longer.

His thick hands wrap around my hair, pulling it tightly into a small ponytail and keeping a hold of it while he uses it to move my neck any way he demands. First to the left, then to the right, teasing me and making sure I'm completely submissive to him.

Moving my head to the left, he leans down lightly licking my shoulder and moving up my neck, pulling my hair back to give him better access to the front of my neck.

Calmly, I sit as still and submissive as possible. Letting him have his way with my body and loving every second. My head is moved to the right as he continues his licking, biting and sucking on my neck.

Heat fills my body as a deep craving starts to melt my core. My head is turned to the right more and is met with his lips crashing onto mine. Kissing them passionately, keeping one hand still in my hair and the other wrapping around, gripping by breast firmly.

Too soon he pulls away, making me whimper from his loss. Taking both hands he wraps my hair up again, running his fingers through it first, tugging me, checking on my submissiveness one more time.

I am his. In this moment, I want nothing but to be whatever he wants me to be, as long as I get him in return.

His sexual game starts over with tugging my hair to the left and kissing all over my shoulder, my neck, my lips and my breasts. All while I sit completely still, facing the counter in a sexual induced haze.

Finally, his lips attack mine, forcing his tongue around my own, moaning at our touch and yanking my hair back even harder. My chest is thumping, my pulse running, my panties soaking.

I try to turn more, needing to feel his body against mine but am stopped by him releasing my lips and pulling my hair to the other side where he starts his show all over again.

I can't take it anymore, I need to feel something before the ache between my legs explodes. I move my hand down, reaching for the sensitive spot just as Preston grabs my hand, stopping my movement.

Breaking our kiss, he whispers, "No. That is mine. All of your pleasure is mine tonight."

My chest tightens to a sharp point at the thought as I pule from his words.

Thick hands wrap around my body, picking me up and walking me to my bedroom. Gently, he stands me up, stripping me of my clothes. Here I stand, completely naked, offering myself to him, in my bedroom, in a non-kink way, and being totally ok with it.

"Lay down on the bed, my beautiful Eurydice," he says through his dark eyes. "Face down. I want to see that beautiful ass of yours."

I do as he asks and look over my shoulder as he climbs on top of me, rubbing my back, down to my ass, gripping it tightly with both hands before pulling it up slightly, giving him better access.

I feel the tip of his cock swirl around my entrance before moving in at a deliciously slow pace. Both of our mouths unconsciously release a deep moan before he starts to move, slowly taking my body and making it his.

The familiar pull fills my core as his hand reaches around, sneaking its way in between my body and the mattress, finding my clit just in time. His fingers work their magic, swirling around the tight nub as I explode, clenching hard around his cock as I feel my body pulse with its release.

I'm mush, floating high above the clouds as he continues his thrusts in and out. Before I know it, his legs are wrapped around me and my body is flipped around so I'm on top of him, my back to his front, in one swift movement.

The new position hits a completely different location bringing me back to reality and preparing my body for the need to release again. His large hands wrap around my tiny waist, holding me still as he pounds his hips up, filling me roughly, making me scream in response.

My legs fall to the side but I'm too weak to hold myself up. Preston doesn't seem to mind that my entire weight is on his as he easily holds me up while sliding in and out of me.

"I want you to reach down, feel where our bodies connect, keep your hand there and feel how wet my cock is as it slides in and out of you," Preston whispers in my ear which sends chills down my body.

I do as I'm told and the feeling of him sliding my lips apart, filling me deeply then pulling back out, leaving my hands slippery fuels my need as my body starts to tighten, ready to release at any moment.

"Now rub yourself. Show me what you would do if I weren't here. How can you make yourself cum?"

My hand reaches up slightly, slowly circling my clit, moving it around in tight circles. Instantly my legs clench, this little movement was all I needed and my body starts to convulse on his as I press my hand firmly down on my clit. Holding it there tightly as I ride the wave of my orgasm.

"God, that was so fucking hot," Preston says through clenched teeth as his release floods from his body and into mine.

I fall to the side as his body encloses mine; holding on to me tightly as he kisses my shoulder, whispering, "Please let me stay the night."

I don't argue, I don't fight it; I just grab his hand, pulling it closer to my chest as I close my eyes to drift off to sleep.

Chapter TWENTY-ONE

Kamii

My phone ringing awakens me but that's not why my heart is pounding hard through my chest. No, that's caused by the man that is wrapped around me tightly, like he's holding on for dear life. I hadn't noticed it all night. In fact, I slept harder than I think I had in years.

Looking at the clock, I see it's past nine. I haven't slept in that late since college. I'm an early riser. For years I have woken up with an anxiety that was too much to handle, forcing me out of bed just so I can breathe.

Even though my heart is pounding, it's not from anxiety. No. Not today. It's from the happiness and excitement I feel waking up next to Preston.

Trying not to wake him up, I reach for my phone to see who it was that just called. Thankfully, they left a message so I press play and hold it up to my ear.

"Morning Ms. Schafer. This is Rick from CSI San Francisco. I have your results back on the cells we found under the victim's nails and the hair found on her clothes. Without getting into too big of details on your voicemail, I can tell you that the two tests came back positive as a match to each other and we can tell you that it is a female. Call us when you have a chance and we can go over things in further detail. Thank you."

Holy shit! Yes. This is the break we need!

I turn around so I'm face to face with Preston. He looks so peaceful as he lies there fast asleep. His breathing is calm and steady and I can't help myself from bringing my hand up to touch his face and the short stubble that's covering his jaw line.

He jolts slightly from my touch then relaxes as I bring my lips softly to his, whispering, "Good morning."

"Morning my beautiful Kamii," he smiles.

"I have good news for you."

"Besides the fact that this is the second time I've gotten to wake up with you next to me?"

I smile, knowing that the thought made my morning as well. "No, we finally have the break we were looking for in the case."

That got his attention. He springs up right in the bed. "What? What did you find out?"

"I just got a call from CSI San Francisco and they found both hair and cells under Becca's fingernails and they not only are a match for each other, but they are to a woman. This can prove there is doubt that you were not the last person she was with and there was a struggle between her and someone else."

He drops back on the bed, sighing heavily. "Thank God. Ok, so what do we do next?"

"Now we have to find out who this is but at least we have some clues to start with. We know it's not Trevor because he was in jail but there was a woman at his house when I went to check on him. Any clue who that could be?"

"No. Knowing him it's some crack head whore."

"Hmm, she didn't strike me as a crack head. She had dark long hair, similar to what they found on Becca. And really Preston, similar to the woman I saw trying to get with you at the club each time we were together."

"What are you talking about? What woman?"

"Preston, I told you before. The woman that tried to be with you every time we were together. I noticed her staring at us a few times. She wanted you. Bad. And that last time I was with," I pause, looking down, not wanting to finish my sentence and feeling ashamed all of a sudden for the last time I was there with those two other men. "She came up right away like she was staking her claim on you. I thought you were with her and was surprised when I saw you sitting by yourself, watching us."

"You noticed me sitting there?" he says with hope that kills me even more.

"I did, Preston," I reach for his hand, "But what if this woman that I saw at Trevor's place is her and even though he didn't get a membership, she did. If I'm right, I'll need for you to give me those names."

He yanks his hand from mine, before sitting up and turning to leave my bed. "We've had this conversation…"

"Fine, Preston." I reach to stop him, "I'll go back out there today. See if I can get her to talk. Maybe I won't need you to tell me who she is and I can figure it out on my own."

"No, that's not safe. We'll send a police officer."

"Are you kidding me? Policemen are not welcome in the neighborhood he lives in. They'll get us nowhere."

"That's my exact point. If policemen aren't welcome there then that's nowhere you should be."

"Preston, this is my job. I've been in much worse situations. Trust me."

"Fine, I'll go with you though."

Two hours later we pull up to Trevor's house. "Damn, talk about a shit hole," Preston states as he puts the car in park.

I don't say anything as we get out of the car, walking up to the front. There's a For Lease sign in the front window and the few things that were sitting on the front porch before are gone.

We bang on the door a few times but no one comes. Peeking in the window we see the place is empty.

"Shit. How come I don't think this is a coincidence?" I say under my breath.

"Because there are no such things as coincidences," Preston replies, while smirking at the fact that he seems to constantly be reminding me of that.

I see a neighbor walking out of her front door. She's an older woman, someone I can tell has lived here her whole life. Her house is a little nicer than the others though still run down.

As I approach her she gives me a warm smile so I give her one in return, hoping I can get some info out of her. "Morning Ma'am. Can I ask you a quick question?"

"Oh lord, who's gotten themselves into trouble now?" she replies. I'm sure she's seen her fair share of trouble living in this neighborhood.

"We were hoping to speak to the woman that was living here. Do you have any idea when she moved out?"

"I'm sorry but you must have the wrong address sweetheart. There was only a man living there. His name was Trevor. Never had a woman there."

"Well, I came here a week or so ago and there was a woman that answered the door."

"No my dear. The place has been empty since he went to jail at the beginning of the month. The owner just came and emptied the place last night since he not paying rent being in jail. I spoke to them myself. They said they couldn't have it sitting there empty as they need the rent and all."

"So you never saw a woman there?"

"Nope. No woman was ever there and I haven't see a light on for quite awhile now."

I shake my head, "Ok, thanks for your help. Have a great day."

"You too dear." She grabs my hand, giving the top of it a pat with her other hand before she walks back into her house.

I look at Preston who shakes his head looking down as I proclaim, "This case just gets weirder and weirder. I swear I spoke to a woman the other day. That's how I knew he was in jail so I know I was at the right house."

"So what now? That lead is gone."

"Well, next is Trevor. Let's go pay him a visit."

Preston looks at me with his eyebrows scrunched up, "You're kidding me right?"

"Nope, come on. Let's head back to the City."

I've never liked visiting the city jail and believe me, I've been here more times than I would like to admit, visiting clients or trying to gather evidence. Since I'm not the attorney of an inmate this visit is treated differently.

We don't get a private meeting with Trevor. No, we are ushered into a big room with a glass wall in the middle and seats on either side. There are partitions up in between chairs offering us a little privacy but not much.

The room is cold. All concrete floors and slate walls. The chairs are even a hard metal making any visit totally impersonal. It's sad that there is nothing warm and inviting for people to come visit their loved ones.

There are two chairs per partition but not enough room for us to sit side by side so I sit in front with Preston behind me.

Coldness rips through me as I watch Trevor being ushered into the room on the other side of the glass. He eyes me with a shit-eating grin on his face that makes my skin rise like goose flesh, sending a chill through my body. No wonder Preston doesn't like this guy. He puts off an aura that more than rubs me the wrong way.

He doesn't take his eyes off of me, or that shit-eating grin off his face, as he grabs the phone, holding it up to his ear so we can have a conversation. "Well, well, pretty lady. To what do I owe this honor for your beautiful face to pay me a visit?"

I guess he was too focused on me and didn't notice Preston behind me because once he stands up, making his presence known, Trevor's entire demeanor changes and the grin on his face turns to that of pure hatred. "What the hell are you doing here?" he barks out at Preston.

I turn, placing my hand on Preston, getting him to calm down before turning to talk to Trevor.

"My name is Kamii Schafer. I'm representing Preston in a case we're working on."

"Yeah. I heard all about a certain murder he committed."

"That's why we're here. I have some questions for you."

"Ha! Questions for me?" He starts to laugh out loud. "Well, well, well. Look who's coming to me now for help? And here you always treated me like a piece of shit you wanted nothing to do with. Well, you know what?" He stands up, looking Preston straight in the eye, "Go fuck yourself."

He drops the phone and walks away from us. Signaling to the guard that he's done with the visit.

Preston pushes his chair back so hard it falls with a loud bang on the ground as he storms out of the room, too.

Shaking my head in defeat, I put the phone back on the wall hanger and walk out behind him.

Chapter TWENTY-TWO

Kamii

My head pounds from the day's stress. After leaving the jail I came back to my office to go over the CSI evidence that they dropped off while Preston went to his office to check in on things.

We definitely have enough here to form a shadow of a doubt that Preston didn't murder her but just because I'm working on the case of my best friend's murder, I need to find out more. Normally my only goal is to make sure my client is off but this is different. This case I want to, no, I need to find who did this.

I need those names.

I know it's not the right thing to do but I'm cornered and right now this is my only lead. So gripping my hands tightly around my purse, I head out of my office before I change my mind, and head straight to Bridge.

It's amazing how different it looks during the day. I still park in the same place, away from everything and look around as I walk down the alley to the entry. To my surprise, the place has a very simple padlock holding the warehouse door from swinging open. Reaching up, I pull the bobby pin that's holding my hair back at the front and head to work on trying to pick the lock.

After only a few attempts the lock pops open, sending nervous chills of excitement through my body as I question if I should really go through with this? Preston could hate me at the end of this but at the same time, if I don't get him off this murder charge he could be in jail for the rest of his life.

It's a risk I'm willing to take.

The door pops open and an eerie feeling washes over me as I enter the room that's only lit from the small cracks in the window coverings that cover two of the four walls. I'm not even sure what I'm looking for so I walk around, looking behind the bar or around the room for any closet that could hold some information.

A door at the back catches my eye and I walk up to it, slowly pulling the door handle open to see a small desk and a filing cabinet.

Jackpot.

The cabinet is locked so I try my magic at picking the lock again, successfully getting it open only after a few minutes. Inside I find folder after folder with a name on each one. Pulling out the first ten or so, I turn to sit as his desk and go over who each member is as quickly as I can.

My hand reaches for a tiny lamp that sits on his desk and when it switches on a vision of myself stares back at me. On his desk, laying flat is a picture of me. It's my Facebook profile picture that he's printed out and placed under a clear mat that lies on his desk with nothing else underneath it.

I'm not sure whether I should be extremely touched or feel even more guilty right now for breaking his trust. He keeps saying that he needs me but I didn't realize like this. I've been telling myself that it's only sex that he *needs* but lately I can't deny the truth I see in his eyes and this just proves it even more. And if I'm honest with myself, lately I'm having an even harder time not spending every waking moment thinking about him.

Before I look at any of the names, I grab the files and put them back. I've already lost someone important to me from not being truthful. I'd be lying to myself if I said Preston wasn't becoming important to me and I'm not about to risk losing that special someone again.

As quickly as I can, I close the door and walk out of the office, then the building, securing the lock behind me, walking away hoping Preston will never find out.

Once I'm back at my office, a familiar music beat coming in from outside my closed office door catches my attention and before I know it, my door opens up to Angie dancing her way inside, clapping her hands as the song demands.

Breaking out in an instant smile, I stand up singing, "I'm gonna love ya. Until you hate me!"

Angie sings back, "I'm gonna show ya, what's really crazy!"

And just like that, Angie and I are repeating our office dance party from a few weeks ago, dancing our hearts out, jumping around and singing at the top of our lungs.

Preston

When I got notification on my cell phone that the silent alarm from Bridge had been tripped, instantly I thought whoever was trying to frame me was inside Bridge. Even though the place is behind my showroom, it's around the corner and not so easy to get to quickly. I ended my phone call with a client quickly and headed straight toward the door to finally nail whoever this was.

What I didn't expect to see was Kamii coming out of the door, looking suspicious as hell and getting in her car to leave in a hurry. Thankfully, she didn't see me but I sure as hell saw her. *Why would she break into Bridge?*

Whatever she wanted from there she got fast. She couldn't have been in there for more than a few minutes. Now what do I do? Confront her? She broke my trust, in a time where I feel like I can't trust anyone.

I walk to the door of Bridge and notice it's locked up and if I hadn't installed that alarm I would have no clue the door was tampered with at all. Reaching for my keys, I unlock the padlock and enter, searching for any clue as to why she was here.

Then it hits me. The names.

Every member has a file here and I pray to God she didn't break the trust that every member here has in me by revealing their names. When I open my office and unlock the cabinet, I can tell the files have been tampered with and blood boils up my face, beyond pissed off. *How could she do this?*

I have to confront her about this so I head straight to her office.

No one is at her assistant's desk and her door is slightly propped open so I open it all the way only to see Kamii dancing around the room to the music beat that I've been haunted with ever since Becca's murder.

"What is going on in here?" I yell, spitting my anger toward her.

"Oh, Preston," she laughs.

She laughs? What the fuck? "What's this song? Are you fucking with me?"

Yeah, she senses my anger now and so does her assistant who stops the song instantly and shows herself out of Kamii's office.

"Preston, what are you talking about? Why are you so angry?" Though her words are strong her body language is shifty and I know she's nervous.

I walk up to her, ready to accuse her of everything. "You are aren't you? You're the one fucking with me?"

She snaps away from me, ready for this fight to happen and I promise, I'm not backing down.

"Have you lost your mind? What are you talking about?"

"It is you isn't it? You're the one who killed Becca? You knew all about how to fake fingerprints and hell, you've had more than your share of opportunities to get my sperm. Fuck, how did I miss it? Of course you *found* her… Goddamn girl, you had me fooled. But why, why would you kill Becca?"

"Ok, you need to stop right there. I have NO CLUE what you're talking about but you have lost your mind? How dare you accuse me of killing my best friend."

"I bet you did do it. I can't trust you for anything. Why the hell did you just break into Bridge?"

Oh yeah, guilty as hell. That face says it all. "Preston," she holds up her hands in defense, "look, I'm sorry. I'll admit that. I did break into Bridge, but I'm just trying to help you. I wanted those names but I promise, I didn't look. Once I was there, breaking your trust meant more to me than finding out those names so I didn't look. I promise."

How can I believe anything she says right now? "But now you're haunting me with that damn song."

"What? *Black Widow*…?" she points her hands up like she's pointing to the ceiling and the music that is no longer playing.

"Ha! Black Widow. Fuck. That can't get any better. That's the name of this song? That's what you are, aren't you? A Black Widow."

"What the FUCK does that mean?" she bites back at me with pure evil radiating out of her pores.

"You heard me. That is you, huh? Why don't you tell me what really happened to your precious husband?"

"How dare you bring up my husband and how dare you accuse me of murdering my best friend. Get the fuck out of my office!"

"No! I'm not leaving until you tell me the truth. You killed her just like you killed your husband."

"How. Dare. You. Who do you think you are? Here I am saving your ass and you accuse me like this. All because of a song? You have officially lost your mind. Maybe you do deserve to rot in hell!"

Holy shit. She's right. What the fuck am I thinking? Did I really just accuse her of killing Becca? Because of a song?

Officially deflated, I sink into the chair in front of her desk placing my head in my hands. "Shit, I'm sorry."

"Damn right you are! Look, I know you're going through a lot right now but how dare you come into my office and talk to me that way."

"I know. I know. It's just. I saw you at Bridge, and I still can't believe you broke into my place. Why?"

She sits down next to me, "I know. I'm sorry, too. But I did. I went there to find those names. I need to find out who that woman is. Right now she's our only lead and I think she's tied to Trevor."

My eyes are heavy with guilt as I look at her, "Please, just don't. You know I can't. And please, forgive me. I'm under a lot of stress and that damn song is haunting me." I place my head in my hands, shaking it back and forth.

"What are you talking about? How is a song haunting you?"

"At first I thought I was losing my mind but it kept happening and I didn't know what to think."

"Preston, you aren't making any sense."

"I hear the beginning of that song, that Jamaican drum beat but there's no clapping. It plays, over and over again every time I'm home. I hear it so faintly, like it's coming from the other room but when I go to that room it sounds like it's coming from the room I was just in."

"What are you talking about?"

"That's the problem. I have no clue. I thought it was some crazy ringing in my ear since I couldn't figure it out but when I heard it right now when I walked into your office I just snapped. It's been driving me nuts and I had that crazy ah-ha moment the second I heard it. I'm so sorry you were on the other side of it."

"I get you're under all this stress but that doesn't explain what's going on. What do you mean you're hearing this beat play in your house?"

"I know… it's crazy right? But I hear it and it seems like it moves throughout my place."

"Has anything else odd been happening?"

I pause, trying to think when something finally clicks, "Now that I think of it, yeah. Every time I walk in my place I have the weirdest sensation come over me. I can't explain it. It's a smell or a feeling, I don't know. It's something I've felt before but I just can't put my finger on it. It reminds me of something though."

Kamii just looks at me like I'm crazy. I'm starting to think I am, too.

"Wait, I've noticed other things, too. Really little things that at first I didn't think much of but now that you mention it, I'm wondering if things aren't just a coincidence."

"There's no such thing as a coincidence," she says my words back to me.

"Exactly," I smirk.

"So what, what's been happening?"

"Small things, like two of my wine glasses sitting upright, not hanging on my under cabinet holder when they're always hanging there. Or my alarm going off at 3 a.m. when I know I set it for 8. Or my remote control I found sitting in my shoe by the door when I *always* leave it on my bedside table. And a couple of times I came home to a light on in my hall closet that I know wasn't on when I left since I don't go in there. Oh and my car… It was parked on the left when I always park it on the right."

"Sounds like someone's getting into your house, is that possible?"

"Fuck, I don't know. They were such minor things that I never put much thought to it. Of course I thought it was weird but, shit, do you think?"

"Yeah. I think someone is messing with you. Who has access to your house? Have you noticed any sign of a break in?"

"No. Nothing. No one has a key but me."

"Well, someone's getting in."

"But why? Why would they break in my house to move my wine glasses or turn on a light?"

"I have no clue but really, this entire case has been a crazy mystery. It's like they're playing a game and you're their pawn. I think they're doing it because they can."

I look up and truly see her for the first time since I walked into her office and ruined her little dance party. She's not the same girl I once met. Her eyes don't light up the way they used to but I saw a glimpse of her still there as she danced around the room with her assistant.

I can't believe I came in here losing my mind on her and calling her a Black Widow. I don't know anything about her dead husband because she hasn't shared anything with me.

The thought hits me harder than I wanted. *I really know nothing about her.*

I reach out for her hand, "Shit, Kamii. I'm so sorry. I really shouldn't have said anything to you like what I did."

She sighs, placing her hand over mine, "I know you are under a lot of stress."

"It's not ok. I promise, I'll never, ever talk to you like that again. How about I make you dinner tonight? My place."

"You're not afraid of whoever this is and being at your place?"

"No. If they are getting in, and they wanted to harm me, they would have done it by now. I'm not going to play their little game or let them run my life."

I'm so glad Kamii forgave me for my actions today. I can't believe I accused her and brought up her husband.

God, I'm such a dick!

I know dinner doesn't make up for it but at least she agreed to come over. When there's a knock at the door I rush to answer it, eager to see her again, that is until I see the look on her face. A darkness I've never seen on her before covers her beautiful face. My heart sinks, afraid of what's on her mind.

"It was the morning after our wedding night," she states in a low, calm voice as she stands in the door, not moving or stepping into my house.

"No, no, Kamii. You don't have to do this."

She looks into my eyes, "No, I want to." She walks in, walking straight to my couch, sitting down before she continues, "I had just become Mrs. Nick Schafer. God," she looks up to the ceiling fighting the tears that are building in her eyes, "he was the man of my dreams." She shakes her head, looking down before she continues, "He was just trying to make our honeymoon start off on the right foot by going to my favorite bakery to get me something special to start my day off right before we went to the airport. I laid back in bed, instead of going with him, I decided to be lazy and enjoy dozing in and out of sleep."

I watch as her eyes fill with more tears that start to fall this time so I place my hand over hers, "Really, you don't have to tell me."

"No," she wipes a tear, "I want to. I haven't told anyone really what actually happened."

I pull her in, holding her tightly, giving her all the time she needs. The fact that she's willing to share her life with me means more than I could ever explain. I've never wanted anyone in my life as much as I want her and the fact that she's sharing her past with me feels like she's handing herself over that much more.

After pulling back from my arms, she looks me in the eyes, "I had just started working for Whitman, Osborn and Steinhorn. Before that I worked as a public defender. To say I hated it was an understatement. I worked crazy hours, defending people who I knew were guilty but the State had to give them a fair trial. There was one case that went too far. I knew, without a doubt, that this guy was guilty but because of a technicality, I was able to get him off. It made me sick and I knew I wanted out. Thankfully, Michael Whitman was following the case and hired me on with their firm once they saw how I got the guy off. Yes, I was good at what I was doing but I wanted to defend people I knew where *not* guilty. I wanted to truly help people."

I interrupt her, "And you are. Look at what you've done for me."

She smiles sweetly before continuing, "Well, the case was against a child. The family was devastated and," she wipes tears that fall freely down her face, "and they blamed me."

Bending over, she sobs as tears fall heavily from her beautiful eyes. It takes her awhile but finally she continues, "Nick opened up our front door, only to be shot, point blank by the father of the child."

I sit, frozen in shock as she stands up, walking to the window as more tears fall. "When I heard the gunshot, I ran to see what had happened. I saw the dad, standing in my door way, shocked at what he had just done, not moving, just frozen in my door way. We caught eyes and he ran off. I bent down to help Nick but it was too late. The bullet hit him directly in his heart and he was dead."

I walk to her, wrapping my arms around her waist and pulling her in, holding her tightly, trying to give her the strength she needs.

"I never told anyone that. I just couldn't. I helped ruin that family by getting that guy off. I couldn't ruin their family even more by sending their dad to prison. I saw it in his eyes. He was sorry. He didn't mean to do it. Not really. The case is still unsolved to this day. It was God's way of punishing me for helping bad people get off."

"No, Kamii. Don't say that. You can't think his murder was your fault."

She turns, looking me dead in the eyes as tears flow down her face. "But it was. If I didn't let a man free that I *knew* was guilty, all because of a technicality, none of that would have happened and Nick would still be alive."

I can't help but think, *But I wouldn't be here with you now if he was*, but I can't say that. I just wrap my arms around her, holding her tightly and try to comfort her as much as I can.

Murderer

Who does this bitch think she is? How dare she come over to his house, opening up about lord knows what, making him look all caring and shit. No. This has to stop. She has to go.

Chapter TWENTY-THREE

Kamii

I spent the night at Preston's last night. That's two nights in a row that I slept curled up in his arms and I'd be lying if I didn't say I loved every minute. I'm screwed and I know it. No matter how much I fight not wanting to be with him, I'm just drawn to him more.

With my head in a fog, I walk into my apartment, tossing my keys on the entry table as my life flashes before my eyes.

Everything. My family. Nick. Preston. Becca. Everything flashes in a second as I see a gun pointing directly at my face.

"Who. The. Fuck. Do. You. Think. You. Are?" a woman's voice questions slow and methodically.

All I see is a gun barrel, as I stand, frozen.

This is it. My life will end just like Nick's. This is what he felt the last few minutes of his life as well.

"Answer me," she demands.

"My name is Kamii."

"I don't want your fucking name. How do you know Preston Babcock?"

"I'm his attorney."

"Bullshit. I've seen you with him."

"So you do belong to Bridge?"

"Ha! Wouldn't you like to know?"
"But why? Why did you kill Becca?"
"Don't you mean why am I going to kill you?"
I feel my stomach drop and my knees wobble. I'm too scared to respond.
"So again. Tell me, who you are to Preston before I kill you?"
A tightness in my chest rips any breath away from me that I try to take. I think I'm going to be sick but my brain doesn't compute to tell my stomach how to push the contents up. It's like everything in my body doesn't function at all. My lips part but no words come out.
"Tell me NOW!" she screams, pushing the gun further into my face.
Finally, my brain functions and I stutter out, "I, I don't know what we are."
"But you fucked him?"
"Yes."
Black. All I see is black.

Preston

One week. One fucking week Kamii has been in a coma. If I thought my life was hell before, I had no clue what hell really was.

I haven't left this hospital in a week. I've showered here, I've eaten here and I've slept here. There was no way I was leaving her side. She's lucky to be alive. Even though she's not out of the woods by any means.

When a neighbor heard the gunshot go off, they called 911 and Nicholas was the first on the scene. I'm still surprised he called me but I'll be forever in debt to him that he did.

The bullet shattered her cheekbone and just barely missing her spinal cord. Whoever shot her was, thankfully, taller so the bullet angled down and out instead of straight and up. Otherwise she would be dead for sure.

I've felt her grip my hand more than once and I made a promise to be by her side the moment she wakes up.

She has to wake up.

I can't take knowing that two of the most important women in my life were killed only because they knew me.

Whoever is doing this tried to frame me again but that back fired, big time. Since I'm out on bail for murder charges, I have to check in with the police department once a week and I just happened to be sitting at their desk at the time she was shot. Talk about an iron clad alibi.

Kamii's office has taken over my case, or what is left of it, and handed everything over to the police department. They believe now that I'm being framed and are tracking down leads that Kamii was working on. All coming up with nothing, yet.

I should be relieved that my chances of jail time have completely vanished but really that is the least of my worries. I'd rather have to face a trial than see Kamii lying helplessly in bed like this. I hate that her attempted murder is what's getting me off of my charges.

As I sit next to her, I hold her hand and lay my head on her bed, praying. Yes, I know I'm not religious but I'm praying like I have never prayed before.

I hear a sigh, a moan, and a cough that jerk me out of my prayers, making me reach up, touching her face. "Kamii, sweetheart."

Her face is bandaged around her cheek and secured around her head but her left eye is clear. Tears fall down my face as I watch her eye flutter slightly before slowly opening.

"Kamii, I'm here. Kamii, can you hear me?"

"Preston…?"

I drop my head back on her bed, fully sobbing at the sound of her saying my name. After I compose myself I grab her hand, whispering, "Yes, baby. My beautiful Kamii. I'm here."

"Where am I?"

"You've been shot. I can't believe you're alive." I grip her hand tightly as I lean down to lightly kiss her lips like I have over a hundred times trying to wake her up. Only this time my wish has come true. She's come back to me.

"A woman," she whispers. Her eye flutters shut, then open again, then shut.

"Shh, don't talk. It's ok."

A few hours later the doctors have done all kinds of tests on Kamii and she's sitting up a little more straight. After everyone leaves and we're alone again she looks at me, "Preston. I remember. It was a woman. She asked me about you."

"Kamii. Not now. Please. You're alive. That's all that matters."

"No, it's not. We need to find this person. What if she comes back?"

"Well, she hasn't so far."

"So far?"

"Kamii, you've been in a coma for a week."

She jolts slightly; shocked to hear how long she's been out. "How was I out for that long?"

"Kamii, you're lucky to be alive. That bullet barely missed anything that would have killed you immediately."

"Yes, she wanted to kill me. She told me so. And she shot me after I admitted that I had sex with you."

Now I feel like I was shot, but in the heart. *She tried to kill her because she's had sex with me. Why?*

Thankfully, the door opens and her assistant, Angie, walks in.

"Oh my gosh sweetie! I'm so happy to see you're awake."

I watch as Kamii tries to smile but her face doesn't move like it used to. It will be awhile before she is back to my same Kamii but I don't care. She's alive and the woman I love it still there, on the inside.

And yes, I said it. I'm so in love with this woman I can barely breathe without her. I knew what I was feeling was intense but now I have no doubt in my mind. She is my one. My only. The one thing I thought I would never feel again.

The doctors removed some of the bandages so we can see her more and, even though her face doesn't move, her eyes still light up with that kindness that fills my world as Angie approaches her bed, leaning down to give her a hug.

"Thank you for coming to see me," Kamii greets her friend.

"Are you kidding me? I've come everyday. I would have stayed if this handsome guy right here wasn't hogging the good seat," she smiles at me before turning back to Kamii. "Seriously though, I missed you. You had us scared there for awhile."

"I know. Thank you. I think I'm going to be ok now though." She looks directly at me with that smile in her eyes I love so much.

Chapter TWENTY-FOUR

Kamii

If I have to stay another day in this hospital I might scream. The food here stinks, my bed is uncomfortable and I am dying for fresh air. Because my wounds were so severe they've made me stay much longer than someone else with a gunshot wound.

Total, I've been in the hospital for a month now. Of course, a week of it I don't remember though. Preston has stayed by my side as much as he can but otherwise I've been bored out of my mind. I've caught up on the new releases of books that I missed because, come on; I was actually living my fantasy instead of just reading about it.

It's funny how the books have a different feeling to me now. Don't get me wrong, I still love them but now, instead of them just being a fantasy, I'm actually taking notes, counting down the days to when I can live these fantasies with my own real boyfriend.

Yeah, you heard that right. Boyfriend. I love him. Told him, too. Of course, after he told me first. So crazy how we got to where we are but I'm more than thankful for him in my life. And I owe it all to Becca.

Not a day goes by that I don't think about her and how much my life changed just from knowing her. I owe her my life and lord knows what I would give to have one more day with her.

Preston walking into my room with a wheelchair takes me out of my thoughts. "Are you ready to get out of here?" he says with a smile on his face.

"You have no idea," I smile back, well, as much as I can smile. The big bandage finally came off yesterday only to be replaced with a smaller, more manageable one. I lost a lot of feeling in the right side of my face. They think with physical therapy and a surgery or two, I'll be able to look semi-normal again.

I don't know. It doesn't bother me too much. I have the man I love already next to me and really; it just reminds me of how lucky I am to be alive. I know my best friend wasn't as lucky as I am so I like having the reminder along with her memory.

Preston insisted that I come stay with him for at least a little while. He didn't want me to be alone and since the police still have no clue who tried to kill me, I agreed.

I'm not sure what's more odd, the fact that I'm staying at his house or the fact that it doesn't feel weird at all?

I love how comfortable we are with each other and how loving he is toward me. I'm in absolute heaven. He's constantly taking care of me, making sure I have everything I need and helping me take care of my bandages.

The most amazing part, we haven't even had sex yet. I've been here a week now and we just cuddle. Wrapped in each other's arms sleeping all night.

His work is, thankfully, starting to pick back up and he was able to secure some of the contracts that started to stray when everything happened, so, for the first time, he's leaving me alone to go in for a meeting.

I can tell he's nervous about leaving me but I'm not afraid. I'm actually excited because I have a plan. Don't get me wrong, I love spending this time with him wrapped in each other's arms but it's time for us to get back to who we truly are. There is no way we're going back to the club, at least not yet, so I'm going to turn this place into the club. I think I need it just as much as he does.

I think he's afraid he'll hurt me but I'm ready to prove to him that I'm back, and that starts with removing these bandages for good.

I stand in front of the mirror, examining the new me. Inhaling deeply, I remove the last bandage and stare at the scar from my eye down to my mouth. It's deep, red and my face is slightly caved in.

Tears fill my eyes as I quickly wipe them away. I will not let this ruin me, or the woman I was so happy to finally become. This scar doesn't change anything about who I am inside. If I've learned anything, it's that Preston wants me, bandaged, scared and all.

So that is what he'll get.

His meeting is only supposed to last an hour so I don't have much time to make this place special. I know he would be ok with us having sex on a bed, like normal people, for our first time back together but I want it to be more like who we are. I need to bring that part back into my life.

For me, for us and for Becca.

I want him to know that he doesn't have to be different with me now, or even gentle. I want the exact man who first caught my attention all those months ago and rocked my world every day since.

My idea is to set up a semi dungeon room with ropes, floggers and a spanking bench. I've been peeking around, looking for ways to make it happen and I think I've got it all figured out.

With ropes from the draperies in the living room and a flogger I found in a drawer when I was putting my clothes away, my scene is almost set.

Figuring out the spanking bench was the hardest part but I found a box up in the hall closet that was full enough that I don't think it will collapse from my full weight on it. I placed a pillow from the couch over it and covered it with a dark red, very soft blanket I found in a trunk in front of his bed.

The room is dark, minus the lit tea light candles I have covering the dressers, making the room glow.

After dressing in black lace lingerie with a garter belt and silk stockings pulled up high with lace wrapped around my upper thigh, I pull my mask down over my eyes, completing my entire scene.

When I hear the door open, I crawl into position, securing my wrists as well as I can and putting myself on display for him to enjoy.

"Hey Preston, can you come to the bedroom please?" I call out sweetly to him.

I position myself so my ass is the first thing he sees as he walks through the door. With my head down, I'm able to see behind me and that's when I see it.

My man has come back to me.

His eyes turn dark instantly. His lips part as his tongue lightly slips out, wetting his lips before a small smirk fills his face.

"Well, hello there my beautiful Eurydice."

"Hello, Eros," I say as slow and meaningful as possible. "Do you want to play?"

He walks over to me, slowly moving his palm over my ass, rubbing, caressing, then slapping it hard, sending a smacking sound into the quiet air.

Chills fill my body as the sting turns to power, lighting my nerves on fire and making me want more.

More from him.

Dropping to his knees, he caresses my ass more before leaning down and kissing it, licking straight to my center.

I wasn't expecting him to go straight there and I jump from the sensation, instantly wanting more and sad that my hands are secured so I can't hold him there again.

My body obviously winces from need as I moan loudly and shake my ass toward him, trying to put my pussy directly in front of his face.

Thank God he complies and reaches out, licking me again. Slowly, softly, teasing me from the tip of my clit, around my entrance and to my backside.

I didn't realize how long it's been and how bad I've missed it until right this second.

Oh my God I want him now.

The sounds coming out of me are ones I've never heard before. I can't hide the need or the lust that is ripping through me, needing more.

Needing him.

Wiggling my ass more, he grabs me, stopping me as he bites it softly, "But you asked if I wanted to play. Not if I wanted to fuck you."

My head drops in frustration as he pulls away, picking up the flogger and running it softly over my body. The flogger helps light my nerves on fire more as every strand runs over my body before he lifts it up and hits me with a soft whack.

Again, sounds I've never heard release from me with no control. My mind is in a sex filled fog and Preston is the only person that can clear my way.

"You sound so sexy with those noises. I know you need my cock more than you need to breathe right now and I fucking love it."

"Yes, Sir. You're correct, as always, on exactly what I need."

"I see you've tied your hands, what if I want your hands to be on me?"

"I wanted to offer myself to you fully, giving you all control so please, do as you wish, Sir."

He leans down, whispering in my ear, sending chills down my spine, "Do you know what I wish?"

"No, Sir. Will you show me?"

He takes the flogger, running it down my back, teasingly slow before slapping my pussy with it.

"I wish I could make you cum multiple times."

I sigh, dropping my head, more than willing for him to try.

"Then," he leans down, placing his finger under my chin, raising it slightly so I can look him in the eye. "Then I want to flip you over and fuck you so hard you scream my name. Do you think I can do that?"

"Yes, Sir. I believe you can."

"So how shall I make you cum first?"

"My body is yours, please do as you wish."

"God, you have no clue how fucking hot that is."

He walks around, touching me here, rubbing me there. Teasing me wherever he can. I'm desperate for more, more of him, more of this, more of us.

Reaching around, he grabs my pussy, spreading it with his fingers, running the length softly up and down before circling my clit. His touch is so soft, it's driving me wild making me want it more and more. I swear, if he gives me just a little more pressure, I'm going to explode.

I get my desire when he wraps his mouth around my clit, sucking hard and pressing with his face, making my body rush and spasm releasing my first, very over due, orgasm.

Before I come down from the waves crashing over me, he pushes his finger inside, instantly bringing me high again from the inside now. First one finger, then two, he slides them in and out, taking his thumb and circling my clit once more.

If I thought the first one was intense, then this is going to rock my world. The feeling of having him inside me is pushing me to places I've never been before.

Just when I can't take it any more, he thrusts his large cock inside, filling me deeply as I scream with another orgasm, clenching him from the inside. I feel myself spasm around his cock, holding on for dear life and never wanting to let go.

Gripping me tightly, he releases my hands from the rope, pulling me up to him and turning me around. Reaching up, he removes my mask and smiles sweetly, "Now get in my bed."

"Yes, Sir," I smile.

I lay down on my back, opening up wide for him, as he crawls over me. I expect him to continue his attack on me but he completely takes me off guard when he slowly lowers his lips to my face and kisses every centimeter of my scar.

His loving touches melt my soul, and warm my heart, more than he could even imagine.

After he's cherished my entire face, telling me how much he loves me after every kiss, he pushes himself back inside while looking straight into my eyes.

Sensation floods through me as he fills my body, my life, my world. My eyes close on their own accord as I moan deeply, loving his body tied with mine.

"Open your eyes, look at me," he whispers as he slowly thrusts in and out.

I do as I'm told and look directly into the soul of a man that's bringing me to my third orgasm quicker than I thought possible.

"My beautiful Kamii," he whispers, rubbing his hand down my face as he increases his pace in and out of me.

It's the first time he's used my real name while we we're having sex and it's just what I need to push me over the edge as I scream out his name, frozen in ecstasy, as waves ripple through my body.

Chapter TWENTY-FIVE

Preston

"Thank you." I lean down, kissing Kamii on the back of her head, as she lies wrapped in my arms.

"For what?" she asks turning around to look me in the eyes.

"For that. For being you. For offering yourself to me."

"I should be thanking you. You've taken such good care of me and that was amazing."

"I'm impressed with how you set up this place," I admit, looking around the dimly lit room.

"I see you found my flogger and is that really the rope from my curtains?"

Kamii shyly smiles shaking her head *yes*.

"I see I've taught you well," I smile, kissing her lips softly. "The spanking bench there was pretty inventive. What's under that?"

"You like? I found a box in your hall closet. I took it down, placed a pillow over it and covered it with a blanket."

"A box... wait, from my hall closet?" I ask, almost afraid for her to say yes.

"Yeah, I hope that's ok. It seemed pretty full so I thought it could hold my weight. I didn't open it or anything."

I sit up, not caring that she's still wrapped in my arms so she falls back onto the bed.

She sits up, grabbing my shoulder. "I'm sorry. Is it something important?"

I look down, not wanting to have this conversation here and now. Without saying a word, I get up, moving everything off the box and walk out of the room.

"Preston," she calls after me, following me down the hall. "I'm sorry. I didn't know it was so important."

Shit. I don't want her to feel bad about this. What she did was amazing. Exactly what I needed.

I drop the box right as we get to the closet and turn to her. "No, don't feel bad. It's just." I look down, "This is the last of the stuff I kept of Kim."

Her look says it all. She knows I'm talking about my dead wife and I look down, ashamed.

"Oh Preston. I'm so sorry. I didn't know."

"No, please, don't feel bad. I shouldn't have this stuff anymore. It's time for me to move on."

She places her hand over mine as I reach for the box. "Don't ever say that. Don't ever forget her. She was your wife. I get it. I had a husband, remember? They are a part of us and I don't ever want to take that away from you."

I stare into her beautiful eyes, more thankful than ever that I found her. Someone who gets it. Who gets me.

"Do you have a picture of her in there? I'd love to see what she looked like."

"I do." I open the box, digging a little ways down and pulling out the most recent photo of us that was taken the year before she committed suicide. After a heavy sigh, I hand it to her, "This is her. This was Kim."

Her face turns pale, as she looks at me, back at the picture and back to me again but doesn't say a word.

"What's that look? What's wrong?"

"Preston. No. No. This can't be Kim, your wife who committed suicide."

"Yes, this is her. What's wrong?"

"No Preston. This can't be," she's stuttering and I can visibly see the photo start to shake in her hand.

"What? Why?"

"Preston. This is the woman that was at Trevor's house that I spoke to that day. She's not dead. She's alive. And looking at her now, I see it. This is the woman who shot me."

"No Kamii. She's dead. I watched her jump."

"She's alive Preston. I promise you. How could anyone forget those eyes? And it's not a coincidence that someone looking just like this was at her brother's house."

"Stop. Stop saying that. She's dead."

"Did you ever find her body?"

"No, of course we didn't. She jumped off of the Golden Gate Bridge. Her body was probably eaten before it could wash to shore."

"I'm telling you. She's not dead. And she's who is framing you for murder."

"No. I said STOP! She couldn't do something like that. We loved each other." There is just no way she would ever do anything like this. *To me.* I'm her husband. No, she's wrong.

"Preston. She killed herself, or pretended to at least. All of this is making more sense now. You said someone was doing weird things inside your house, right? Well, she probably still has a key. She knew you donated your old shoes, she could have easily gotten your sperm and fingerprints. Preston… she's alive."

"There's no way. This can't be," I say in absolute disbelief, turning to walk away from her.

She grabs my arm to stop me. "Wait, why did she say she wanted to kill herself?"

I look down, hating myself for the truth, "Because I wanted to live a more sexually free life and she didn't want to."

"Exactly! Oh my god. It's her. That's why she killed Becca and then came after me, all framing you for it. She hated the fact that we were sleeping with you."

"I still can't believe this. There's just no way!"

"Believe it, Preston. This is her," she holds up the photo, trying to prove her point.

"Why? Why would she do it? This is all crazy!" I pause, remembering the last thing she said to me. "Holy shit."

"What?"

"The last thing she said to me. Shit, I thought her killing herself was what she was talking about but no. It was this. She was planning all of it. She knew I had thoughts of opening my own club. I talked about wanting to do it just for the safety factor for her. I didn't plan on having it all anonymous then. She started that Facebook account then for the application. Shit. She actually asked me for my sperm sample. Oh my God!" I throw my hands up in the air. "How could I be so stupid? We were trying to get pregnant. It wasn't happening so she had me give a sample and said she was taking it to the lab for testing. I was so busy with work that I just believed her and did as she asked."

My heart feels like it's been ripped in two, permanently this time. I thought losing her was hard but putting all of this together now is completely debilitating. I loved her and I thought she loved me. We were together for ten years. How does someone you think you know do something like this? How could she kill Becca? This is not the Kim I knew.

My body falls against the wall and slides down to a sitting position on the floor as I rest my head on my arm that's resting against my knees. Here I thought she was dead this entire time and I don't know what's worse, knowing she's alive or knowing she killed someone I cared about because of what I wanted with our lives?

Breathing becomes a harder task than normal and just the feeling of Kamii's hand resting on my back makes my mind a little clearer.

"So what did she say before she killed herself?" Kamii quietly asks while rubbing my back.

I look up at her, "She said, 'I'm gonna show you what's really crazy.'"

She gasps, "The song! Holy shit. You said the song *Black Widow* had been haunting you. The beat right?" I nod. "Well that's a lyric from the song. Preston, it's her and she's been here. She has to be watching you some how which means she knows I'm here, too."

"We have to call the police," I demand, moving to get up to grab my phone.

"No, wait. We need more proof. We don't have actual proof that she's alive yet."

"How do we do that? We already know that she's not at her brother's house anymore. She could be anywhere."

"Yes, but she wants me dead so she'll be coming back for me and when she does, we'll be ready this time."

"Kamii. No, I'm not putting you in any harms way."

"We have to do this. For Becca. For you. She's not going to stop until she gets what she wants."

Chapter TWENTY-SIX

Kamii

It took some convincing but we came up with a plan. Preston has not left my side for more than a second for the last couple days but I can't say I'm complaining. We're hoping we're correct in thinking she's watching us. That's the only way this will ever work.

Thankfully, Becca's brother, Nicholas, is on board with helping us now that he knows Preston is innocent. It took some convincing for him to believe it's Kim setting up Preston and he's still a little skeptical. We kept it quiet from anyone else. We can't have any slip ups if this is going to work.

Since we know she's been in the house we think there might be cameras placed around watching us so we put on a little play, acting like Preston has to go on a trip and pack his bag with Nicholas posted across the hall at Preston's neighbor's house, watching from the peep hole for anyone to approach.

"Are you sure about this?" Preston whispers as he hugs me goodbye.

"I'm a big girl. I can take care of myself," I whisper back.

"I love you."

"Love you, too," he leans down and kisses me on my lips before turning around and walking away with his luggage in tow.

The plan now is to go about my business like nothing is up so I make myself dinner, and curl up with a good book and a glass of wine. It should be a perfect night for me, if only my nerves weren't completely shot as I sit here like fish bate.

If she didn't come by eleven then I'm supposed to get ready for bed and crawl under the covers, so when I see it's that time, I get up to wash my glass and brush my teeth.

Nothing seems out of the ordinary, so I head to the bedroom, removing my shirt over my head as I flick on the light. When I turn to the closet I'm startled by the dark hair, crystal blue eyed woman staring back at me.

"So, we meet again?" she says with no emotion.

Holy shit, how did she get in here? How long has she been here? How is Nicholas going to know she's here?

"I know who you are," I say, speaking as clearly as possible so she doesn't sense my fear.

"Yeah. So you know that you're fucking my husband."

"He thought you were dead."

"Doesn't matter. He would have fucked you anyway. I wasn't enough for him, so you should know you never will be either. Especially when you're dead," she raises a gun to point at me once again. "This time I'll make sure the bullet hits your heart, just like you've driven a bullet through mine."

"How are you going to frame him for this?" I ask, trying to get her talking to stall, for what though I have no clue.

"I don't give a shit about that anymore. I've seen the way he looks at you. He used to look at me that way. I'll have more fun knowing he lost his precious Eurydice."

"But why?" I plead.

"Ask him that. Oh wait, you'll be dead. I guess you can go to hell with Becca and wait for him to answer you there."

"Kimberley?" I hear Preston say in disbelief. He's standing in the doorway of the bedroom, staring directly at his wife that he thought was dead. "Why?"

"You know why. Then stupid Trevor screwed everything up, I could never trust him. Can you believe he went to the wrong house?" she shakes her head with a smirk on her face. "Idiot. I guess it was for the better though. It felt good, killing the woman that had fucked my husband."

"How could you do this? She was innocent," he pleads.

"You promised to love me. You promised to be with only me. Yet you said I wasn't good enough and you had needs."

I look at Preston as the pain that he's caused his wife washes over him. "But I thought you were enjoying it, too."

"No Preston. I wasn't. I did it for you but I've never felt so dirty and disgusting in my life. Yet there you were, getting your dick sucked by another woman and loving every minute. When you stuck your cock in them as I watched it literally killed me. So you know what. It's your time to die." She moves the gun from my face to pointing directly at him.

Preston doesn't seem fazed by the gun, only hurt is written all over his face as he reaches out to her. "You could have told me. I would have understood. You were enough. I loved you and a part of me did die when I thought you jumped off that bridge."

"You didn't love me. How could you love me and fuck those other woman?"

"It was just sex. It's a release. A way to have a good time. I only fucked them. I made *love* to you. I came *home* with you. I wanted a *family* with you. You're the one that ruined that. If you would have just told me you didn't want to go anymore then I would have realized what was really important and stopped."

Calmly, he takes a step forward, reaching for me to move behind him.

"But you said you had needs," Kim says as her voice starts to shake slightly.

"Yes, but my needs also involved having you in my life."

"So you would have stopped?" Her arm drops a little as her tight grip fades slightly around the gun.

I watch silently as he takes a closer step toward her, "Yes. I would have. The night you jumped I made up my mind quickly that I would. There was no question to it really. My needs for you were much bigger than my needs for a sex club. I only kept going after you died because I didn't have you."

"How can you say that? I asked you to stop and you said no."

"Kim, you never said anything until you stood on that bridge. If you would have just talked to me, told me how you felt. I never wanted to put you in a situation that made you uncomfortable. I can't believe you weren't honest with me and told me that you didn't like it. God Kim, that's heart breaking to hear. I was your husband. The one person you should have trusted in the world and I led you to do things with your body that you didn't like. I'm so ashamed and so sorry."

I watch as Kim stares blankly at Preston, completely emotionless.

"Now please. Drop the gun. This is not the way to settle this," Preston says as he reaches out for her.

"It's too late. My life was over a year ago. I guess it's finally time for it to be over for good," she responds.

I watch in horror as she raises the gun to her head and without a second thought, pulls the trigger.

"No!" Preston yells as he reaches toward her but it's too late.

Her body falls like a cut down tree, landing on the ground with a loud thump. Preston falls around her, lifting up her lifeless body as he starts to cry.

I walk up, rubbing my hand on his back not sure what to say. I've been in his shoes. Even though it's been a few years, and with everything she just put him through, I know this is still the hardest moment in his life.

Thankfully, Nicholas comes running in the door after he heard the gunshot. I hear him call 911 and tell them there's been a shooting and someone was dead but everything else is a blur.

I stare as Preston cries over her lifeless body saying things like, "Why?" and "This didn't have to happen," and "I loved you."

The last one hurt but I know I can't take it personally. I love my husband to this day and a part of me always will.

After the paramedics are gone and the place is cleared out, I look at Preston who's got a look of complete loss on his face.

"Are you ok?" I ask as I wrap my arms around his body, showing him that I'm still here and not going anywhere.

Thankfully, he hugs me back. "Yeah, I'm so sorry you had to witness that. I still can't believe she was alive this entire time."

"Yeah. Pretty crazy, but I want to know how *you're* doing?"

He looks me in the eyes, "Thank you. Thank you for caring about me. For understanding what I'm going through right now. For wanting to help me. And for loving me."

I don't need to say anything. It's all been said so I lean over, kiss his soft lips and hug him as tightly as I can.

EPILOGUE

Kamii

"I don't know if I'm ready," I say to Preston as we park in front of Bridge. Preston reaches over, grabbing my hand, "This is what Becca would have wanted. You know that just as much as I do."

I smile up at him, knowing if she were here right now she would kick my ass for doubting getting out of the car. I laugh to myself as I picture it in my head. Preston's right. We owe her this.

Life has been good these past six months. I ended up buying the place I had my eyes on and, not only is Preston helping me remodel it, but we're making it our home together. Both of us are ready to move forward together and forget about our dark pasts.

Only we're not alone now. I'm five months pregnant and we just found out we're having a girl. There was no question as to what her name would be. Rebecca Lynn Babcock is due on June 23rd. Though it was a complete surprise, both of us are ecstatic to welcome a baby girl into our lives.

It's amazing how things worked out. Preston and Kim tried to have a baby for years and they could never make it happen, while Nick and I froze his sperm with hope of a day that never came. Preston and I weren't even thinking about it and surprise! It was the best moment of my life when I saw that plus sign, clear as day, telling me I was going to be a mommy.

Pregnancy has been good to me and I only have a slight baby bump so I promised Preston we'd go to the club again before I started to look like I was about to pop. We don't plan on playing with anyone else though, tonight is just for us.

I slip my mask down my face as we slip out of the car and down the dark alley. It feels so good to be back.

We're greeted with a knowing grin by the security guard at the door. Though the club is still private with no names and masks, Preston introduced me to the staff once I officially took over Becca's role.

They're not to greet us in a different manner or let people know who we are but the smile I get in return soothes my nerves, welcoming me back home.

Even though I've been back in the building, it was during the day so it didn't feel real. But as I walk in now, I'm taken back to my first time with Becca. The night I met Preston, and my life was changed forever.

A calmness wraps around me making me smile. I feel her. She's here with us, forever.

The next morning, while I'm waiting for my drink at Starbucks, I run through how much my life has changed. How I went from being a lonely, workaholic, basket case to a confident, sexy, woman who is madly in love and pregnant in the span of a few months, will forever baffle me. I'm so thankful for everything my life has become.

"I have a dirty chai for Rebecca on the bar," I hear the barista call out.

A bubbly woman, with short brown hair gives me a warm smile as she walks up, grabbing her drink and walking out the door.

I have to laugh as I whisper up in the air, "Love you, girl."

Playlist

Lost In You by Three Days Grace
• This song came on when Kamii turned on Pandora, listening to music for the first time.

Blow Me Wide Open by Saint Asonia
• Preston plays this when he's trying to drown out the steel drum beat.

Comatose by Skillet
• This plays after Preston first spends the night with Kamii.

Black Widow by Iggy Azalea
• Ha! I'm hoping I don't have to explain this one ;-)

Acknowledgements

Writing *Black Widow* was an extremely different process than both *Unwritten* and *Rewritten*. When I wrote those books, I only had dreams of one day publishing them and I worked on them for over a year before they were actually released. With this book, I knew it would be released and that made me somewhat more nervous.

I started *Black Widow* before *Unwritten* was actually released, on a high of my author debut. Not knowing yet, truly, of the high and lows of publishing. One day you're seeing sales and five star reviews, the next everything slows down and you don't know why. My books were named best book of the year by three blogs on the same day that someone left a review saying *Unwritten* was the worst book of the year… Talk about a rollercoaster of emotions!

This is where Jeannine Colette was my savior. She was the one person I could contact any time and she knew exactly what I was going through and, more importantly, knew the perfect thing to say with her, "Say it with me, I suck!" and a link to a *Friends* episode in a text. I couldn't have a better author bestie than her!

I'd also like to thank the wonderful people I've met online who have made this entire process worth it. Especially Giovanna Bovenzi Cruz, Aubrie Brown, Laurie Breitsprecher, Nancy Butler, Dale Gardiner and Nancy Parken. A special thank you to Ana Rita Clemente who was my biggest supporter in finishing *Black Widow* and would check in to see how I was doing and encourage me to finish it.

None of my books would have gotten out there without the help of Wordsmith Publicity and Autumn Hull along with blogs who read my books and helped promote them. A huge thank you to Marina Skinner of MI Bookshelf, Kimberly Lucia from Kimmy Loves to Read, Christine Tovey from Sweet & Spicy Reads, Tanya Baikie from I <3 Books, Wilmari Carrasquillo-Delgado from The Sisterhood of the Traveling Book Boyfriend, Naomi Hopkins from Naomi's Paranormal Palace, Arabella Bright from RedRoom Bookreviews, Innergoddess Booklover and Maryse's Book Blog for posting the sales of both *Unwritten* and *Rewritten*. A special shout-out to Cassandra Delorie from Nerd Girl Official who I met online and it randomly turned out that we lived in the same hometown! What are the crazy odds?!

And of course, I always have to thank my family and friends the most who put up with my endless talks of books, hours of working with my laptop and what my husband calls "the blogisphere." To Amy Gentili, Lacy Pryde and Sonia Aguero who got the first few chapters of *Black Widow* and text me with amazing comments, encouraging me to finish it. And to my amazing new beta reader, Stefanie Pace, who was the first person to finish the entire book and wasn't afraid to tell me it needed more. Her one small suggestion turned into 13,000 more words and the book that you hold today. Stefanie, I can't thank you enough for your support!

Lastly, to every reader who's contacted me, bought my books and left me reviews. I couldn't do this without you. Thank you!

About the Author

Lauren Runow is the author of two other Adult Contemporary Romance novels, *Unwritten* and *Rewritten*.

When Lauren isn't writing, you'll find her listening to music that speaks to her, at her local CrossFit, reading, or at the baseball field or skatepark with her boys. Her only vice is coffee, and she swears it makes her a better mom!

Lauren is a graduate from the Academy of Art in San Francisco and is the founder and co-owner of the community magazine she and her husband publish. She lives in Northern California with her husband and two sons.

Sign up for her newsletter through her website at www.LaurenRunow.com to keep up to date about new releases.

She'd love to hear your comments and feedback. Please take the time to leave a review on Goodreads, Amazon, iBooks or wherever you purchased *Black Widow*.

You can also stay in touch through the social media links below.

www.facebook.com/laurenjrunow
www.twitter.com/LaurenRunow
www.instagram.com/lrunow
www.goodreads.com/author/show/14168280.Lauren_Runow

Join her street team at https://www.facebook.com/groups/1628591530724682/

Want more books by Lauren Runow?
Check out *Unwritten* and *Rewritten* that are both out now.

Made in the USA
Monee, IL
04 April 2021